## *"In my experience, women say one thing and mean another,"*

Linc told her. As an agent, he thought, honesty certainly wasn't *his* policy. It could get him killed. Still, his conscience nudged him where Brie was concerned. She seemed incapable of lying—so far.

She turned to him. "And I suppose you've never said one thing and meant another, Tanner?"

He reached out, his fingers outlining her cheek and delicate jawline. He saw her lips part beneath the unexpected caress. "One thing you'll find out about me: I'm honest," he lied. "The truth may hurt, but it's better than the alternative."

He scowled. Somehow, she'd gotten under his skin. He ached to continue his featherlight exploration of her. His body was going rigid just from that fleeting touch. What the hell was happening here?

Dear Reader,

Welcome to the Silhouette **Special Edition** experience! With your search for consistently satisfying reading in mind, every month the authors and editors of Silhouette **Special Edition** aim to offer you a stimulating blend of deep emotions and high romance.

The name Silhouette **Special Edition** and the distinctive arch on the cover represent a commitment—a commitment to bring you six sensitive, substantial novels each month. In the pages of a Silhouette **Special Edition**, compelling true-to-life characters face riveting emotional issues—and come out winners. Both celebrated authors and newcomers to the series strive for depth and dimension, vividness and warmth, in writing these stories of living and loving in today's world.

The result, we hope, is romance you can believe in. Deeply emotional, richly romantic, infinitely rewarding—that's the Silhouette **Special Edition** experience. Come share it with us—six times a month!

From all the authors and editors of Silhouette **Special Edition**,

Best wishes,

Leslie Kazanjian
Senior Editor

# LINDSAY McKENNA
## Come Gentle the Dawn

*Silhouette Special Edition*

Published by Silhouette Books New York

**America's Publisher of Contemporary Romance**

To my sisters
Ruth Gent, René Anderson, Ann Roher,
Betsy Lammerding, Cinda Garland, Linda Dubnicka
and Karen Mylnar.

And to our Mother, the Earth,
who needs our protection.

SILHOUETTE BOOKS
300 East 42nd St., New York, N.Y. 10017

ISBN: 0-373-09568-6

First Silhouette Books printing December 1989

Printed in the U.S.A.

**Books by Lindsay McKenna**

Silhouette Special Edition

*Captive of Fate* #82
*\*Heart of the Eagle* #338
*\*A Measure of Love* #377
*\*Solitaire* #397
*Heart of the Tiger* #434
*†A Question of Honor* #529
*†No Surrender* #535
*†Return of a Hero* #541
*Come Gentle the Dawn* #568

\*Kincaid trilogy
†LOVE AND GLORY series

Silhouette Intimate Moments

*Love Me Before Dawn* #44

Silhouette Desire

*Chase the Clouds* #75
*Wilderness Passion* #134
*Too Near the Fire* #165
*Texas Wildcat* #184
*Red Tail* #298

## LINDSAY McKENNA

spent three years serving her country as a meteorologist in the U.S. Navy. She is also a pilot. She and her husband of fifteen years, both avid ''rock hounds'' and hikers, live in Ohio.

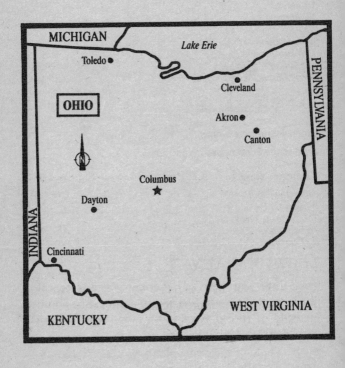

## Chapter One

There's no way in hell I'm working with a woman in hazardous material," Linc said. He got up from the leather chair and faced his superior, Brent Cramer, who sat behind the massive oak desk. The scowl on Linc's lean face deepened as he gauged Cramer's unruffled reaction to his caustic statement. He didn't care. He was bone tired from his last assignment and hadn't been given enough time to recoup before Cramer had decided to throw him on another one.

"She knows what she's doing, Linc." Cramer lifted his narrow shoulders beneath the three-piece gray pinstriped suit. "I'm getting plenty of heat from the senator from Ohio to do something about this pronto. The Hazardous Material Bureau is his pride and joy politically. He can't have haz-mat people being blown away with no suspects. It won't look good to the voters in that state. And he's up for reelection soon."

Linc Tanner stopped pacing and threw his hands tensely on his lean hips. He glared out the window through the venetian blinds. He stared unseeing at the other government buildings surrounding them. *I need rest. I don't need a damn broad who's fingered to be blown apart,* he thought savagely. He twisted his head in Cramer's direction and, with barely veiled anger, said, "I don't care about the senator's voting problem in Ohio. My job and his politics don't mix."

Cramer calmly steepled his fingers. "I know you could care less about politics. That's my job. Yours is to go into the field and assume an identity. I chose you for this assignment because you're the best, Linc."

Tanner shot him a venomous look out of the corner of his eye. "Spare me the platitudes, Cramer. Chances are, if I look at the roster, I'm the *only* available agent for this mess."

A hint of a smile curled Cramer's thin mouth. Ever since Linc had joined the Bureau of Alcohol, Tobacco and Firearms, he had been considered a master of sorts. Of sorts, he reminded himself sourly. A few well-chosen adjectives summed him up: acerbic, a loner and damn good at his job. He knew it was the last reason that kept Cramer from firing him outright for his constant insubordination.

"You're probably right," Cramer acknowledged. "Now, let's talk about this problem with the haz-mat team in Ohio."

Linc tensed. "I just got off a heavy assignment. I want a couple of weeks' rest. I almost got exposed on this last one, and you want me to stick my neck out a week later. This time I'm saying no."

Cramer unsteepled his slender hands and leaned forward, a crafty gleam in his gray eyes. "You take this one, Linc, and it will earn you that desk job you've been wanting for some time. Think for a moment. Six years out in the field as an ATF agent is a long time. You crack this case, and I'll get it for you. Anywhere in the United States, Linc."

Linc studied his boss in the taut silence. It wasn't like Cramer to promise him a plum just like that. No, Cramer was a politically savvy animal on the Hill who manipulated others as easily as puppets. But Cramer had never promised him something and not delivered. He rubbed his square jaw, considering and weighing the offer. Finally, he sat down opposite Cramer.

"One of two things has happened. Either this is a hell of a lot bigger than both of us or you're getting political pressure even you can't control."

"A little of both. The senator from Ohio just happens to be on the Appropriations Committee, which holds the purse strings to our budget. We've got some big requests coming up before them soon. If I don't give him what he wants, he could turn on us. We're strung out too thin in the field and we need to hire more agents."

"Tell me about it. I'm so used to leading a double life my real one was destroyed years ago."

Cramer nodded, looking grim. "I know."

"You've got my attention," Linc muttered. "Go on."

"You'll take the assignment?"

"I didn't say that. I want to hear the details," Linc countered.

Cramer smiled and opened the file beneath his hands. "The players involved are the Ohio State Fire Marshal's office, the Hazardous Material Bureau, one

murdered haz-mat tech, one suspicious explosion—
and no answers.''

Linc scowled. ''A murder?'' Who would want to
blow away a haz-mat tech?

''Yes. A man by the name of John Holcomb, who'd
been employed by the FM's office for five years,
bought it. His partner nearly went with him, but she
managed to pull through and is now back on the job.''

''Who's playing rough?''

''No leads. Your guess is as good as mine.''

''You said 'she.' Was that Holcomb's partner before he died?''

''Yes.'' Cramer pulled out a large black and white
photograph and handed it to Tanner. ''Meet Brie
Williams, the unknown quantity in this puzzle. She's
a qualified haz-mat tech. Been working for the FM's
office for the past three years. Report is, she's very
good at her job.''

Linc studied the photo intently, missing nothing. It
showed a tall woman in a one-piece dark uniform directing several fire fighters toward what appeared to
be a haz-mat accident involving a derailed tank car.
Linc looked closer. Brie Williams was not what he'd
call a beautiful woman. Her face was square, holding
large, expressive eyes, an aquiline nose, full lips and a
mildly stubborn chin. The high cheekbones emphasized her eyes, which were her best feature, in his
opinion. Her hair was dark and short. Linc halted a
smile, thinking that with the baseball cap on her head,
she could almost pass for a man. Except for her
rounded breasts. Her shapely rear and hips would also
persuade any man that she was definitely female. His
gaze came back to her face, and he waited for his gut
impression, which had never led him astray and had

often saved his life. Despite the tension in her face, the intentness reflected in her eyes and thinned lips, she didn't seem all that tough. Maybe on the outside, but Linc would bet his life she was vulnerable beneath that exterior. He fervently hoped so or there wouldn't be a prayer for them working together as a team.

"How did a woman get that high up in the state on something as specialized as haz-mat?" he asked.

Cramer pulled out another paper and held it out to him. "Here's Williams's bio. Read it and you'll see why."

"She was a fire fighter for five years?" Linc muttered in disbelief. Another rarity. Out of one million, three hundred thousand fire fighters in the United States, only one percent were women.

"Williams has paid her dues," Cramer defended. "When the FM's office hired her on, she was a lieutenant with her fire department up near Litton, Ohio."

Another unique quality, Linc thought. What were the odds of a woman fire fighter becoming an officer? One in a hundred thousand. She was sure beating a lot of odds. Tiredly, Linc rubbed his face, tossing the papers on the desk. "That's all I need: a woman who's in male territory."

Cramer's eyes grew hard. "Look, I know you think all women belong barefoot and pregnant, but this one time, you'd better put your opinions aside. Williams has nothing but commendations in her file."

Linc raised his chin. "Is she a suspect then? A pawn? The next victim? What?"

"We don't know. That's what you're going to find out and tell us. Her partner was murdered, judging from all the evidence that was gathered. Although officially, it's being soft-pedaled as an accident with an ongoing investigation."

"So?" Linc challenged. "Did she walk away from it and let Holcomb get killed or what?"

"No. She was going back to the haz-mat truck to get some tools when the explosives detonated. Williams was in the hospital for three months afterward."

It wasn't making sense to Linc. Either he was as tired as his thirty-three-year-old body felt or Cramer was being handed a royal gift that could blow up in several directions. And he didn't feel like teaming up with a woman who might be a suspect herself, and becoming a target in the bargain. "For all we know, she could have had Holcomb fingered. Maybe they were lovers. Maybe she got scorned and blew him away."

Cramer's mouth tightened. "Always the woman's fault, isn't it?"

Linc glared at him. "That's been my experience."

"The odds point to her innocence. According to the FM, she's a possible target, too. They don't want to lose their highly skilled people, Linc, regardless of whether they're males or females. I know it makes a big difference to you, but that's tough. If you take this assignment, you're going in to protect Brie Williams."

He snorted. "More than likely, from herself. She'll probably get me killed screwing up a detonation."

"Well, now, that's your problem. You're the explosives expert. I'm sure you'd speak up and let her know if she was doing something wrong."

"You bet I would. Women have screwed up too much of my life already. I'm not going to let another one finish off the job and get me killed."

Cramer held his angry stare. "So you'll take it?"

"Do I have a choice?"

"Realistically, no."

Linc rose. "Protect Super Woman, huh? Okay, I can do that. The price is high, Cramer. You'd better come through with that desk job or else."

Cramer grinned. Linc knew the older man was used to his bark, which was generally much worse than his bite. "You name the city and state, and you'll have your desk job, Tanner. Now go home and shave, will you? You look like hell."

Linc picked up the folder marked Williams and tucked it beneath his arm. He'd get home to his dingy, rarely used apartment, shave, take a hot shower and read her file. No, on second thought, he'd catch up on sleep first, then read the file. He didn't want any nightmares.

"You what?" Brie stammered in disbelief.

Chief Craig Saxon obviously girded himself internally. He must have known without a doubt that there was going to be a minor explosion in his large, well-appointed haz-mat office. He nodded his craggy head, the silver in his hair giving his bulldog face a saintliness it didn't deserve. "Calm down, Brie," he soothed in his gravelly voice.

"Calm down!" Brie repeated, whirling and planting her hands on her hips. "You call giving me a *second* rookie nothing? What are you trying to do to me, Chief?" There was an odd catch in her voice. "I've got one trainee right now. Jeff is coming along fine, but he won't be fully qualified for another month. Why a second trainee? Give the guy to Jim McPeak over in Quadrant Two. He's got the nice, quiet sector of Ohio.'' She ran her fingers through her sable-brown hair. Saxon had requested her to come down from Canton for a meeting on her only day off that week. Brie had arrived in a peach-colored dress of silk instead of her haz-mat uniform.

"Sit down, Brie," Saxon tried again. "Come on," he entreated, giving her that fatherly look that always got to her.

Brie's green eyes narrowed speculatively on her superior's face. Saxon was like a father to her in one way. Ever since she had been hired by him three years ago, she had never made him sorry for that decision. Brie recalled the furor that had hit the newspapers over the appointment of a woman to the haz-mat team. There wasn't a fire chief interviewed around the state who didn't parrot the same tired old spiel: she was a woman, she couldn't do a man's job. Well, she had proven them all wrong. Just as she had when she had been one of the few female fire fighters in the state.

Reluctantly, she acquiesced to Saxon's plea. "Okay," she said, sitting down and smoothing the silk over her long thighs.

Saxon smiled benignly. "I'm sorry to have to call you down here to the Fire Academy on your day off, Brie. I know it's a three-hour drive one way. But I've received orders directly from the FM to assign—" he raised the official-looking paper, squinting at it through his bifocals "—Linc Tanner to you."

Brie digested the information, feeling as if she were being torn apart. She knotted her cold hands in her lap, the knuckles whitening, as she tried to control the fear eating away at her. Few people saw Brie Williams down and out, but for the good of all, she had to level with the chief.

"Ever since the—" Brie choked and lowered her gaze. Blinding tears stabbed her eyes. Her voice had been low and unsteady, which wasn't at all usual. Groping for control Brie sat silent a long time before she spoke again. "What are you trying to do? Pressure me out of my job, Chief? Because if you are, I'll hand in my resignation now. I can't take—"

"No," Saxon uttered in astonishment, his gray eyebrows raising in alarm. "My God, no!" He got to his feet, pushing the chair back.

Brie winced beneath his whiplash tone. Neither of them was overtly emotional, but ever since the—accident? murder?—of John Holcomb, she had been riding a daily roller coaster of vitriolic emotions. She knew the Chief felt responsible for John's loss almost as much as she. But not quite. At least Saxon could sleep at night. She couldn't. Desperate to regain some calmness, Brie forced words out. "Look, you pushed a green kid on me one week after I got out of the burn unit up in Cleveland and you asked me to train him to be my partner to replace...John." She paused, still fraught with recent pain and nightmarish memories. "So, in the past three months I've trained him. Now you're telling me Jeff isn't going to be John's replacement. Jeff's going to the southeast quadrant. And this—this..."

"Tanner," Saxon provided softly. "Linc Tanner is his name."

Brie jerked her head up and looked across the desk at Saxon. "He could be the archangel Gabriel and I wouldn't care, Chief!" She tried to still her rising temper. Licking her lips, Brie concentrated on breathing more slowly before she went on. "Jeff's doing fine. He's enthusiastic and he learns fast. I need someone up in the northeast quadrant who's quick and alert. I don't need a rookie to babysit again."

Saxon looked down at the file on Tanner. "Brie," he murmured apologetically, "this one is out of my hands. If it were my decision, Jeff would stay. You've been through hell. I can see you need more time to recover, but it simply isn't possible under the circumstances. I need you and your experience back up there now."

"Since when does the FM stick his nose into our business? You've always had total control of haz-mat. Why now? I could understand if things were getting worse up there, but they aren't. Since you created this unit three years ago, Chief, we've accomplished so much."

Saxon gave her a sad smile. "The FM feels you need someone with better credentials than what Jeff possesses. Tanner has a BS in chemistry like yourself. He's got six years with a fire department as an officer—"

"Paid or volunteer?"

"Paid. Does it make a difference to you?"

Brie grimaced. "You know it does. Paid fire fighters always think they're better than volunteers." She was unable to sit any longer and began to pace the length of the office in her low-heeled sandals. "That will be just one more hurdle I'll have to deal with him on. Once Tanner finds out I came up through the volunteer ranks, he'll challenge me." She turned. "Paids hate volunteers. It's pounded into their thick, Neanderthal skulls."

"Well, the way you're talking, you sound a bit prejudiced yourself, Brie."

A sour smile touched her lips, and she halted. "Guess I do, don't I?"

"It's commonly referred to as a chip on the shoulder, I think."

Her mood lightened momentarily at Saxon's gentle teasing. "Touché. I'd better look at myself first before I start hurling hand grenades at others."

"Perhaps, perhaps."

"Chief, why does the FM feel we need Tanner over Jeff, aside from the degree he holds?"

"They want the best for Quadrant One, Brie. Things are heating up. You know that," he answered quietly.

Her green eyes narrowed. "Because of John's murder?"

"We don't know if it was a murder yet, Brie. At least not officially."

"That's a bunch of—"

"Facts, Brie, facts. Until we have proof from that ongoing investigation, John's death has been officially listed as accidental."

"That call we answered was rigged! I saw the photographs that were taken right after John got killed. Freshly painted fifty-gallon drums sitting by an old warehouse in Cleveland where only rats lived is suspicious. You'd expect rusted drums instead. I saw those wires leading to the drums, Chief. It was murder." She took a deep, ragged breath. "Is that it? Tanner's older, more mature? They don't want someone of Jeff's age with me. They want me to defer important decisions to the man?"

Saxon must have heard the edge to her voice because he frowned. "If you remember nothing else from this conversation, Brie, remember this: *You* are in charge. Tanner is a rookie, as far as I'm concerned. The moment he disobeys you, he's done." He opened the file. "And I intend to make that particular point very clear to him, believe me. I won't have you hassled in any way."

Her shoulders sagged, and suddenly feeling the stress of the last three months, Brie wearily sat down. "You don't deserve my anger or frustration over this whole thing."

"It's all right," Saxon admitted unhappily, also sitting. "At sixty-five, maybe I'm getting too old to handle this job any more. It used to be that a haz-mat spill was bread and butter. Now, with a probable murder of one of my best people, the rules of the game are changing. I feel like a fish out of water." He folded his hands and gave her a sober look. "I was a fire chief for thirty-nine years, Brie, not a cop. And with this situation, we need law-enforcement direction. Fire fighters aren't policemen. John Holcomb's death has proven that." He released a long sigh and sought out her intelligent gaze.

"Look, Tanner comes with top recommendations. Maybe the FM's right: you need a more mature, older partner. John was three years younger than you, Jeff is four. Tanner is thirty-three to your twenty-nine. He's been around. Here, take a look at his file."

Brie reluctantly took the file and settled back in the chair. She groaned, giving Saxon an I-don't-believe-it-look. "Ex-Marine lieutenant? Oh, wonderful, Chief. Now I know he'll be a male chauvinist hunting for me!"

"He was a mine and explosives expert in the service, though," Saxon pointed out, but that angle didn't soothe her distress.

Brie gave him a flat look. "There's no war going on, Chief. We aren't hunting bangalores, land mines or rockets. Just hazardous material."

She knew Saxon wasn't so sure with the powerful criminal element in the Youngstown-Cleveland area, which was part of her territory to protect and cover. And despite all her objections, she could see Saxon only wanted her safe at any cost. After the explosion in Cleveland, Brie had been in a coma for nearly five days before becoming conscious. Saxon must have seen with brutal clarity the third-degree burns that had scarred her back, right shoulder and arm. She had also suffered internal injuries and had spent three months recovering in a hospital.

Brie couldn't hide from Saxon the emotional scars that had resulted from the incident. He'd felt it best to get her a new partner in order to take her mind off the horror. Jeff Laughlin's youth, idealism and lack of chauvinism had helped her get back on her feet. Still, she knew the chief worried.

"Tanner does have a good background," Brie grudgingly admitted, handing the file to him. The initial resentment in her voice had disappeared.

Saxon breathed a sigh of relief. "If it makes you feel any better, Brie, I know how hard it's going to be on you dealing with two trainees at once." He spread his hands in a gesture of futility. "I tried to reason with the FM on this assignment, but he's made up his mind."

With a grimace, Brie leaned back in the chair. "Instead of sixty hours a week, it will now be seventy," she uttered tiredly.

"Maybe after the first month, you can get a couple of days off and let Jeff run the show with Tanner."

Brie pursed her lips. "By that time, I'll probably need it." She cast him a grin, rising to her five feet, eight inches. "So when do I meet Superman?"

Saxon opened his appointment book and peered at it through his bifocals. "Next week. Tuesday to be exact. Meet us over at Lock 24 Restaurant for lunch at noon, and I'll introduce him to you."

"You buying?"

He matched her grin. "Sure."

"I think I'm gonna have a cardiac arrest. This Tanner must really be important or you'd never spring for lunch, Chief."

Saxon escorted Brie to the door and opened it for her. "Now you've went and hurt my feelings. I occasionally buy you lunch when you get down our way.

Brie was barely able to suppress her growing smile. She felt her tension dissolving in the good-natured teasing. "Okay, I'll see you next Tuesday. Fair enough?"

"Fair enough."

Brie swung her white leather purse strap across her shoulder. At this time of year, when the May weather was turning mild and sunny, Brie usually wore pretty sundresses that showed off her shoulders and back. But since the explosion, she never wore anything that might expose her scars. She knew she'd retreated into a shell. Would she ever emerge?

As she began to walk away, Chief Saxon called out, "Hey, be careful out there."

"Yes, sir, boss," she said, throwing him a mock salute and a halfhearted smile. The smile disappeared almost immediately as she stepped through the air-conditioned modern building that included the Ohio State Fire Academy and the FM's office. Brie gave the place a tender look. She had taken her two hundred hours of fire training here. She had loved every minute of the grueling and demanding classes that turned her into a fire fighter. That was so many years ago.

She went out into the sunny afternoon, and a breeze ruffled her hair. Her mind swung to Linc Tanner. She formed his name on her lips, saying it softly. She could often get a feel for the individual by rolling the name off her tongue. His was a strong name, one that had no obvious weak facets, not like her name or how she felt presently. The murder of John had destroyed so much of her confidence. She wished she could change her name to connote a stronger facade. Maybe Gertrude. Now that was a strong, immovable name. Or Dagmar, another name that vibrated with strength. A gleam came to her eyes as she opened the door to her silver Toyota. At least her sense of humor had survived the explosion.

She slid in and closed the door, hungering for the warmth the sun provided. She dug the sunglasses from her purse and put them on. The headache throbbing in her temples was increasing: another gift from the explosion, she groused to herself, starting up the Toyota then backing out.

It was a long drive to her small house near the outskirts of Canton, and as Brie pulled into traffic, she wondered what kind of man Linc Tanner was. She prayed he had a streak of humanity in him because if he didn't, she wouldn't be able to cope with him.

Linc looked discreetly at his wristwatch. He had learned a long time ago to mask his impatience. Chief Saxon sat next to him at a table for four in a sunny corner of the restaurant. He gave Linc an apologetic look.

"Brie must be running a bit late," he said.

Like every woman I've ever known, Linc countered silently. "I think it's part of the female mystique."

Saxon's gray brows drew downward slightly. "Brie is normally on time to the second."

Strike one, Linc warned himself. He had met the grizzled, white-haired chief only a half hour ago, and he wasn't sure where Saxon stood on the subject of women in men's careers. It appeared Saxon was not a chauvinist, despite his age. Folding his hands and leaning his elbows on the table, Linc tried to cover his tracks. If Williams wasn't going to show up on time, he might as well buttonhole Saxon and find out the lay of the land a little more.

"It must make things a little more interesting having a woman in the ranks, chief."

"In what way, Mr. Tanner?"

Careful. Linc shrugged his broad shoulders beneath his red polo shirt. He was damned if he was going to climb into a business suit to meet Williams. He wore a suit to impress his date, not his boss. "I would imagine Ms. Williams adds a different perspective to things around here."

"Oh." Saxon grunted, reducing his defensiveness. "Brie gets along with everyone. The men in the hazmat unit treat her like a sister." Saxon chuckled. "To her, they're like brothers." His voice lowered. "Do me a favor, Mr. Tanner?"

"What?" Linc never promised anything before hearing what the request was.

"Don't mention John Holcomb's death to her. I know you and the FM had a closed-door meeting earlier, and I don't know what was discussed, but Brie is still very sensitive to John's death."

I wonder why? Was she his lover? Linc mentally cataloged all the possibilities. A woman didn't grieve like that without it having a sexual angle. "All right," Linc agreed slowly.

"If she brings it up, fine. But don't hit her on it. Frankly, I'm worried about Brie. I'm afraid you're meeting her at the worst possible time, and that's not fair to either of you. Brie is—well, how do I put it? She's a confident person with plenty of experience to back her up in the haz-mat area. There are few who can equal her savvy, enthusiasm and dogged adherence to principle."

Linc's brows fell. "What principle, Chief Saxon?"

Saxon watched the door, waiting to see Brie appear. "Northeast Ohio is the armpit of toxic waste problems mainly because it's the most industrialized part of the state. A lot of steel mills, chemical companies and tankers transporting the stuff make it a highly active area. Three years ago when she agreed to head up that quadrant, she made a promise to me. Brie knew of the waste disposal problems and the cheating that goes on up there by many of the companies. She wanted to clean them up."

Wonderful, now I have a raving fanatic on my hands to boot. "Go on."

"She and John made a great inroad on that promise. She has a list of chemical companies and facilities that use chemicals that she visits every month. Of course, none of the officials for any company are going to deny her access to their records because she can get a court order at the drop of a hat and force them to show her their files. They're running scared of her now. It used to be that some of these companies would send out their trucks loaded with toxic waste and order the drivers to dump then in some unsuspecting farmer's field, a roadside ditch or in a stream in the middle of the night. Reports of that kind of activity have fallen off almost seventy-five percent since Brie has put the pressure on these companies to produce records of when a truck hauling toxic waste is sent out and where its destination is, and then checking that destination to make sure it arrived and dispensed with the chemicals on its bill of lading.'' He smiled grimly. ''Brie has handed out a hell of a lot of citations, and the attorney general of the state has backed her to the hilt and prosecuted these companies. The fines these companies have had to pay run into the millions, and now they're wising up and deciding to play by the law and not get caught dumping illegally. They can't afford it anymore.''

Linc rubbed his jaw. ''Maybe that's what got Holcomb killed.''

Saxon gave him an unhappy look. ''There are over a hundred people whom she's had heavily fined. Holcomb's death could have been an act of revenge, a warning, who knows? She's too valuable to our continuing efforts to clean up waste disposal and toxic substances in our state. Oh, here's Brie now,'' Saxon said, and rose.

Linc tried to mask his surprise as a tall, slender woman made her way through the heavy noontime trade of the popular restaurant. Her sable-colored hair gleamed with gold highlights; wispy bangs barely brushed her brows. The one-piece uniform of dark

blue sporting patches on both arms, a gold badge over
her left breast pocket and gold name tag over the right
one made her look like someone in authority, Linc
decided. His gaze moved up to her face, and he decided to modify his first opinion. Although Brie had
a square face and that stubborn-looking chin, he
found himself staring into her huge dark green eyes,
which appeared almost catlike. And when his gaze
dropped to her delicious mouth, he felt his body
tighten with unexpected heat.

Shocked at his initial response to her, Linc main-
tained an unreadable expression on his face. What a
mouth, he thought: full, corners softly curved upward and lushly red. When he realized she wore no
makeup and that was the natural color of her lips, he
gave himself an internal shake. He'd thought there
wasn't a female alive who didn't plaster herself with
foundation, gobs of mascara for almost nonexistent
eyelashes, rouge for cheeks and lipstick. Brie had a
natural flush on her cheeks, which emphasized her
large eyes. And her lashes were so thick and long that
at first Linc would have sworn they were false. But
they weren't. Brie Williams wasn't like other women,
he grudgingly admitted, and grimaced, displeased with
his physical reaction to her. There wasn't much not to
like about her upon first meeting: nice body, attrac-
tive in an arresting fashion, and she moved like a gazelle. What the hell was she doing to him?

Brie risked a glance at the tall, ruggedly built man
in a red polo shirt and faded, well-worn jeans that
emphasized his superb build. He was scowling at her,
and she tried to gird herself against his obvious dislike of her. She turned her attention to Saxon.

"Hi, Chief," she said breathlessly, "I'm sorry I'm late. There was a tanker on I-76 without placards indicating what chemicals he was hauling, and I pulled him over."

Saxon patted her hand. "See, Mr. Tanner? I told you there would be a reason our Brie was late."

Linc slowly inclined his head toward her. He saw a great deal in her suddenly darkened eyes: distrust, wariness and fear. Why fear? Did he look like an ogre to her? More than likely. He managed a sour smile. "So you did, Chief Saxon, so you did."

Brie matched his scowl, immediately on guard against the insinuation in Tanner's carefully modulated voice. Had he accused her of being late because she was a woman? Brie felt anger surge through her, and she swallowed hard, holding his dark blue gaze.

"Brie, I'd like you to meet Linc Tanner, your new partner. Linc, this is Brie Williams."

Linc extended his long, tapered fingers. "Ms. Williams."

Brie slid her damp hand into his, very aware of his blatant maleness. "Mr. Tanner."

The waitress came up, shattering the icy tension. "Something to drink?" she asked them, smiling warmly at Linc.

"Coffee for me," he said.

Brie hadn't missed the waitress's moon-eyed reaction to Tanner. He wasn't pretty-boy handsome. No, his face had been molded by experience. Harsh experience, she would bet. There were deep lines at the corners of his eyes and grooves on either side of his well-shaped mouth. Despite his unshakable arrogance, Brie found herself liking Tanner's mouth because it wasn't as hard as the rest of his rugged

features, which could have been hewn out of stone.
"I'll have a vodka gimlet," she told the woman. It was
one of the few times that she would use alcohol to settle her taut nerves. One look at Tanner's disapprov-
ing look and her stomach automatically knotted.

"Drinking on the job?" he queried softly.

"It's my day off, Mr. Tanner. Do you object?"

Linc heard the warning in her husky voice. Strike
two. "I'm not your keeper, Ms. Williams. You drink
whenever you feel the need."

Brie gave him a sizzling glare, locking with his cobalt eyes. The arrogant bastard. He was gunning for
her. And right in front of the chief. Pulling the napkin into her lap, she fixed a brittle smile on her lips.
"I'm glad we agree on one thing, Mr. Tanner."

"So am I, Ms. Williams." He wanted to kick himself. He had stepped into it with her and he hadn't
meant to. Most women wouldn't have challenged his
innuendo. But she had. A part of him admired her
gutsiness. Not many women—or for that matter,
men—took him on.

Saxon cleared his throat, thanking the waitress
when she returned with their drinks and the menus. He
gave Tanner a warning that spoke volumes. "Brie
works fifty to sixty hours a week, Linc. It's rare she
gets a day off. And when she does, she's on twenty-
four-hour call for haz-mat accidents up in her quadrant. She made a special trip down here today to pick
you up and take you to Canton to start looking for an
apartment."

Linc inclined his head, a hint of amusement in his
eyes. "I owe the lady an apology then, plus thanks for
going an extra yard on my benefit." The car he had
driven from the East Coast had developed transmis-

sion trouble. The garage said it would take at least a week to repair, leaving Linc without any transportation. An auspicious start, he thought, to the whole assignment.

He saw her eyes widen momentarily, as if shocked by his sudden good manners. Good God, he wasn't an animal! And when Brie quickly averted her gaze and picked up her drink to take a healthy gulp, Linc felt a tinge of guilt. He missed nothing from being an agent for so many years. The fact that her long fingers trembled made him feel like a heel. He was supposed to protect her, get her confidence, not make life rough for her. If Cramer saw how he was behaving, he'd yank him off the case. Fortunately, Cramer wasn't around to see his spectacular hoof-and-mouth act, and Saxon didn't know his true identity, so he was safe. This time.

They ordered lunch, and Linc noticed Brie wanted nothing but a salad. The uniform she wore hung loosely on her, telling him she had lost weight. Of course, if he had been nearly killed, he wouldn't have much of an appetite, either. There were hints of shadows beneath Brie's eyes. She didn't get much sleep. Was it due to the trauma or just the fact that Saxon was working his people to death?

Linc folded his hands, resting his chin on them. "Fifty or sixty hours a week is a lot," he said to no one in particular.

"It doesn't do much for your personal life, either," Brie said, sipping her drink and hoping he would take her comment as a joke, which would ease the tension between them.

He met and held her nervous gaze. "Do you have one?"

He was taking her seriously! "If I did, it wouldn't be your concern, Mr. Tanner."

"Call me Linc. I don't like standing on formality any more than necessary."

"I would think with your military training, you'd enjoy it."

He picked up his cup, holding it to his lips. Saucy, aren't you? He took a sip of coffee. "What I learned in the military can't be applied too much in civilian life, Ms. Williams." Linc waited for her to drop her guard and ask him to call her by her first name just as he had done. But she didn't.

"That's what I told the chief: you can't apply war games to haz-mat."

Tanner smiled slightly. Okay, I'll let you play with me. I spat and hissed first, so now you get your turn. I'll take my lumps before the chief has a cardiac arrest in front of us. "From what I understand, haz-mat is taking on certain aspects of war."

Brie stiffened at his inference, her spine going rigid. "I hope you left your Marine Corps training where it belongs, in the past."

"I try to. But sometimes, in some situations, it comes in handy."

"One thing is in your favor for being in service, Mr. Tanner."

"What's that?" he asked amiably, deciding a friendlier tone might have a soothing effect on her.

"You know how to take orders."

His blue eyes gleamed as he held her gaze. "I also know when to question them, Ms. Williams. I don't just blindly walk into a situation without first assessing it properly.''

Brie was stung. Was Tanner hinting that she hadn't properly analyzed the situation in Cleveland that had gotten John killed?

## Chapter Two

Halfway through lunch, Chief Saxon's emergency beeper went off. He gave Brie and Linc an apologetic look and went to find a phone.

Linc leaped at the opportunity. Since his last idiotic comment, Brie had sat there pale and shaken. The fork she used to push the salad around in her bowl trembled from time to time.

"Listen, Brie," he said, using her first name deliberately, "I do owe you an apology. We got off on the wrong foot." He gave her a lopsided grin, trying to figure out how to dissolve the fear he saw in the depths of her jade-green eyes. "I think we've both had a pretty rough week, and we're a little more sensitive and jumpy than usual." He raised his hand, holding it out to her. "Forgiven?"

Brie stared at his large, well-shaped callused hand. The nails were short and blunt, the fingers beautifully tapered. Searching his pensive face, Brie tried to see if this was all a game with him. There was some undefinable nuance about him that made her instincts go on guard. Was it the look in Tanner's eyes? The glint in them told her on a gut level there was more to him than what he presented. He was a man of secrets. But what secrets? He made Brie uncomfortable. "You've got a razor for a tongue."

Linc winced. "Yeah, I know I do. Usually it gets me out of trouble, not into it. When I'm tired, I get crabby. My ex-wife would gladly tell you that." He kept his hand extended. "Well? Am I forgiven? Can we shake hands and start over?"

Some of her terror began to disintegrate, and she firmly shook Linc's hand. "Forgiven," she said, quickly retrieving her fingers. Had he noticed how damp and cold her skin was? If he did, he said nothing.

"But not forgotten," he added.

"I'd like to forget everything," Brie said, "and settle in for a long, hot bath and ten hours of uninterrupted sleep."

A glimmer came to his eyes. "Is that an invitation?"

Brie gave him a flat stare. It took her a few seconds to realize he was baiting her and wasn't serious. At least she didn't think he was. "Like I said before: you join haz-mat and you have no personal life to speak of, Mr. Tanner. It's probably just as well you're divorced because your wife wouldn't be seeing much of you anyway except late at night and in bed."

Linc speared a few French fries with his fork, his gaze never leaving Brie's. She was an open book, he realized. There was a translucence to her every expression, and her lovely eyes reflected everything she was feeling. That was good. He wouldn't have to work at prying things out of Brie. All he had to do was drop a verbal bomb, and she'd react plenty. "Is there anything more important than a night in bed? I could live with that."

"I'm sure you could, Mr. Tanner."

"You're beginning to sound like a prude, Ms. Williams. I didn't realize there were any left."

"I'm hardly a prude. What happens between two people should be private, not a topic for a luncheon meeting."

Linc grinned. "I've been told I have a terrible case of hoof-and-mouth disease. Think there's any truth to it?"

The man was impossible! But Brie found a grudging smile inching across her lips. "I don't mean to sound like I'm perfect, Mr. Tanner. I know I've got my share of faults, maybe not as obvious as some of yours."

Linc gave her a long, appraising look. "You look pretty perfect to me." When he saw the color rise in her cheeks, something wrenched inside his heavily guarded heart. Didn't men compliment her on her good looks? Not according to her reaction. "Bet you had to chase the boys away from your door when you were in college."

Brie managed a shy smile. "Being an honor student through four years in chemistry didn't leave me much time for anything else."

Linc rubbed his jaw, his smile warmer. Brie had a nice trait of being unassuming, which was a plus in his book. "Ouch. I barely scraped through."

"I imagine because you had the girls knocking down your door to get to you."

His laughter was free and rolling. How good it felt to laugh again. "What are you? A mind reader?"

Brie shook her head, her shoulders slowly relaxing. Maybe Tanner wasn't so arrogant after all. More than anything, Brie wanted to believe that he was just tired and out of sorts from his long trip from Washington. "With your good looks, it's pretty easy to figure out."

"Logic in a woman. A rare find," he murmured.

"A lot of women have logic, Mr. Tanner," she said stiffly, some of her defenses moving into place.

Careful, Linc. "Most of the women I've been around have little ability to add up one and one and make two. It's not an insult. Just an observation."

Brie toyed with her glass, enjoying the beaded coolness on her fingertips. "In this business, we go by the numbers and by the rules," she put in with an edge of warning. "I'm not going to automatically assume you have that capability, Mr. Tanner. Just because you're a man and men are supposed to be logical won't wash with me. You'll have to prove that out in the field to me before I believe it."

Linc sat up, frowning heavily. "I'll stack my logic up against yours anytime, Ms. Williams."

Brie gave him a tight grin. There was something within her that loved challenge and competition. And Linc Tanner had just triggered it. "Fair enough, Mr. Tanner. Just as I'll be assessing your abilities day in and day out, you can do the same to me." She leaned forward, all business. "With one major difference: the final decision rests with me, not you. Jeff Laughlin, the other rookie, will tell you that I openly encourage your input and observations, but in the end, the responsibility is mine.''

He didn't know whether to be angry with her or admire her. Now she was talking like a hard-nosed businessman, and not a woman. "That's damn democratic of you, boss."

She held his stormy gaze calmly. "I'll give you the chance you deserve, Mr. Tanner. I only hope you'll extend that same courtesy to me and try to overlook the fact I'm a woman."

"That's going to be hard to do."

"You haven't worked around many women, have you?"

Linc was unsettled by her insight into him. "I never mix business with pleasure. Anything wrong with that?" he drawled.

Brie colored beneath his digging inspection. "In this case, yes. I'm a woman dealing with you in a business function. Something that I'm sure has never happened to you before, since you were a fire fighter and there are few women in the ranks."

"Right again, Ms. Williams. But in your case, I see no reason we can't mix a little business and pleasure."

"Am I supposed to be flattered, Mr. Tanner?"

Linc gave her a disarming smile. "I would hope so."

Brie saw Chief Saxon returning, his face serious. She blotted her mouth with her napkin. "I would never have thought you were a dreamer, Mr. Tanner."

He shrugged his broad shoulders. "Who knows? I like to learn from every new situation. Maybe I'll find out logic and fantasy do mix."

Brie shot him a withering look meant to deflate his ego. "Now who's being illogical?"

Linc was about to answer when he caught Saxon out of the corner of his eye. The chief sat down and directed his conversation to Brie.

"Looks like McPeak has a good one going down near Dayton."

Brie was relieved to get back to what she knew best: haz-mat. In that area, she felt safe and secure. Or she had before the explosion. Still, it was an escape from Linc Tanner's challenging blue gaze and the dangerous parrying with him. "Oh?"

"Yeah, train derailment. Seems a couple of tank cars carrying some nasty chemical combinations have overturned and are burning. Jim's having to call in quite a few of the surrounding fire departments to help coordinate a mass evacuation near Englewood where it occurred."

"Sounds pretty serious. Any loss of life?"

Saxon blotted his forehead with his handkerchief. "None so far, thank God."

Brie gave Tanner a glance. "Well, there goes the rest of my day off."

"What do you mean?" Linc asked.

She patted the beeper that was hanging from her right pocket. "When McPeak gets a bad haz-mat incident, we get one, too. Don't ask me why. It just seems to happen that way."

"Better not," Saxon said gruffly, handing the check and some bills to the waitress.

"Why?" Linc wanted to know.

Brie rose and slipped the strap of the purse across her shoulder. "Because Jeff's over in Pennsylvania visiting his folks until Sunday afternoon. That would leave just me to handle the call. Chief Saxon believes in two heads being better than one in handling a haz-mat incident, and I agree." She held up crossed fingers. "Chief, let's hope McPeak's curse doesn't land on us like the bluebird of happiness."

Saxon grinned, putting his hand on her shoulder. "Is that like cows flying, Brie?"

Her laugh was full. "One and the same, Chief. Thanks for lunch. I'll get Mr. Tanner's gear, and we'll head for Canton."

They emerged from the restaurant and found the sunlight blinding and the bright blue Ohio sky sporting a few puffy clouds. Linc followed a bit behind Brie, openly admiring her. She was built more like a cat than a gazelle, he decided. There was definitely a feline grace to her walk and a nice, easy movement to her swaying hips. Maybe this assignment wasn't going to be as horrendous as he had first thought. Despite her defensiveness, Brie had a decent sense of humor. And she looked like an ingenue of twenty-three, not twenty-nine.

"Well, here's your home away from home, Tanner." Brie stopped and gestured to the large white van sporting huge red letters on each side that said: Fire Marshal's Office, Hazardous Material Team. "This van is affectionately called the white whale because it looks like one." She looked up at his serious face.

"Any relation to Moby Dick?"

She smiled. "I hope not. We don't need haz-mat trucks gobbling up people. Is your gear at the Fire Academy?"

"Yeah. With my car in for repair, the chief let me put my suitcases at the dormitory."

Brie unlocked the passenger side door and opened it for him. She saw him grin. "Chauvinism is dead, Tanner. You might as well get used to it."

He chuckled indulgently. "If you say so, Ms. Williams."

Brie ignored his irreverent humor and climbed into the driver's seat. She put on the safety belt and started up the van, all the while noticing that Tanner was looking over the various supplies inside. She headed out of the parking lot.

"Impressive," he murmured, gesturing toward the rear. "Air packs, holding drums for toxic waste, gas suits. I can see no expense was spared to put this baby together."

"When you realize Ohio is number two in the nation for toxic spills, you know why, Tanner. Chief Saxon single-handedly created the concept of splitting the state up into four quadrants, manning each one with a truck and two haz-mat techs to protect our people." She pulled out into the lazy Saturday traffic, heading for the Fire Academy, which was located only a few miles away.

Linc faced front, and his gaze swept across the complex radio equipment that had been installed in the dashboard. There were special radios for the state police and for sheriff and fire departments. "There must be twenty thousand dollars wrapped up in this equipment alone," he said, whistling.

"Close to it. If we have a full-scale haz-mat incident, it's imperative we be able to get hold of all agencies in order to help evacuate the people who might be harmed by a spill."

He nodded. "I'm impressed as hell."

A slight smile appeared on Brie's mouth. "Wait," she told him softly, catching his glance. "There's a natural high you get from coordinating such a massive effort. Not that I wish for those sorts of spills, but I like the knowledge that from this truck, we can mobilize an entire county, if need be, from Disaster Services right up to the Red Cross in a matter of minutes."

Linc digested her fervor. She loved her job. It was obvious from the luminous quality that had suddenly sprung to life in her bleak-looking eyes. "I can tell you've handled a few of those."

"A few. And so far, my record is clean. Well, almost," Brie said, stumbling.

"What do you mean?"

"Before John was murdered, in every call we answered in the past three years, there had been no loss of life." Her voice dropped to a whisper. Brie hadn't meant to discuss John with Tanner, but her enthusiasm for her job opened the guarded door to her grieving heart.

"I'm sorry it happened, Brie."

She trembled; his husky voice was like thick, golden honey soothing her aching heart. "Thanks, Tanner."

"Don't you think we can begin to act civil with one another and call each other by our first names?"

He was right, Brie realized. She had been deliberately holding him at arm's length because of the red flag her instincts had waved in front of her face. There was a searching quality to his voice. He wanted to smooth the waters between them, too. "Okay," Brie agreed reluctantly. "Call me anything you want as long as it isn't derogatory."

"How about if it's provocative?"

She glanced at him, again aware of the amusement in his eyes. With a laugh she said, "You're incorrigible, Linc Tanner."

He settled back in the seat, a pleased expression on his face. "So I've been told, Ms. Brie Williams, so I've been told."

Brie stifled a yawn. The interstate stretched long and boringly in front of her as she drove the haz-mat truck toward Canton.

"Want me to take over for a while?" Linc asked, realizing how tired Brie was becoming. Those faint shadows beneath her eyes were darkening.

She shook her head. "No, thanks. We've only got little over an hour to go. Why don't you get us some coffee from that thermos down there. I filled it before meeting you at the restaurant."

Linc picked up the battered aluminum thermos, noting its quart size. "Who drinks this much coffee?" he asked, twisting off the cap.

"Me. There have been times when all I've lived on for three or four days were coffee and nerves." She looked at him, offering him a slight smile. "Comes with the territory."

"Saxon didn't warn me about that," Linc groused good-naturedly, handing her half a cup of the steaming coffee.

"Thanks," Brie said. "He probably didn't tell you too much for fear you'd turn down the job."

"Then you weren't stretching the truth about putting in sixty hours a week."

"Stick around and find out."

He rested one booted foot on the dash. "I intend to do just that."

"Real masochist, aren't you?"

"Nah, I'm a red-blooded American man who believes in Mom, apple pie and Corvettes."

"Corvettes?"

He gave her an innocent look. "Sure."

"Expensive taste."

"Superb," he agreed contentedly, pouring himself a cup of coffee then recapping the thermos.

"Bet you've never eaten any humble pie."

His grin tore at her senses.

"I said apple pie, not humble pie."

She joined his laughter, sensing that Tanner's arrogance shielded a solid layer of confidence. She fervently hoped so. Maybe Chief Saxon had been right. She needed a partner who was more mature than her own twenty-nine years. Still, Tanner wasn't exactly the answer to her dreams. He was a chauvinist of the first order, and she knew they would butt heads on just who was the boss. He was a man with secrets, possibly. She'd have to sit back, use her considerable patience and watch. With time, he'd reveal parts of his real self.

"I can tell you from lots of experience that humble pie isn't as good as apple pie," Brie said.

"I don't see you eating too much of that."

She shrugged, gazing at the rolling green countryside of Ohio. She always enjoyed the drive to and from Canton; most of it was comprised of farms, silos, dairy herds and hundreds of acres of corn. "A long time ago, when I joined the fire department in Litton out of college, I used to think I was really something."

"What happened to change your mind about that part of yourself?"

Brie was pleased with his interest in her as a person. "Anyone ever accuse you of asking good questions?"

Linc sipped his coffee. "Not recently. Ask my ex-wife, JoAnne, that, and she'll give you a very different answer."

"That's the second time you've mentioned your divorce. It must be pretty fresh."

"Am I that obvious?"

"Mack trucks usually are," Brie said, giving him a warm smile meant to take any sting from her comment.

"Guess I drove into that one, didn't I?" Linc returned, thinking her whole face became breathtakingly beautiful when she genuinely smiled. He saw a glimmer of light in her eyes and for no reason, it made him feel good, even if the joke had been at his expense. *Where are your claws, little cat? You're a woman, and I know you have a set.*

"Just shows you aren't perfect, that's all."

He feigned a hurt look. "Most women think I am."

"All except JoAnne, remember?"

Giving her a sober glance, Linc agreed. "In all honesty, it wasn't Jo's fault. I was gone too much of the time."

"The fire service is tough on marriages," Brie agreed.

Linc said nothing. In the bio given to Chief Saxon, he had been a lieutenant in a fire department for the past six years, with specialization in the field of hazardous material. For some reason, he didn't like lying to Brie. There was a freshness to her that he'd never encountered in a woman before, and he didn't want her to think negatively of him. At some point in the future, she would eventually be told who he really was and his reason for being with her. Linc studied her profile for several minutes, wondering how Brie would take that information. Would she hate him? Distrust him?

And then he pulled himself up short. Why should he care what she thought of him after this case was out in the open and solved? One look at her and those soft lips curved gently upward and Linc knew why but refused to acknowledge the answer.

"Tell me, what's a marshmallow like you doing in a job like this? It's got to be tough on you emotionally."

Brie pushed her fingers though her short hair, giving Linc an unsettled look. "You calling me a marshmallow?"

Linc sat back, arms across his chest. "It's not an insult, you know. I pride myself in knowing people pretty well on first meeting. Despite your tough act, you're basically a pretty gentle woman. The two don't mix chemistrywise with a job like this."

Now he was playing amateur psychologist, Brie thought, a bit of panic racing through her. No one had ever been able to see the real her beneath her uniform and title. She had never allowed anyone that privilege. And now, Linc Tanner had peeled her open, and she didn't like it. "Even if I was that so-called marshmallow you accuse me of being, who said it matters?"

Linc treaded carefully, hearing the challenge in her voice. "Far be it from me to say a marshmallow can't be effective in a job."

Brie cast him a look. "That's big of you, Tanner."

"So you are a marshmallow."

"I didn't say that."

He grinned widely, which made him look boyish suddenly, instead of hard. "If the shoe fits, wear it. In this case, you practically admitted you're a marshmallow."

Disgruntled, Brie pulled a map of Canton from the side pocket on her seat and handed it to him. "If you want something to do, open this up and take a look at it. It's a map of Canton. You have to decide where you want to look for an apartment or house."

Unfolding the map, Linc was still grinning. "What's wrong with being a marshmallow? Did I say there was anything wrong with them? I happen to like marshmallows. They're all soft inside. And sweet—"

"One more word out of you, Tanner, and—"

He gave her an innocent look, realizing how delightful she was to tease. "Okay, boss lady, I'll read the map." He pretended to study it, then after a few minutes he lifted his head and murmured, "I like hot dogs roasted over an open fire. Nothing like a few well-toasted marshmallows for dessert—"

"Tanner, you're really bucking the odds."

He met her flashing green eyes. "If I say I'm sorry, would that count?"

"No, because you wouldn't mean it."

Linc suddenly laughed. "Has anyone told you, Ms. Williams, that you're fun to tease?"

"On second thought, you're not a masochist. You're a sadist."

He had the good sense to bury his head in the map, giving Brie the space she needed from his unmerciful prodding.

Quiet settled into the van, and occasionally Brie would steal a glance at Linc. He had scrunched his well-built frame down into the seat, one foot resting lazily against the dash. She liked his ability to be laid back, and hoped that he would apply the same easy-going attitude to his dealing with haz-mat incidents.

Her heart beat hard when Linc turned his head and met her gaze with a heated look. Embarrassed that he had caught her inspecting him, Brie looked away. He could have needled her about it, but he said nothing, thank God. When had she ever met such a self-assured male? Never, her heart whispered. Somehow, that knowledge steadied her brittle confidence.

Over the years, Brie had met many fire fighters. Some of them had that unique confidence that emanated like a beacon from Linc. But Linc's strength, or whatever it was, was deeper, and her womanly instincts knew that. Brie smiled. She could just imagine what Tanner would say if he knew how she relied more on her gut instinct than on her so-called logic. That was all right, he'd find out soon enough. In the past three months, she'd gotten Jeff to switch to that life-saving internal equipment each person possessed.

Sadness engulfed her as Brie recalled with aching clarity that her gut instincts were screaming at her the day she and John approached the drums sitting just outside the abandoned warehouse on the seedy side of Cleveland. When the call had come in, her stomach had knotted instantly, which wasn't normal. John had smiled, shrugging it off.

"We'll be more careful," he had told Brie. And they had been, parking the haz-mat truck farther away than usual and using binoculars to size up the situation. When it didn't look dangerous, they decided to cautiously approach the freshly painted drums. Unconsciously, Brie rubbed her stomach, trying to shake off the dread that had nearly suffocated her as they walked toward them. It was only when they had changed the angle of their approach that she had spotted several red and gray wires coming out of the bottom of the center drum. The wires disappeared beneath the corrugated aluminum wall of the warehouse wall. She had pulled John to a halt, pointing toward the wires.

They had stood there staring at the drums that were still a good hundred feet away, talking over and assessing the new development. Her stomach was knotted so hard that Brie was in pain. Her heart was galloping in her breast, and her throat was constricted.

"What's your gut say?" John had asked softly, his hand coming to rest on her upper arm, as if preparing to pull her away from the drums.

"To get out of here. It's not right, John. I feel real bad."

"Okay, Brie. I'm going to keep the same distance from them and see if I can spot where those wires lead while you go back to the truck and get the nonsparking tools. This might be a job for the Cleveland bomb squad, not us. But we're going to have to get closer to find out."

"John, why don't you come with me? I don't feel good about this at all. Let's call the police instead and let them investigate it."

"I won't get any closer. I promise. Now go on. Get that box of tools for us."

Brie closed her eyes for a second, dragging in a ragged breath. Her insides felt like quivering jelly, and she broke out into a sweat.

"Brie?"

She jerked her head in Linc's direction, hearing the concern in his voice. The normal hardness was not in his face as he silently met and held her gaze. For a second, Brie wanted to cry. The feeling caught her off guard: she hadn't cried since getting out of the hospital. She had cried for John. She had cried for his wife, Carol, and their two-year-old girl, Susie. But she had never cried for herself. Hot, blinding tears stung her eyes, and Brie swiveled her head to face front. Trying to concentrate on the task of driving, she was mortified that Tanner had caught her with her guard down. What would he think if she suddenly burst into tears? He'd grumble something about it always being just like a woman to cry at the drop of the hat or some such garbage. Her fingers tightened on the wheel until her knuckles whitened.

Linc rested the map on his lap, directing all his attention to her. He had glanced over moments before and saw Brie visibly pale and a light film of perspiration glaze her flesh. What had triggered that kind of reaction? At first, he thought he had caused it by teasing her too much. But when he had softly called her name and she had swung toward him like a startled doe caught in a hunter's cross hairs, he knew differently. He saw genuine terror in the pools of her luminous eyes. He was no stranger to terror himself and recognized that whatever Brie carried within her was tragic and profound because it was affecting her physically.

He watched her expressive face close up and become unreadable. If he hadn't seen the transformation, Linc would never have believed it. Was this another facet to Brie? The embattled veteran of one too many horrifying accidents? Linc had seen fire fighters gradually lose their nerve to fight fires or peel injured or dead people out of gruesome auto wrecks. He recognized that same look in Brie's eyes, and his throat tightened with sudden emotion. The urge to reach out and place his hand on her tense shoulder and tell her everything was going to be all right nearly overpowered him. It took a supreme effort for him to sit quietly.

"I—I'm all right," she forced out in a low, strained voice.

He gave her a gentle smile meant to support her. "I don't know about you, but I could use another cup of coffee. Want some?" He held up the thermos. His ploy worked—he saw the terror slowly drain from her eyes, and her shoulders dropped to their normal position.

"That sounds like a good idea, thanks."

You're pretty cool, aren't you? You're in a lot of pain, but you hold your own. Linc's mouth tightened as he mulled over how Brie was able to shift gears quickly, from being frightened by something inside her to being calm and returning to the outer world, where she had to continue to function. That was good. Was her terror due to the accident? John Holcomb's death? He handed her the coffee, their fingers briefly touching. He felt how cold hers were, and again, to his own disbelief, he felt the urge to hold her in his arms and protect her.

You're getting old, Tanner. Let a woman with big, beautiful green eyes that are marred with pain come near you, and you want to protect her. What's gotten into you? Separate, pal, separate. She's supposed to be protected from a possible criminal element. No involvement. It will screw up your reflexes, and that won't be good for her or you if someone's gunning for her.

Linc settled back, sipping the hot coffee. He repeated the litany in his head several times before all those new feelings Brie had brought to life in him had been erased.

The silence in the truck was broken by a call coming over one of the radios. Which one? Linc wasn't sure until Brie reached for the mike closest to the driver's seat.

"Remind me to kill McPeak the next time we see him," she muttered, switching one of the dials to a new position.

Linc sat up. "Why?"

"This is the Ohio state police calling. The only time they contact us is when there's a haz-mat accident on our turf."

He listened with interest to the radio conversation. Without being told to, he picked up the small clipboard that swung from a hook on the dash, and wrote down the location of the accident, the types of chemicals involved and the numbers on the truck placards.

Brie's scowl deepened as the trooper read off the numbers.

"FM 26, he's got two placards. One is 1050 and the other is 9161."

Linc started to reach for a small manual entitled Hazardous Materials Emergency Response Guidebook to find out what the numbers meant. But before he even opened the booklet, Brie was saying, "Sergeant, that's anhydrous hydrochloric acid and zinc sulfate."

"What kind of danger does that present?"

Plenty, Brie wanted to answer. Instead, she kept her voice impersonal and calm. "What's the status on the tanker carrying the chemicals?"

"It's resting on its side along the berm."

"From your position, can you see any of the contents leaking out?"

"Not that I can see. I have the driver with me. He escaped injury and ran from the truck."

Brie turned to Linc. "I would, too." She switched the mike on. "We'll be on scene with you in—" she glanced at her watch "—twenty minutes, Sergeant D'Onofrio. Until then, block that entire stretch of road one-half mile away on either side of the actual accident. If there is a leak, the fumes from the hydrochloric acid, if breathed in, can kill. Alert the nearest fire department and have them on the scene and standing by."

"Roger, FM 26. We'll be looking for you shortly."

Grimly, Brie hung up the mike. "Well, you wanted some excitement, Tanner, you've got it."

Linc held up his hands in a gesture of surrender. "Hey, this is McPeak's fault, not mine."

Brie managed a slight smile, dividing her attention between driving and rustling through a series of manuals between the chairs. "Cross your fingers that tanker hasn't sprung any leaks. If it hasn't, clean up can go pretty smoothly and quickly."

He reached for the manual she placed her hand on. "How quick? I'm beat."

"It's five o'clock now. If we're lucky, maybe three or four hours. Take this manual and look up those two chemicals. Acquaint yourself with the safety procedures regarding each of them."

"You know them by heart, don't you?"

"Backward and forward, but that isn't going to help train you. We've got time before we arrive on scene, so bone up, Tanner."

He began paging through the thick index of more than a thousand chemicals. "Yes, ma'am," he drawled.

Brie reached up to a panel overhead and flipped on a switch. The red and white light bar came on, whirling brightly above the cab. She pressed more firmly on the accelerator, making the van move at a brisk sixty-five miles an hour. Time was of the essence.

Silence settled into the cab again, but Brie's mind was working at a feverish rate. Her heart was pumping hard. The very thought that the serious accident could erupt into a full-scale explosion and loss of life shook her deeply. Before John's death, Brie had never felt worried like this. Now, her hands were damp and sweaty and her breathing came fast with each call. She was scared. Swallowing against the burgeoning fear, Brie forced herself to focus on the contingency plans that might have to be initiated once they arrived.

Linc watched Brie change like a chameleon before him as they drew up next to several white state police cars that blocked the two-lane highway. Troopers in gray uniforms were directing traffic to turn around. In the distance, Linc could see an eighteen-wheeler tipped over, its elliptical tank rusty looking. Not a good sign, he thought, climbing out of the truck with Brie.

Brie met Linc at the back of the van. As she unlocked the rear doors, she said, "Stick close, watch and listen."

He nodded, settling his hands on his hips, noticing the crowds of interested spectators who had pulled their cars over to look at the accident. "Any other way I can help?"

"I wish," Brie answered fervently, pulling the doors open and slipping a pair of high-powered binoculars out of their case. She gave him a quick look. "Thanks just the same."

"I feel like a three-legged dog—useless."

A bare hint of a smile touched her mouth as they walked toward the four state troopers. "I happen to like dogs. They're good companions."

He looked down, openly admiring Brie's demeanor. With a job like this and all kinds of pressures on her, she could have been cold, huffy or defensive. Instead, she was trying to put him at ease and make him feel needed! Grudgingly, Linc admitted that was a good sign of leadership, something he hadn't ever seen in a woman before. With that new lesson, Linc decided to relax slightly and learn from her. Sergeant D'Onofrio gave Brie a look of relief as she approached him. Did Brie have that kind of effect on all men? he wondered, suddenly a bit jealous.

Brie gave the sergeant a nod. She listened gravely to his report, all the while scanning the tanker through her powerful binoculars. Above all the confusion, the crowd and the blaring radios, she was wildly aware of Linc beside her. Some of her fear abated because she felt an overwhelming sense of protectiveness emanating from him. How was that possible? They had known each other only three or four hours. Unable to give the thought more attention, Brie tucked it away for a later time when she would be able to examine the discovery more closely.

She handed Linc the binoculars. "From all signs, I don't see any cracks in the tanker's skin, and the lid on top looks secure. Sometimes they get sprung, and that's where most leaks will occur."

Linc scanned the wreckage. He was flattered that Brie gave him the binoculars. That implied a certain amount of trust, and he was at once surprised and pleased. Another sign of a good leader—make your people feel involved and important to the total effort. How could a woman know so much about leadership?

Brie stared at Linc, watching his mouth purse as he studied the tanker. Now she would see how he responded under actual working conditions. If anything, he had grown quieter and calmer. A good sign. "Do you see anything?"

"Nothing," he said, handing her the binoculars, "but that tanker is old and rusty. I wouldn't trust it."

"Right." She turned to the trucker who stood nearby. "Have you contacted the tanker's company?"

"Yes, ma'am, I have. They're sending out another tanker from a local company to come and drain the contents from the truck when you give the word."

"Are the cables leading to that truck battery still attached?"

"Yes, ma'am, they are." He was a short man with an ample belly beneath his white T-shirt. "Ordinarily, I'd cut them, but I didn't know if the sparks might set the chemicals on fire if there was a leak," he apologized.

Brie nodded. She'd have to go in with the non-sparking tool kit and cut the wires leading to the battery, or a fire could occur if conditions were right. "Fine," she answered absently. "We'll take care of it. Linc, let's go."

Linc followed her to the rear of the haz-mat truck. She climbed into the back—she was almost able to stand up in it—and took a silver suit with a hood from the wall.

"What are you doing?" he demanded, scowling.

"I'm going to get suited up and go in there to cut the cables, then inspect the tank."

"Well, where's my suit?"

She sat down on the bumper, nudging off her low-heeled shoes and slipping her long legs into the attached boots of the one-piece suit. "You don't have one yet. Your measurements were taken only today. It's still on order for you."

"What about that suit?" he protested, pointing to a second one hanging on the wall.

Brie shook her head, sitting again. "That's Jeff's, and it won't fit you. You're too big for it, Tanner. Here, help me get the air pack over my shoulders."

Muttering a curse under his breath, Linc lifted the forty-pound air pack off its holder and spread the array of nylon straps aside so that Brie could struggle into it. "I don't like this, Brie. You shouldn't be going in there without a partner. That's the law of fire fighting: you always work on the buddy system."

She felt the weight of the air pack on her shoulders and pulled the nylon straps to tighten them. She snapped the latches closed across her breast and stomach, then shrugged a few times to settle the tank comfortably against her. "Normally, I'd agree with you. But I can't allow you to go near that tanker without being properly protected. You might breath in hydrochloric acid or step in it, or it might explode. You need the safety this suit offers."

Running his fingers through his hair, Linc said, "Let me put on an air pack and go in with you." No woman could handle a task like that alone. How could she recognize battery cables from other cables in a huge truck engine?

Brie was grateful for his help in getting the bulky suit up and over the air pack. The silver-colored material of the gear glared in the dying rays of the sun hovering on the western horizon. She closed the crotch-to-throat Velcro and tested her breathing apparatus. Everything worked fine. Linc held the silver hood in his hands. "I appreciate your concern, but it's impossible." Her voice turned grim. "I've already had one partner die, and I'll be damned if you'll be the second because I overlooked a point of safety." She slipped on the oxygen mask, which fitted over most of her face. She tightened the rubber straps on either side until it was sealed, keeping her from breathing any poisonous fumes.

Linc suspended his protests, realizing this wasn't the time or place to argue. Brie needed his support, not his dissension in the face of a crisis. He lowered the hood and sealed it to her shoulders. A large glass plate showed her beautiful green eyes and thick lashes and nose behind the clear plastic of her oxygen mask. "How can I communicate with you?" he demanded, raising his voice.

Brie pointed to a small radio inside her suit and to a similar one on Jeff's. "Just put on the headpiece and take Jeff's radio off his suit," she shouted, her voice muffled.

At least he'd have radio contact with her! Linc slipped on the slender headpiece with the mike close to his lips. She picked up the toolbox, and he followed her around the van.

"Are you sure you know where the battery cables are located at the back of that truck?"

Brie almost laughed but had the good sense not to. "Yes, I know where they're at."

Linc rubbed his jaw, giving her a dubious look. "You sure?"

"Look, I know by now you don't think women are of much use beyond the bedroom."

"I didn't say that."

"Yes, you did." She met and held his cobalt gaze. "Put your prejudice aside and maybe you'll find out that women can understand mechanical and electrical things, too."

Linc clamped his teeth together, his jaw rigid. The looks she received from the bystanders made him want to laugh: the people were reacting as if a Martian had landed. The bulky silver suit did resemble something from outer space. Brie walked with surprising agility in the cumbersome outfit, but then, she was a feline.

Linc went with her as far as the troopers' cars. He gripped her arm, gently swinging her around. "You be careful out there, kitten. You get into trouble, you call me. Understand?"

Brie's eyes widened momentarily as his raspy voice came through the headset she wore. A heady warmth suddenly blanketed her, and she felt an exquisite sensation at his concern. A tiny shiver of pleasure raced up her spine when his voice dropped intimately at the word kitten. "I will, Linc. And thanks." She smiled. "See, even three-legged dogs are valuable."

That was her last contact with him for the next ten minutes. Linc paced back and forth, watching as Brie made her way toward the tanker with the small toolbox in her left gloved hand. When she finally reached the rusty, battered truck and leaned into the truck engine and cut the cable wires, his heart began a slow, uneven pounding. He stood, legs apart, binoculars to his eyes, watching her every move. Brie, be careful! he told her silently. The what ifs overwhelmed him. What if there was a leak in some unknown place? What if there was a spark if she cut the wrong cable and it caught fire? She could easily be killed in the resulting explosion. What if her air pack suddenly stopped working? She could suffocate in minutes if she couldn't get out of that suit to fresh air. What if the breathing apparatus developed a leak and she breathed in some of those deadly fumes? She could be dead before he would be able to race that half a mile to rescue her.

Muttering another curse, Linc swore violently that this would be the last time Brie would ever go anywhere by herself. She needed a man around in case anything happened! She wasn't able to handle a situation like this by herself! He punched down the radio button. "Talk to me, Brie. What's going on? What do you see?" His voice came out in a low growl of impatience.

Brie felt immediate relief when she heard Linc's voice. Talking used too much oxygen. If she were breathing lightly and evenly, she would have twenty-five minutes of air. If, like today, her breathing was choppy and erratic, she had perhaps twenty minutes.

She climbed down from the rear of the truck and approached the tanker. Her eyes narrowed as she quickly took in the condition of the rusted tanker. "I don't see anything yet. I'll let you know, Linc. Got to conserve my air. Out."

With painstaking care, Brie examined every square inch of the overturned tanker. The tank was badly dented, and she got down on her hands and knees to slide her gloved hand along the area where the tank rested on the berm. If there was any leak, the dirt would be dark and damp.

Brie knew that it was possible the entire truck might shift down unexpectedly. If it did, her fingers, if not her entire hand or lower arm, would be caught and crushed. Then she could be trapped, and in far greater danger. Sweat trickled down her brows and into her eyes. She shut them tightly, then blinked a few times. The sun was still warm even at six o'clock, and sweat was running freely down her body. The suit acted like a sauna. It was a great way to lose five pounds in a half hour's time. Except she needed to gain weight, not lose it.

As she neared the top of the tank, she stood up and minutely inspected the hatch and shoring mechanism, making sure it wasn't sprung. The lid was plenty tight. Brie got back down on her hands and knees, continuing her inspection. Finding no change in the dirt, she went to the other side of the truck and crawled in between the huge tires and axles, hunting for leaks. Her breath was coming in ragged gasps. She had to be careful not to tear her suit on the jagged metal sticking out at odd angles from the truck. If there was a leak, one tear could be her death. Chemicals were quickly breathed in by the pores of the skin, and that could kill her just as though she had breathed them in through her mouth and nose.

"Brie?"

Linc's voice was quietly furious. He's probably lost sight of me, she thought, making her way toward the cab of the truck on all fours. "Nothing so far. Lid's secure."

"You've got five minutes of air left." That wasn't a comment, it was an order for her to get away from the truck.

Brie smiled and slowly made her way out of the tangle of wheels and torn truck cables and stood near the cab. "Roger. On my way out now. Tell Sergeant D'Onofrio that the truck's secure. There's no danger of a leak."

## Chapter Three

Linc's eyes were burning with obvious concern as he walked the last hundred yards from the barricade of police cars and met her. Without a word, he helped her out of the hood. The fresh air felt heavenly, and Brie closed her eyes as she loosened the rubber straps of her face mask. She pulled it over her head, breathed in deeply, then gave him a welcoming smile.

"I never lose the wonder of taking the first deep breath after wearing this gear."

Linc's mouth was a thin line as he walked at her side toward the van. "You may be the boss, lady, but that's the *last* time you ever go into a situation by yourself." He still didn't believe she had been able to cut the battery cables by herself, much less make sure there was no leak.

Brie gave him an understanding look. "If it makes you feel any better, I didn't like the idea of going in alone, either."

He tried to ignore the natural warmth that emanated from her. The crisis had brought them together as a team, and he found himself reacting like a team member. "Like I said, it's the last time that's going to happen. So many things could have gone wrong." His jaw tightened and his mouth worked as he wrestled with emotions he refused to share with her.

"They'll have a suit for you by next week, Linc," she soothed. "Chief Saxon will give us a call when it's ready."

Partly mollified, Linc nodded. "For whatever it's worth, you really bring out my protective side, lady."

She smiled, amusement in her dark jade eyes. "Don't look so distraught over it happening, Tanner. It's not a disease, you know."

Linc didn't have time to respond to her obvious teasing. Brie was hounded by a television camera crew and two local newspaper reporters the moment she stepped beyond the line of state police cars. He hated reporters with passion and stepped in front of her to protect her from their rabid charge, placing his bulk between them like a wall. Brie gave him a silent thank-you and escaped to the rear of the van to change. The reporters were behaving like spoiled children because he was an unknown who had broken up their charge.

"Hey, buddy," one freckle-faced reporter with carrot-red hair called, "who do you think you are? We have a right to interview Ms. Williams!"

Linc stood with his arms crossed. Sergeant D'Onofrio joined him, looking equally menacing.

"You'll get your interview when we're done coordinating this haz-mat cleanup," Linc growled back.

"If you're with the haz-mat people, why aren't you in uniform?"

Linc glared at the pushy little reporter. "It was my day off. Now do us all a favor and stand back. When we're done, you'll get to talk to Ms. Williams. But not now."

"But," the television reporter cried out, "I've got to make the eleven o'clock news!"

"You're breaking my heart. When are you reporters going to learn you can't interfere in a crisis like this? You wait your turn."

The trooper at his shoulder allowed a hint of a grin to appear as they watched the newspeople reluctantly disperse.

"Couldn't have said it better myself, Mr. Tanner. If I did that, my post would get accused of being uncooperative with the news media."

Linc snorted, dropping his hands to his sides. "I hate those people, if you can call them that. They're always underfoot."

The sergeant smiled, looking past Linc. He spotted the tanker that had been dispatched to come and pump the contents from the damaged one making its way slowly toward them. "I've worked a couple of times with Brie, and it's my opinion she allows those reporters too much time. She gives in to their demands."

"She won't any more," Linc promised, turning and walking to the back of the van. Brie was putting on her shoes when he rounded the corner. Her hair was dark with sweat and plastered against her head, the bangs hanging limply over her eyebrows. The heavy, protective gear, had made her perspire, and her one-piece uniform clung to her body as a result. He appreciated her slender lines.

"Do me a favor?" Brie asked, lifting her head as she tied her shoelaces.

"Name it."

"In the front, between the seats, is a jug of water. I'm dying of thirst. Can you—"

"I'll get it. You just sit there and rest for a minute."

Brie swallowed her smile, aware of Linc's exaggerated protectiveness. John had given her a similar, although not as powerful, sense of care. Jeff didn't, but perhaps that was because of his age. Linc came back and handed her a plastic glass. The water was lukewarm but it tasted wonderful anyway. She drank three glasses before her thirst was sated. Thanking him, she stood and touched her hair. With a grimace, she tried to tame the wet strands into some order, then gave up.

"You look beautiful just the way you are," Linc said.

"You have strange taste, then."

He shared her smile, watching the golden flecks of life in her eyes. "I have good taste, though. Does that count, Ms. Williams?" he asked her in a gritty tone.

Brie's heart thumped at the sudden intimacy between them. She felt heat flooding her cheeks, and avoided his intense blue stare. "The tanker's here," she stammered, avoiding his question altogether. "Come on, I want to talk with the driver before the troopers allow him through."

Linc followed, keeping an eye on the restless band of reporters nearby. Good, they were staying out of the way—for once. Brie spoke at length with the driver, and Linc found himself in awe of her knowledge of the equipment to be used, of pumping procedures and of how to safely take the chemicals out of the overturned vehicle. No woman could know that much about mechanics!

Climbing into the van, Brie motioned for him to come inside. She was allowing him to go with her! Then he decided since they were going to the overturned truck, he'd personally check for leaks, not trusting Brie's inspection. The women he knew always glossed over situations, and Brie could have, too.

Floodlights provided by a nearby volunteer fire department illuminated the transfer of chemicals. Linc looked a his watch and realized it was nearly nine o'clock. The day had died in a crimson sunset earlier. He had suspiciously checked the tanker for leaks. To his chagrin and relief, he didn't find any. Brie had caught him at it and broke into a grin, making him feel foolish. And it needled him further that she had said nothing and merely turned away to leave him to complete his personal inspection.

Linc made sure all the equipment was hung up in the van afterward. He said little as the tanker carrying the noxious chemicals slowly drove away. In the floodlights, Brie's features were washed out and taut with exhaustion. He wanted to urge her to forget the reporters, but she doggedly shook her head and went over to them. She answered their barrage of questions for nearly twenty minutes. He breathed a sigh of relief when she finally ended the press conference and walked to the van.

"Why'd you go out of your way to talk to those idiots?" he asked, shoving his hands into the pockets of his jeans.

"Because the people of Ohio need to be informed on what we do. Every little scrap of information through the media to them may help us do our job in the long run, Linc. It helps everyone if we can teach the public to check tankers as they pass them on the highway, see if they have any leaks, then report them, if there are." She stopped near the van, giving him the keys. "You drive, I'm getting tired."

He opened the door for her and saw a shadow of a smile lurking at the corners of her glorious mouth. "Chauvinism is *not* dead," he informed her silkily.

She climbed in. "Does that mean you'll put my seat belt on, too?"

Linc hesitated, very aware that she looked so vulnerable because of her fatigue. "Just say the word. Nothing's too good for you, lady. Not after the way you handled this haz-mat situation."

Brie met his dark eyes, realizing he respected her for the first time. "Get in. I'm not so weak that I can't buckle up. Will I need to put on a crash helmet with you at the wheel?"

Linc shut the door and grinned. "My good friends always called me Captain Crash."

Brie chortled and waited until he climbed into the van before saying, "Is that short for Captain Crash and Dash?"

"Yeah. How'd you know?"

"That's an old fire fighter's pet name for those who crash through a burning structure's door, then fall through the floor into the basement. We never thought much of the crash and dashes in our department, or any other, for that matter. They risk other people's lives with their inability to think coolly under stress."

He got the van on the road and they headed toward Canton. "I'm not that kind," he protested.

Brie slumped into her seat, relaxing and closing her eyes. He wasn't a reckless driver, and she smiled slightly. "So, how many pumpers or tankers did you wreck then? There had to be a reason for the nickname."

He glanced at Brie, alarmed by the faraway tone in her soft voice. Darkness shadowed her features, relieved only by the lights of passing vehicles. "The name Captain Crash was given to me because in certain situations I just lower my head like a bull and charge."

"Wonderful. Now you tell me. What did you do, bully those poor reporters earlier? They didn't have many nice things to say about your handling of them."

His brows drew down. "Tough. I'll never let them at you when you're exhausted or busy coordinating an incident."

Sleep tugged at Brie, and she wanted to give in to it. "Linc, I'm going to knock off for a while. It's still an hour until we get home. Wake me up when you hit the outskirts of Canton, okay?"

Again, Linc was struck by Brie's exhaustion. Didn't she ever get a decent night's sleep? "Are you all right?" Concern was obvious in his voice, and he saw her look at him through her lowered lashes.

"I'm fine. Don't worry, I didn't breathe in any of that stuff at the site. I'm just beat, that's all."

"Okay. Sleep for a while."

"Sure? It's been a long, hard day for you, too?"

He liked her sensitivity and regard for others. "Go to sleep, kitten. I'll wake you when it's time," he told her in a husky voice. Linc tried to tell himself that the care he extended toward Brie was part of his cover, not real concern.

Pleasantly wrapped in the melting honey of his tone, Brie went to sleep. She spiraled quickly into an abyss where nothing except peace existed.

When she awoke, it was to the caress of strong fingers gently massaging her shoulder. Wanting to remain in the arms of sleep, she nuzzled the hand, which she discovered had wiry hairs across it. When it slowly dawned on her whose hand it was, she jerked awake and sat up.

"We're near Canton," Linc said quietly, giving her a worried look.

"What time is it?" she asked groggily, rubbing her eyes.

"A little after ten. How do you feel?"

"Like I've been hit by a Mack truck," she muttered, sitting up. "My neck feels like it has knots in it." She began to rub it gently. Her hair had dried and was mussed, giving her a fragile look that Linc found hard to ignore.

He wondered what it would be like to make love to Brie. She was so responsive, like a hot, spirited thoroughbred. He had spent the past hour mulling over many facets of Brie, making a checklist of what he did or did not like about her. In the minus column, she was his boss. She was either a target or had set up Holcomb to be murdered. Which was it? Linc wanted to discount that Brie was capable of having her partner blown away, but he couldn't that easily. Then again, if she was the culprit why did she risk injury as she did? He had only a few answers, and there were still so many pieces of the puzzle that didn't fit. A plan had formed in his mind as she slept, and now he was going to spring it on her.

"Listen, I've been thinking, Brie."

"Uh-oh, that could be dangerous," she said, digging for the thermos.

"Are you always a tart when you wake up?"

She sat up, the thermos between her hands. "Just with your kind, Tanner. Want some?"

"No, thanks. What do you mean, my kind?"

Brie poured herself a cup of coffee, capped the thermos and sat back, enjoying Linc and her just awakening state. "Your kind meaning the guys in the fire service who are all macho and given to rooster crowing and strutting. They always have a line for the women who come around. Actually, I should thank all those guys I spent my fire fighting years with. They helped me handle someone like you." She glanced out of the corners of her eyes to see how he was taking her teasing.

"You can really dish it out, can't you, Ms. Williams?"

She grinned, placing both feet on the dash. "That's right, any time, day or night. I'm on twenty-four-hour call, Tanner."

"I'm impressed as hell. When I wake up, I'm not sharp at all."

"No? Pity. Here I thought all you ever did was parry your way through life."

He slid her a warning look laced with humor. "Only with smart mouths like you, Williams. Satisfied?"

"Immensely. Now, what did you want to talk about?"

Saucy little cat. I'll corner you someday and then we'll see just how fast you can try and talk your way out of me kissing you. Linc wondered where that thought had come from. "How about if I crash and burn on your couch? We're both beat. There's no sense in driving all over Canton to find a motel open at this time of night. Besides, if you are called out, you'll have to come and pick me up, wasting valuable time."

Brie's good humor disappeared abruptly. She put her cup down, rested her hands on her knees and pondered his suggestion. Panic riffled through her. She didn't want Linc at her house. She had no way of knowing when she would have another nightmare and she'd awake screaming. No, she couldn't risk her image with Tanner like that. She wanted no one to see that weakened side of herself at any cost.

"I think you'll be more comfortable at a motel, Linc."

"I don't sleep well in motels. There's just something about a home that puts me at ease." He glanced at her, seeing the set of her lips. What was going on inside that head of hers? Was she hiding something at her house she wanted no one to see? "I promise I'll stay on the couch. No cute stuff. Okay?"

Brie rubbed her brow, feeling a headache coming on. Great, he didn't sleep well at motels. Neither did she. "It's a small couch. You wouldn't be comfortable on it. Take my word."

Linc softened his features and gave what he hoped was his best puppy-dog look. "We had a rough start. How about if we both get a good night's sleep to put us in good stead for tomorrow?"

She wasn't prepared for the sudden pleading look in Linc's eyes and felt like a heel for trying to turn him down. "Oh, okay," she grumbled. "But I warn you,

Tanner, I won't be your cook or bottle washer. To-morrow's Sunday, our day off. I don't want to have to jump out of bed and feed your growing-boy appetite in the morning.''

Linc tried to look properly grateful. ''No problem. All I like in the morning is coffee, anyway.''

Brie shot him a disparaging look. ''At least we agree on that.''

Allowing a bit of a friendly smile, he murmured, ''Not bad for two people who are opposites, eh? I'm impressed, too.''

''Well, just don't expect the Ritz, Tanner. You make up your own bed on that lumpy couch. I'm going to grab the shower first, then hit the sack. You're going to have to wait your turn. I'm dead on my feet.''

''No problem,'' he said. ''Ladies first, anyway.''

Brie wrinkled her nose, trying to figure out how to short-circuit the nightmares that stalked her. She still had some sleeping pills left from her stay in the hospital. But what if there was a haz-mat call? She wouldn't be able to function properly in that groggy state, and Jeff wouldn't be returning until tomorrow afternoon. Groaning, Brie shut her eyes, trying to think clearly and not succeeding.

Following her directions, Linc found her small white home with green trim on the outskirts of North Canton. The one-story house was hidden by a long gravel driveway lined with oaks, elms and maples. A large overhead sulfur lamp lit the entire front of the house, which was embraced by blossoming white and purple lilac bushes. They stood window-height in some places. Tulips, daffodils and hyacinths were in full bloom in front of the shrubs.

"Nice place," Linc murmured as he shut off the engine. He'd meant it.

"This is Camelot, the place where I go and hide when the world gets too much to take," Brie said, climbing out. She fished for the key from her purse and opened the door.

"Come on in," she invited Linc, who was hanging back. Was it her imagination or was he looking around the entire area as if he were an investigator? Brie shook her head, not caring. Throwing her purse on the Formica counter in the small kitchen, she headed for the linen closet in the hall near the bathroom. She found sheets, a pillow and a blanket, and put them in Linc's waiting arms. "The living room is that way," she said, pointing. "I'm getting my shower then going to bed."

He gave her a nod. "Sounds good. Good night. And thanks"

Brie barely responded, going to the kitchen to pour herself a glass of chablis instead of downing a sleeping pill. In the bathroom, she shed her clothes, dying for a bath, but it was too soon after her burn injuries to subject her tender, still healing flesh to it. With a sigh, she stepped into the warm shower and scrubbed her hair and body. By the time she finished, she was so groggy she could barely stand. After she slipped into a pale apricot silk nightgown that brushed her slender ankles, Brie opened the bathroom door and padded down the carpeted hall to her bedroom. Before the accident, she had always worn gowns that showed off her shoulders. Since then, because of the terrible scars, she wore only gowns with high necklines that hid the telltale scars. Some of them were still visible, but a robe would hide them from her eyes as well as Linc's curious, always penetrating gaze.

Bed had never looked so inviting as she quietly shut the door. Moonlight streamed in through the floor-to-ceiling windows on the east side of the room; the pale ivory sheer curtains lent a radiance to the scene. But Brie couldn't appreciate any of it tonight. The instant she snuggled beneath the quilt her grandmother had made for her, she was asleep.

Linc took a shower and stepped into his light blue pajama bottoms. He tightened the drawstring and opened the door, waiting and listening. Damp dark hair clung to his brow, and he tamed it into place with his fingers. It had been nearly a half hour since Brie had gone to bed. He turned off the hall light, stepped up to her door and carefully turned the brass knob. The door opened without a creak. He waited a few more seconds, listening. Then, he pushed the door open just enough to see. There, lying on one side of the brass bed, was Brie sleeping soundly, the moonlight outlining her form.

Her face was almost radiant and was without a trace of the previous tension around her full, sensual lips or eyes. His heart beat harder, and he took a deep, steadying breath, his body going rigid with need of her. She looked soft and warm, vulnerable and incredibly feminine. With a shake of his head, Linc slowly closed the door. It must be moon madness, he thought wryly. No woman made his head spin like that.

Padding to the living room, which, in his opinion, had so many plants it bordered on being a jungle, Linc went directly to the massive cherry rolltop desk. He turned on the Tiffany stained-glass lamp and, with

painstaking thoroughness, he began his investigation.
He found a stack of letters and committed the names
of the correspondents to memory. If he had time, he'd
read the contents of each later. Another small drawer
yielded several color photos. In one, Brie was smiling
brilliantly, her arm around a man in a haz-mat uniform. He had to be John Holcomb. Linc felt the stir-
rings of envy as he absorbed the happiness evident in
Brie's face. Her eyes were like dead embers now compared to the photo. He pushed aside his personal feelings and noted that Brie was at least fifteen pounds
heavier in the photo, and sported a golden tan. Her
beautiful sable brown hair was curling richly around
her shoulders. Had her hair been burned off in the
explosion? More than likely, and he was suddenly sad
that had happened, because she was lovely with dark
hair framing her face. His throat constricted with
emotion as he gazed at her. Where her cheek had once
been filled out with a rosy bloom, it was nothing but
flesh over bone now.

He cradled the picture between his hands, lifting his
head and staring into the darkness toward the bedroom. The trauma of the explosion had devastated
Brie much more than he had first realized. No one
looked like a prisoner of war as she did now without
the ravages still inside her, still eating her up. His
forehead furrowed deeply as he stared down at Brie.
The report on her had said she suffered internal injuries and burns. Had she sought therapy afterward to
cope with the trauma? More than likely not. Who of
them did? Linc recalled her every move at the haz-mat
scene. Brie had been professional, like a man would
have been. She hadn't lost her touch. So how was the
trauma affecting her?

Having more questions than answers, Linc continued his search of the desk. There were several photos of Brie with Holcomb, his wife and child celebrating Christmas, Easter, birthdays and other holidays. Linc got the impression that Brie was part of Holcomb's family.

Going back to the letters, he opened the one with the latest postmark, which was only a few days ago. It was from Carol Holcomb.

Dear Brie,
How can Susie and I thank you for the lovely flowers? They were such a wonderful surprise and they brightened our day. Susie loves the balloons that came with the bouquet and has them in her room. And whenever I'm down, I go smell the flowers, and it makes me feel better.

By the way, Susie asks me every day, when is Aunt Brie coming over again, Mommy?

We miss you, Brie. And I know how busy you are. Just know we pray for you nightly.

Love,
Carol and Susie

Linc folded the note and put it into the pink envelope. *Aunt Brie.* You endear yourself to everyone pretty quickly, don't you? What is it about you that makes people want to reach out and become a part of your existence?

The next letter was from Steve, her brother.

Dear Fighting Tiger,
How's my ace sister doing? When you gonna come to my base and visit me? I haven't seen you

since visiting you in the hospital. Knowing you like I do, you're licking your own wounds by yourself, as usual. Come on! I may be your kid brother, but I have a pretty broad shoulder that you can lean on if you want.

And, also knowing you, you haven't cried much lately (you'd get more blood out of a turnip) and I'm pretty good at sitting and listening, why not try me? How come you haven't been calling me once a month like you usually do? I know you're busy, but the state of Ohio can't have blown up that much. It's been three months since you got out of the burn unit, and I haven't heard from you.

If I don't hear soon, I'm going to go A.W.O.L. from the Air Force and fly back to see you. How's that for a threat, Big Sis? Seriously, call or write. I'll even accept a collect call from you, Tiger.

Love,
your strong, intelligent, handsome brother Steve

So you've locked yourself up since the accident.

He glanced at the names on the next letter—Mr. and Mrs. Vernon Williams. Her parents.

Dear Sweetheart:

How are you doing? Dad and I are so worried about you. Please come home for a visit. I just have this feeling you need someone, Brie. You and John were so close. And I know he was like the big brother you never had, honey.

Why don't you take some of that vacation you've earned? You haven't had one in over a year. I know you love your job and you believe in what you're accomplishing, but everyone needs a rest now and then. If you'll come home Dad's promised you can help around the farm. You always loved plowing the fields in the spring. He says your favorite old John Deere tractor has been tuned up and is waiting for you.

Of course, if you don't want to work, you don't have to. We just need to see you again, honey. After that awful three months in the hospital and seeing what it did to you, we both think that right now, you need a little T.L.C. Please, Brie, you give so much to others. Don't you think it's time you came home to get some for yourself?

If you can't afford the plane ticket, Dad says we'll spring for it. Let us know soon. We love you, honey.

Love,
Mom and Dad

Linc's mouth twisted as he put the letter in the stack. He stared down at six others. Were they all from friends and family who were worried? Driven to find out and rationalizing that his decision to read them was for the purpose of his investigation and not his personal need to know, Linc spent another twenty minutes perusing them. By the time he was done, his face was grim. The other six letters were from members of the haz-mat team. Some had sent funny cards; others more serious, but they all contained one message: Brie was special, respected and cared for by her family of coworkers. He sat back in the chair, the

Tiffany lamp casting light and making deep shadows around him.

Everywhere he looked, Linc saw life. Huge ficus trees, almost as tall as the eight-foot ceiling, graced two corners of the pale green living room. Behind the bamboo couch with fluffy ivory colored pillows were two tall, slender palms, adding a wild touch to the room. He liked it, realizing he was privy to another facet of Brie's existence. The room throbbed with vibrancy. She had embraced life in ways he had seen few people able to do.

Linc stared at the stack of unanswered mail and returned the letters to their drawer. Framed pictures of lions, cheetahs and other animals graced the walls. Was that how Brie felt? Was she a wild lioness who demanded freedom? He smiled. He hadn't missed the mark on her after all—she was feline...

Why are you running from everyone's offer of help? Is there something they don't know? Are you mixed up with a criminal element and afraid to talk for fear they'll blow the whistle on you, too? Or maybe you really were secretly in love with John Holcomb and are afraid to admit that to anyone. Rubbing his face, Linc got up, running his hand across his chest where an ache had centered.

Brie moaned and tossed violently, throwing the quilt off her. She lay floating between sleep and wakefulness, aware that her nightgown was sticky against her flesh. Her breath came in ragged gasps as she saw herself turning from John to head to the haz-mat van. She felt her heart start a hammer of warning. No! Oh, God, please, no! she screamed silently. Come back, John! Come back! Helplessly, Brie watched the unfolding drama before her.

Just as before, Brie heard the powerful explosion, felt the blast of annihilating heat. Then blackness overcame her as she was slammed to the concrete surface. A scream tore from her lips when she regained consciousness. She rolled over on her back. Her ribs hurt, and she gripped her right side as she sat up. Warm liquid was running down her face, blinding her. A metallic taste was in her mouth, and her nose was bleeding heavily. Brie felt another scream building deep inside her, clawing up through her like a caged animal that had to free itself. She lifted her chin to look at the drums. The raw cry finally tore from her. Brie sprang up, fighting pain and dizziness as she lurched forward, trying to get to where John lay facedown three hundred feet away.

Brie jerked upright in bed, burying her face in her hands, her shoulders hunched and broken. She barely heard the door being torn open; she was not aware of the light being turned on.

Linc froze, one hand on the doorknob, the other on the light switch. Brie was breathing hard, her gasps hoarse. She sat on the edge of the bed as if she were prepared to leap off it. He had heard her scream and thought that someone had slipped into her bedroom and attacked her. His wide eyes traveled from the closed windows to Brie. Without thinking, he started toward her out of some instinct to comfort her. His mouth opened then closed. He tasted the bitterness of bile as he stared at her heavily scarred right shoulder. The upper buttons of the gown were open and moved aside enough for him to see some of her injury. Twisted pink flesh clearly showed the path of destruction the explosion had collected from Brie.

He knelt on one knee and raised his hands to settle them on her shaking shoulders. She was in so much pain that unexpected tears came to his eyes.

"Brie? Kitten?" he began haltingly. Linc berated himself. He was so damn good in a dangerous situation. Why couldn't he be just as good when it came to a genuine human crisis? His hands wavered inches from her shoulders, and he didn't know whether to touch her or not. JoAnne had always accused him of being incapable of expressing emotions openly, of always hiding behind his image as a cool, collected agent. Linc swallowed hard, then called Brie's name again and again until she responded.

The need to touch her, to soothe away some of her pain forced him to settle his hands gently on her shoulders. Her skin was clammy. The moment he made contact with her, she reacted violently, pushing him away, her eyes wide and unseeing. Linc slowly got up, holding out his hand toward her, talking to her in a low, unsteady voice.

"Brie, it's all right, take a deep breath. You're here, in your bedroom. The explosion is past. You're safe now. Take slow breaths..."

Her face was contorted. For several long, agonizing seconds she stared at him. Her breasts rose and fell beneath her nightgown; her hands dug convulsively into the mattress.

"That's it," Linc whispered, seeing her eyes begin to lose their terrified look. "Slow your breathing down. I'm here, and you're safe."

Brie wanted to cry, but no tears would come out! The need to cry was like a knife thrusting deeply inside her, but no tears would come! Linc's face wavered like a mirage before her, conflicting with the image of the warehouse and the flames roaring around her as she tried to get to John. Disoriented, Brie raised her hand. "John . . . John?" she cried hoarsely.

Linc winced and shut his eyes momentarily. "No, kitten, I'm not John. Come on, pull from the grip of that nightmare. You're at home, and I'm Linc. Linc Tanner. Remember? Brie, keep taking deep breaths."

She staggered and fell, the jolt ripping through her. For a moment, she felt blackness swallowing her. Reaching out with her left hand, Brie crawled forward across the blackened concrete toward John. He had to be alive, he just had to be—and yet, the voice she was hearing wasn't John's. Fighting to shake off the powerful nightmare, Brie closed her eyes and concentrated on listening to the instructions to control hyperventilation. When she opened her eyes some minutes later, she found herself staring directly into Linc's tortured features.

Licking her dry lips, she croaked, "What are you doing here?"

Relief flickered in his blue eyes. "Thank God," he whispered. "You had a bad dream, Brie. And you screamed." He looked toward the windows. "I thought someone had broken in and was attacking you, so I practically took your door off the hinges getting in here."

Brie turned slowly to look at the door. It hung by one hinge. She buried her face in her hands because she couldn't stand the look of pity written across his face. "Just leave," she said brokenly.

"Are you sure? I mean—"

"Please!"

Linc started for the door. "Are you sure, Brie?"

Tears struck her eyes. Maybe it was because of the unexpected tenderness in Linc's voice. Or his protectiveness. Brie wasn't sure. She felt embarrassed. With a trembling hand, she pulled the throat of the gown closed. He had seen her ugly burns and seen her down. Not even her own family had seen the extent of her injuries yet, only the doctor. And more than anything, Brie didn't want to be alone. She felt him close to her and lifted her chin. He hadn't left, and old hurt tore loose from her heart. Linc looked exhausted and ravaged.

"M-maybe some water... please?"

"Sure. Just stay put. I'll be back in a minute," he promised.

Brie shakily reached for her apricot robe at the foot of the bed, pulling it haphazardly across her shoulders to hide her burns. The shame of being seen weakened washed over her. Unable to cope with what he probably thought of her now, Brie simply sat there until Linc returned. He shut off the lamp when he entered the room, the moon giving them enough light. Gratefully, Brie took the glass of water he offered her. Linc knelt beside her, one callused hand resting lightly against her elbow. She drank the contents and handed the glass to him.

"Thank you," she whispered, her voice raw.

Linc set the glass on the bed stand. "It's the least I could do. Listen, let's get you back into bed and covered up. You're pretty sweaty, and this cool air isn't going to do you much good."

His voice was like balm, and numbly, Brie did as he directed. As she allowed him to pull up the quilt, she closed her eyes.

"I wish I could have a bath," she murmured, her voice slurring with exhaustion.

Linc stood there, puzzled. "I can fix it for you if you want, Brie."

A broken smile faded from her lips. "Can't... yet...my burns...time, the doctors say it will take time before I can take one. I miss the bath so much. I can relax in it..."

He gently sat on the edge of the bed and took her hand. She had curled up on her side. "You can relax now, Brie," he soothed quietly. "Just hold my hand and you'll relax."

Her fingers tightened slightly around his hand. "I'm so scared," she whispered, "so scared..."

"Shh, that will go away, Brie. Go to sleep, kitten. I'll just sit here and hold your hand so you can sleep. You'll be safe now. No more bad dreams."

The tension began to dissolve from her face, the soft corners of her mouth relaxing. Linc continued to talk in a low monotone to her, speaking from a heart he didn't realize existed within him. He spoke in words meant to heal and take away her pain. He willed her anguish into his hand so that she could sleep in a dreamless world where only peace existed, instead of grief. Within half an hour, her fingers uncurled from his hand; Brie had found an edge of peace in the torn fabric of her universe. Linc wanted to stay with her, but he fought the desire. He could take her into his arms and hold her... and protect her.

As Linc sat there, watching the slow rise and fall of her breast beneath the rainbow quilt, he was able to put all the letters together. Brie had no one she could reach to for solace or healing. Even he knew that at times he needed someone in order to heal himself. Of course, Linc thought with a bitter laugh, he was the pot calling the kettle black. He was just as bad as Brie in that instance. Except he had channeled out all his traumas and cleansed himself, and Brie had not.

Sadness overwhelmed Linc as he reluctantly stood. He leaned over, tucking the quilt behind her back, and noticed Brie had thrown the robe across her shoulders—to hide her scars from him. Against his better judgment, he reached down, barely stroking the crown of her sable hair. It was as soft and silken as he had imagined it would be. That small discovery pleased him as much as if he had taken her to bed and made love to her. True, he hadn't known her very long, but that didn't matter. Just having the privilege of being near her, sharing the haz-mat incident and now sharing her tragedy, had melded him like hot, molten steel to her. The forge of trauma had cast them into one. They held an indestructible link to one another whether they wanted it. He tried to break that emotional bond, because she was still a prime suspect. Brie could be a killer, and he reminded himself he was an investigator, not her haz-mat partner.

Linc forced himself to leave her bedroom, and he left the door hanging at a sad angle. He wanted it open in case Brie started having nightmares again.

## Chapter Four

The morning sun was warm against her back, the soil moist between her hands. Kneeling, Brie lifted her head momentarily, allowing the sun to caress her face. The birds, mostly robins, some sparrows and a pair of noisy blue jays, provided the music that surrounded her in the small garden behind the house. Brie took the hoe and got to her feet. She dug a shallow trench from one end of the plot to the other, the freshly turned soil like a dark scar against the lighter, drier earth.

That's how she felt—stripped. She was cold inside. Her stomach had knotted soon after she had awakened this morning. She tried to concentrate on planting her garden and pushing last night's memories away. But it was impossible. As she knelt and opened her first packet of peas, a flood of embarrassment washed over her. Not only had Linc seen her stripped of all control over her emotions, he'd probably seen a portion of the massive scarring caused by the burns on her back. She gently nestled three peas every few feet until the entire row had been sown. The lulling songs of the birds quelled her screaming nerves, and Brie devoted her complete attention to one of her favorite pastimes of the year—spring planting.

Glancing at the watch on her wrist, Brie saw it was almost eleven o'clock. She risked a glance toward the house. Linc was still sleeping soundly, thank God. She didn't want to have to meet him face to face after last night, but she knew it was inevitable. Her gut had told her not to allow him to stay overnight, and now she was going to pay dearly for ignoring her instincts. Linc was the kind of man who would hold last night against her. More than likely, he'd throw it up in her face at a critical moment, questioning her authority.

Lips compressed, Brie pushed the right amount of soil over the peas and gently pressed it in place with the palm of her hand. Jeff was supposed to arrive around noon. If only he would arrive before Linc woke up. That was almost an impossibility, Brie realized. No one slept until noon. She was surprised Linc had slept this long. Perhaps her screams had unsettled him more than she realized, and he hadn't been able to get back to sleep for a long time afterward. A ragged sigh escaped her as she got up and made another shallow row with the hoe.

Time melted away with the joy of caressing and molding the soil of the earth between her hands. Brie's back was to the house, and she was kneeling near a row in which she was dropping beans, when a slight noise startled her. She twisted her head around.

"Good morning," Linc greeted quietly. He stood there with a cup of coffee in each hand, dressed in a

navy blue polo shirt that emphasized the clean, powerful lines of his chest, shoulders and hard stomach.
Worn jeans hugged his narrow hips and long thighs
like an intimate lover. Brie's lips parted, and her heart
banged at the base of her throat. Her hands froze in
midair as she forced herself to look at him. She melted
beneath his sleepy inspection. If his face had been hard
and unforgiving, as it usually was, she would have died
a little inside. As Brie took in his drowsy features, her
heart wrenched with compassion. She recalled Linc
telling her he didn't wake up quickly in the morning.
Right now, he looked like a little boy with his hair
softly mussed, eyes sleep-ridden and his features vulnerable to her inspection.

Brie returned her attention to the planting, avert-
ing her gaze from the tender flame that sparked in his
half-closed eyes. "Good morning," she muttered.

Linc looked around. The back yard was embraced
on all sides by towering trees and, a strong shaft of
morning sunlight brightened the lawn and garden. His
gaze moved to Brie, who was doggedly paying a great
deal more attention to her planting activities than to
him. Could he blame her? Although he was still
groggy, he noticed the high flush to her cheeks when
he had spoken to her. He sat down on the grass a few
feet from where Brie worked, and put down the coffee cups.

"When did you get up?" he asked, his voice gravelly. He rubbed his face wearily.

Brie shrugged. "A couple hours ago." Please don't
let him start asking me about last night. Please don't!
She didn't know what she would do if Linc did. Even
now, she could feel tears pricking her eyes, and she

was stunned that Linc would bring out that kind of response in her.

Linc sipped the coffee. "You make good coffee."

"I'm glad you like it."

He realized Brie's cool, clipped manner was to protect herself from last night's ordeal, and he tried to steer delicately clear of anything having to do with the episode. "I'm used to concrete, condos and people all jammed together. Not trees, birds and quiet."

She managed a slight smile, continuing down the row. Why wouldn't Linc just get up and leave? If only she could will him to go into the house. "Canton's a nice middle-size city. Large enough to offer you anything a big one has, but small enough to afford the luxury of trees and privacy, if that's what you want."

Linc gazed at the two acres of neatly kept lawn that was guarded by trees. "I think you wanted your privacy."

"I did."

He sipped more coffee, a feeling of contentment filling him. There was something almost maternal in the way Brie was running her fingers through the soil, planting the seeds then patting the soil into place. Dirt had lodged beneath her short nails, her hands were stained with the color of the earth she was lovingly tending, and a small smudge streaked her right cheek. But that didn't detour him from thinking how beautiful she was this morning. Dressed in a long-sleeved pale pink blouse and a pair of loose-fitting jeans, she looked as if she belonged with the land. When he remembered her parents' letter and the fact that they farmed for a living, it all made sense. At least he hadn't caught her in a lie . . . yet.

"This place must have cost you a bundle. Two acres in D.C. would equal our paychecks combined for the next ten years."

Brie took a tiny breath of relief. Was Linc going to have the sensitivity not to mention last night? She got to her feet, retrieved the hoe and began another shallow row. "It didn't cost that much, but it has put a definite strain on my budget."

"Why aren't you like every other modern woman I know who owns an apartment closer to the city?"

Brie gave him an irritated look, then resumed her hoeing. "Modern woman? Is that your concept of one? She owns a condo and parties in town?"

"Sounds good," he mumbled.

"Are you always a comedian in the morning?"

"Hey, slow down, you're getting too far ahead of me. Remember, I'm the one who staggers around after getting up."

She relented, stealing a glance at Linc. There was something about his groping and stumbling demeanor that endeared him to her. He was more open now than she had ever seen him. Still, that alert glint was in his eyes, always making her think he was a wolf stalking a quarry. And that red flag of warning was screaming at her again. She wrestled with the clash between her gut feeling and Linc's vulnerability. He invited her trust, and his actions thus far made it easy for her to trust him. So why was the alarm going off inside her head? "Then refrain from those chauvinistic remarks."

"Ouch." He gave her a boyish smile meant to defuse her abruptness. "Just ignore me, okay? I'm not much good the first hour."

"That's an understatement," Brie murmured, trying to curb her slight smile. She put the hoe down and went through her collection of seeds yet to be planted, trying to decide what should go next to her green beans.

"You're a country gal."

"Yes. I love the land," she admitted softly.

"Is that why you got into haz-mat? To protect the earth? A lot of chemicals are buried in the earth, ruining it for years if not decades to come."

She was pleased with his insight and sat back on her heels, a package of bush beans in her hand. "Being a city boy, you'd laugh if I told you the truth."

Linc crossed his legs Indian fashion, the cup resting on one knee. "No, I wouldn't. Besides, it will help me understand you."

Brie wrinkled her nose and tore the top off the seed packet. "That's what I'm afraid of."

"Isn't it natural for people to want to get to know each other?" Part of him wanted to know because of the assignment. Another part of him wanted to know for personal reasons. Linc was disgusted with his indecisiveness regarding Brie. To hell with it. He wanted to know her more intimately because she was a suspect, he rationalized.

She shrugged and crawled up to the head of the row, carefully putting the seeds into it. "Up to a point," she parried.

"You know, you're like this place of yours: hidden, guarded and mysterious."

"I like it that way."

"Why? What's wrong if someone knows you?"

Brie shifted uncomfortably. The coffee he was drinking must be waking him up; he was sharper and more focused. "Technically, nothing. I'm just a private person by nature. I don't feel it's anyone's right to know all about me."

Linc absorbed the stubborn set of her face. This morning, there was a fragility to Brie. He couldn't put his finger on exactly what made him sense that. The nightmare had left her devastated and wide open to attack. That was why she was behaving defensively with him, he reasoned. Desperate to establish some sort of beachhead of trust with her, Linc shifted the conversation to himself.

"When I was a kid growing up in the city, I often wished I could just pack up and head for the country. I guess it's like that old saying—the grass is always greener on the other side of the hill."

Brie closed her eyes for a moment, thankful Linc was talking about himself instead of trying to needle her. She resumed the planting, needing the warmth of the earth in her hands to soothe her frayed nerves. "Didn't your parents ever take you to the country?"

Linc drank the last of the coffee, then set down the cup and rested his hands on his thighs. "I grew up between foster homes and orphanages in New York City, so I saw a lot of skyscrapers, glass, steel and concrete." At least that part of his life wasn't a lie. Linc laughed at himself. Why should he care? Brie had a soft side, and he wanted to cultivate it in order to make her trust him. Ordinarily, he never spoke about his childhood to anyone.

Brie lifted her chin, her eyes dark with compassion as she met and held his blue gaze. "Orphanages?" she uttered, a catch in her voice.

"Now don't go getting soft on me," he warned. "Plenty of brats got dumped by mothers who didn't want them, and they ended up kicking between foster homes or an orphanage. It's no big deal.''

Her hands stilled on her thighs. She could imagine him as a dark-haired, blue-eyed little boy who strutted around pretending he was tough and could take anything. Perhaps that was why he came across like that now. It was the only way he knew how to protect the vulnerable inner core of himself. "I—I had no idea..."

"Come on, Brie, it wasn't a life sentence. Quit giving me that sad, soulful look. You aren't going to cry on me, are you?''

The right blend of sarcasm laced with disbelief effectively tamped her flow of feelings toward him. He was still that tough little boy, she thought, her heart wrenching in her breast. And somehow, knowing that about Linc made him less of a threat to her. But she'd never tell him that. "No," she whispered, "I won't cry." She never cried, and she needed to. The tears might crowd into her eyes, but they'd never quite spill out and release the pent-up grief that she carried within.

"Good," he said.

She went back to planting. "So you were raised in the city in a series of foster homes?''

"Yeah. I lived in a jungle, too. But it wasn't like the jungle you have inside your house or surrounding you out here.''

"I see. A concrete jungle?''

"Something like that.''

Brie compressed her lips. "What parts of New York City did you grow up in?''

"The Bronx. A good blue-collar community that's been eaten away by street gangs.''

She heard the disgust in his voice. "Did you belong to one of those gangs?"

"Yeah. If you were anybody, you were part of a gang."

"And you wanted to belong..." Brie said gently, meeting his eyes.

He shrugged. "I was bored. The Panthers gave me someplace to go and something to do."

"What did your foster parents have to say about that?"

Again a shrug. "Let's put it this way, Brie. One set of foster parents took in brats like me to get the money. They really didn't give a damn about us. All they wanted was the monthly allotment check."

Her heart twisted. Linc had been rejected from the day of his birth. My God, how would she have felt if that had happened to her? Brie's hands stilled over the warm earth. Her voice was almost inaudible. "My growing up years were very different. I have wonderful parents. They have a three-hundred-acre farm in Iowa." She gave him a wry look. "I grew up working alongside Dad and my younger brother, Steve, fixing tractors, hay balers, wind rowers and trucks. We didn't have the money to send them to a garage in town to be fixed, so we did all the repairs ourselves."

Linc gave her a sour look. "So that's why you knew where the battery cables were located on that truck yesterday?"

Brie swallowed a smile. "Yes."

He gave her a disgruntled look. Brie could have rubbed his face in it with that piece of information, but she continued to plant her beans. Linc knew more than a few people who would be delighted to make a first-class fool of him if they had the opportunity. But Brie hadn't. His brows drew together.

"You're a strange bird, Ms. Williams."

She rose, dusting off her knees. "I could say the same of you, Mr. Tanner. Well, do you feel up to seeing a truly strange bird?"

Linc enjoyed looking at Brie, at the way the sunlight made her hair a brown halo laced with strands of gold. He had touched that hair last night and felt how silky it was. Emotions woven with desire deluged him as he absorbed her in those fleeting seconds. Somehow, with dirt-stained hands, her hair loose and free, standing in a pair of patched jeans, she looked beautiful. Was she like Ceres, the mother of the earth from Roman mythology, giving life to everything she touched? Linc thought so, responding to the wry smile on her full, provocative lips.

"What surprise do you have for me," he asked, rising to his full height.

Brie's eyes glimmered with mirth as she stepped carefully between the rows and walked toward the house. "Come on, and I'll show you."

After removing her tennis shoes at the door, Brie stepped inside and led Linc down the hall. The moment she opened the door to the right of the bathroom, an excited whistling sound emerged. Frowning, Linc followed Brie into the room. He saw a sewing machine in one corner with some peach-colored fabric that resembled a blouse. Turning toward the whistling sound, he saw a small gray bird flapping its wings madly in its cage on a desk across the room.

"What's that?" he asked.

Brie smiled, sat on a chair and opened the cage. "This is Homely Homer, an orphaned baby pigeon the kids down the street brought to me two weeks ago. Apparently Homer fell out of her nest, and they couldn't get her back into it." She gently picked up the pigeon, which had no feathers on her breast. Looking at Linc, she could see his scowl deepening. "Come on over here. You wanted to see what it's like to live in the country, now you're going to find out."

Linc came and stood near the desk. "He's the ugliest-looking thing I've ever seen."

Homer perched on Brie's finger, flapping her wings and whistling shrilly. Brie laughed and stroked Homer's few feathers, which were beginning to grow out on her back. "Homer's a she. Don't insult her like that, Linc. Here, sit down. You can let her perch on your finger while I get her the baby food."

"Baby food?" he echoed, not sure at all that he wanted that ugly-looking, buck-naked bird with its long, oddly shaped beak on *his* finger.

Brie motioned for him to sit on the edge of the desk, which he did with great reluctance. "Hold out your finger," she urged.

"What if—what if that thing decides to take a dump on me?" he protested.

She chuckled. "I have papers spread over the desk. Just hold Homer away from you. She'll be a lady and sit nicely on your finger." Without waiting for him to say no, Brie placed the squab on his finger. She turned and headed for the door.

"Hey! Wait a minute. Where are you going?"

"To the fridge to get Homer's breakfast. I'll be right back."

Linc's face fell. "But—what if—"

"I'll be back in a moment," she promised airily, disappearing. He scowled at the pigeon. "You're ugly,'' he growled at the bird. Homer blinked her big brown eyes at him, whistled through the nostrils of her long beak and gently flapped her gray and black feathered wings, as if to dispute his comment. Linc sat there uncomfortably. What had he gotten himself into? He glared at the bird. Relief rushed through him when Brie came back minutes later.

''Here, take this thing,'' he growled. ''I'm no good with animals.''

She placed the small jar of baby food on the desk and twisted off the lid. ''That's only because you haven't been around animals much, Linc. You're doing just fine. Look at Homer, she's very contented on your finger. You can tell she's happy because she barely flutters her wings and she's talking to you in that soft whistle of hers. She's accepting you as her parent.''

''The whistle is driving me crazy,'' he said tightly. ''And I'm not going to be some bird's foster parent.''

''You'll get used to it after a while. Okay, I'll take her now. Thanks.''

Grudgingly, Linc watched. He was fascinated with Brie's understanding of so many things—first battery cables, then a garden, now a pigeon. Who had that kind of broad spectrum of knowledge? No one he knew. He saw her in a new light and decided she was like a well of unfathomable and unknown depth.

For the next fifteen minutes, Linc was taught a lesson of interaction between a human and an animal. He'd seen nothing like it. Brie talked and chatted with Homer as if the bird were human, and occasionally reached out and petted the pigeon's back or short, stubby tail. The bird dived into the jar of baby food, flapping her wings wildly, whistling shrilly, dancing around it as she gobbled down the food and had a great time. Linc crossed his arms against his chest, sourly admitting he was enjoying the odd spectacle. More than anything, he saw Brie's pale features glow with a breathtaking radiance as she communicated with the orphaned bird through voice and touch. Linc actually felt a bit envious. What also fascinated him was that a pigeon was responding to Brie with joy because of the attention.

There was a heavy knock at the back door, and Brie's face registered relief. "That's probably Jeff," she told Linc. "Come on in," she called, raising her voice.

Linc scowled. "You always just tell someone to come in without first finding out who it is?"

"I always know who's coming here. Why should I leave Homer half fed and go find out?"

"Look, this place is in the sticks, Brie. What if it was a burglar? Or someone else up to no good?"

She shook her head, confused by the sudden tension in his body and voice. Again, her instincts begged her to be on guard toward him. Linc's reaction was ridiculous under the circumstances. "I've lived here three years, and nothing has ever happened."

He was about to give her a lecture on the topic when a string bean of a man with a narrow face appeared before them. Linc's scowl remained as he sized up Jeff Laughlin. String bean was a good word to describe him, Linc decided irritably. Laughlin was his height and a third his weight. Dark brown hair lay neatly against his skull, emphasizing his large, twinkling eyes of the same color. There was a relaxed quality to the twenty-five-year old man, and Linc decided the hazmat tech wasn't darkly handsome enough to interest

Brie. That particular thought surprised him because he didn't normally assess another male in that manner. And on the heels of that thought came a bizarre realization: he didn't want Brie to have any romantic relationships right now.

"Hey, Brie!" Jeff greeted, throwing her a wave.

"Hi, Jeff. I'd like you to meet our second trainee, Linc Tanner. Linc, this was going to be my partner, Jeff Laughlin."

Linc shook the smiling man's slender hand. "Nice meeting you," he said. Liar.

"Same here. Welcome aboard, Linc." Jeff leaned over Brie's shoulder. "You feeding the Bottomless Pit again?"

She laughed fully. "Remember what I told you. Homer is sensitive. What if I called you the Bottomless Pit? How would you feel?"

"But it's the truth! I keep trying to fill out and look like Linc here to impress the women, but it just doesn't happen."

Brie's jade eyes lightened with genuine happiness. "Maybe you ought to start eating baby food and see what happens."

"Ugh!"

Linc sat there for the next ten minutes listening to the easy banter between them. And he was uncomfortably jealous of Jeff Laughlin. Brie's lovely green eyes were sparkling with happiness. He had begun to wonder if she was always in a serious state, but now he knew differently. And he didn't like it each time Jeff reached out and touched her arm or shoulder. Brie didn't seem to mind it, but Linc did. She and Jeff sounded like the best of friends, and Linc's scowl deepened.

"Listen, Jeff, I've got a favor to ask of you," Brie said, gently placing Homely Homer in her cage.

"Name it. I'm yours forever anyway."

"You've got problems then. Seriously..."

Jeff grinned lopsidedly and rocked on his heels, his hands resting on his narrow hips. "I'm always serious where you're concerned, Brie. You know that."

"Oh, go practice those lines on the women you're stalking, and not on me!"

He had the good grace to blush slightly. "I'm still too chicken to go after Elaine down at the FM's office. Gotta keep polishing my lines until they sound genuine and not like a line," he complained.

Brie rested her hand on Jeff's shoulder, giving him a playful shake. "I'm sure Linc can help you in that department. Listen, I want you to take Linc around Canton and help him find an apartment or house this afternoon. Will you do that for me? I've got a lot of paperwork to catch up on here while you're gone."

Jeff cast Linc a conspiratorial look. "Now we've got her where we want her," he said in a dramatic stage whisper.

"What are you mumbling about, Jeff?" she demanded, placing the lid on the baby-food jar.

"Linc, tell Brie that if she doesn't have her world-famous chicken barbecue ready tonight when we get back, we aren't going anywhere. We'll just sit here underfoot all day and drive her buggy."

Brie groaned. "Jeff!"

"I want an apartment, not chicken barbecue."

"Man, do you have lousy taste. Anyway," Jeff said archly, centering all his attention on Brie, "no chicken barbecue, no driver for Linc."

"Laughlin, you're such a—"

"Yeah, I know. And you love me anyway, don't you?"

With a shake of her head, Brie slipped past him. "All right! You're such an arm twister, Laughlin."

Jeff leaned against the doorjamb, watching her move down the hall. He turned to Linc, a loose smile on his face. "I'll tell you what, Linc. You got the best person in the world to train you. Brie is one of a kind. She's special. Actually, I'm envious you're getting her for a partner and I'm not."

Linc remained sitting lazily on the desk, hands resting against his thighs. "Luck of the draw, I guess," he said in a neutral tone. Brie reappeared, drying her hands on a towel. It struck him deeply how domesticated she really was, and that knowledge sent a ribbon of warmth through him.

"Hey, Brie, what happened to your bedroom door?" Jeff asked. "Did you run into it last night?"

Brie froze, all the happiness slipping from her eyes, her face draining of color. She flashed a pleading look at Linc.

"When we got home last night it was stuck shut," Linc lied in an off-the-cuff tone, rising to his feet. "I used a little too much force unsticking it and nearly took it off the bottom hinge."

Jeff nodded, standing. "This is an old house. I told Brie one day it would start shifting on its foundation and then the windows and doors would start jamming."

Linc saw relief flood Brie's waxen features. Obviously, Jeff knew nothing of her emotional problems from the explosion. He reached out, guiding Jeff out of the room and away from the sore spot of conversation. Brie didn't need any more stress than was already hanging over her head like a scimitar. "Look, there's the Sunday paper on top of that rolltop desk in the living room. Would you mind getting it for me?" Linc asked Jeff.

"Sure. Tell you what. My pickup is parked out front. I'll get the paper and meet you out there so we can start your house hunt." Jeff leaned over, kissing Brie's cheek. "See you later, doll face."

Brie barely nodded, her dark eyes centered on Linc as they stood in the dim hall. How easily Linc had lied for her benefit. And if she hadn't known it was a lie, she would have accepted his explanation without questioning it. Uneasy, Brie tried to shake the feeling of wariness toward Linc.

Linc forced a grin. "That's not a good line to pull on the ladies today, in case you wanted to know," he told Jeff.

"Oh?" Crestfallen, Jeff shrugged. "Well, cross that one off my list. How about if I run them all by you this afternoon? You can tell me which ones are in and which ones are out."

"You've got a deal," Linc agreed amiably. He waited until Jeff disappeared before turning toward Brie. She tried to slip by him, the towel clutched in her hand.

"Wait a minute," he called to her softly, gripping her upper arm and bringing her to a halt. He saw the terror in her eyes as he swung her around. "Look," he began, "I know this isn't the time or place to talk about what happened last night, but—"

"Please, Linc," she begged, her voice strained, "not now. Not ever." She tried to shore up her dissolving defenses, barely able to hold his compassionate blue gaze. "Thanks for not telling Jeff the truth. He . . . doesn't know."

No, and neither does anyone else, little cat. But somehow, someway, you've got to let go of all that hell you're carrying around inside of you. Linc was aware of the softness of her flesh and gentled his grip on her arm. He kept his voice low and quiet. "Will you be all right here by yourself this afternoon?"

Brie gave him a shocked look. "Of course. Why?"

He gave her a slight smile. "I'm just being protective of you after what happened, Brie. You're more affected by this incident than I had realized."

Tears ached in her throat, and Brie tore herself away from Linc, blindly moving past him to escape. "I'll be okay. Now just get out of here and find a place to live."

Linc digested the desperation and pain in Brie's tone. He wanted to stay and hash out the nightmare that stayed with her. But another, wiser part of him stemmed this inclination. He would have to get Brie's trust before he could try to defuse that mass of terror she carried. Time, he told himself, heading toward the front door. Time and patience.

Brie tried her best to hide her agitation when they returned. She was in the back yard with the barbecue. Jeff waved to her. What a difference between them, Brie thought. Linc walked with long, deliberate strides, his gaze restlessly scanning right, left then toward her. He was always looking around, checking things out. That wasn't normal for most people, and Brie tried to explain his alertness on his Marine Corps experience. She felt heat move into her cheeks and avoided his intense eyes. Thank God, he wouldn't be staying with her tonight.

"Hey, guess what, Brie?" Jeff said, coming up to inspect the eight chicken breasts that were close to being done over the coals of the barbecue.

"What?" she asked dryly, barely raising her head to acknowledge Linc's presence. Her heart was thundering away at a gallop.

"Linc found a real nice apartment only two blocks from here. Man, we must have gone to at least fifteen places before he found this one."

"Two blocks?" she repeated stupidly. Only two blocks? What kind of bad luck was following her?

"Just one hitch," Jeff said, reaching out and tasting the sauce in the bowl beside the chicken. He licked his lips and smiled. "Man, you make the best sauce."

Brie stared at Linc, but his face was unreadable. "What hitch?" she ground out.

Jeff sat at the wooden picnic table nearby, spreading out the plates, utensils and napkins. "He can't move in for a week. They're still painting it and stuff." Jeff turned. "I'd offer Linc my place, but you know I live up in the attic and it's a one-room studio. I told Linc how you let me stay with you that week when I was trying to find a place to live. So I figured you'd make him the same offer." He gave her a sheepish smile. "Hope you didn't mind me telling him it was okay if he uses your couch for the rest of the week."

The brush trembled in her hand. Had Linc put Jeff up to it? He was capable of that. First anger then despair flooded her. Numbly, Brie brushed the last coating of sauce on the chicken, then started to pick the pieces up with the tongs. If she tried to back out, Jeff would be embarrassed, not to mention herself.

Linc wouldn't care. He'd taken a few on the nose before and survived. But one look into Jeff's animated face and Brie lost the heart to chastise him for his decision. Wasn't she trying to teach him good leadership? He had accurately assessed the situation and come up with what he thought was a good solution. Technically, it was. Emotionally, Brie felt a clawing sensation moving up through her, and she wanted to scream. She knew Linc would corner her sooner or later about her nightmares. And what if she had them again while he was there? She never knew when they would hit.

"No, it's okay," she said in a barely audible voice.

Jeff frowned, getting up and taking the platter of chicken.

"Sure? You're looking might peaked, Brie."

Linc was watching Brie closely from where he had sat down. The tension sizzled palpably around them. He knew and she knew. Jeff was floundering, realizing he had done something wrong, but he didn't know quite what. Linc felt his heart wrench as he met and held Brie's bleak stare, then he savagely destroyed the emotion. Brie was hiding something, and he wanted to get to the bottom of it.

Jeff waved goodbye from his truck and disappeared around the corner, swallowed up by the line of trees. Linc stood on the front porch, hands on his hips. The sun had set and the sky was a lush pink, reminding Linc of the color of Brie's cheeks. She had eaten little of the meal and had kept silent except when spoken to directly. He felt like a first-class jerk for camping under her roof. But it was necessary. It would give him the time he needed to thoroughly investigate her and the premises and, he hoped, come up with some clues on who had killed John Holcomb. He pushed several dark strands of hair off his brow, turning and going inside the house.

Brie was busy in the kitchen, an apron tied around her slender waist. She was up to her elbows in soapsuds, and Linc wandered over. He picked up a towel and began drying the dishes in the drainer.

"If word ever got back to my ex-wife that I'm helping do dishes, she'd die," he said, trying to relieve the tension between them.

"A woman's work is in the kitchen, is that it?"

He nodded amiably, giving her a warm smile meant to get her to relax. It didn't work. "Yeah, something like that."

"I suppose you wanted her barefoot and pregnant, too?"

His grin was genuine. Brie's sense of humor was still intact, thank God. "Maybe at one time."

She scrubbed the bowl hard, obviously trying to hide her nervousness. "Did you want kids?" she asked.

"No."

"Why?"

"I don't know. Maybe because I had such a rotten childhood that I never wanted to see another kid have to scratch and claw like I did to make it."

Brie raised her chin, her jade eyes meeting his. "Your child wouldn't have. He or she would have had you and your wife for parents."

"I was never home because of my job," he grumbled. Well, Linc reasoned, she was responding, and some of the terror was draining from her face. He never discussed his personal life on an assignment. He always fabricated a cover. But if it was going to get Brie to trust him, then it was worth opening up.

"I see," she said.

"I really don't dislike kids."

"I know."

He stopped wiping a plate as he stared at her. "How?"

"At noon, when I fed Homely Homer, I could tell you were enjoying her despite your protests. The look in your face, I guess."

He resumed drying the dishes with a snort. "I'm just a sucker for orphans, is all."

"I like that about you," she said softly.

A shaft of pleasure and shock hit him simultaneously. He was surprised at how happy he was over her admission. "That wasn't a line?" he teased.

Brie shook her head, pulling the sink stopper out so the suds and water could drain. "Jeff is the one practicing the lines, not me," she said, trying to smile. Maybe Linc wasn't going to bring up the nightmare. God, please don't let him do it.

"That's something I like about you. You're honest as the day is long."

Brie met his smiling eyes, sinking into his warmth and absorbing it. "What's the matter, don't you think women aren't normally honest?"

He completed drying the dishes and hung the towel over the handle of one of the drawers. "In my experience, women say one thing and mean another." And as an agent, honesty wasn't his policy. It could get him killed. Still, his conscience nudged him a bit because Brie seemed incapable of lying or being dishonest—so far.

She turned to him, wiping her lower arms. "And I suppose you never do, Tanner?"

Picking up her challenge, Linc reached out, his fingers outlining her cheek and delicate jaw line. He saw shock in her eyes, and her lips parted beneath his unexpected action. "That's one thing you'll find out about me—I'm honest. The truth may hurt, but it's better than the alternative." Guilt pricked at him. Containing the unexpected feeling Brie brought out in him made him scowl. Suspects shouldn't get under his skin, but somehow, Brie had.

He reluctantly dropped his hand to his side. Brie's flesh was soft and pliable, and he ached to continue his feather-light exploration of her. His body was going rigid at just that fleeting touch. The look in her eyes melted his professional intent, and he no longer tried to deny his building hunger for her. "Like now," he said, his voice dark like thick honey. "I've been wanting to reach out and touch you all day. To tell you that everything is going to work out. I don't like what I see in your eyes, Brie." His brows fell. "And I wish there was some way I could help you..." What the hell was happening? Linc caught himself and pulled back.

Brie lifted her fingers, resting them against her cheek where he had caressed it with his work-worn hand. A new ache throbbed to life deep within her, and she recognized the heady warmth that enveloped her. Linc was affecting her, and she didn't have time to sort out anything. She took a step away from him, folding the towel with deliberate movements. "Sometimes you have to go through a particular experience alone, Linc."

He shook his craggy head, holding her brittle eyes, which were marred with confusion. "Listen to me,

Brie. In my thirty-three years of life, I've faced just about every kind of traumatic situation you want to name, including the losing of my partner. I was able to work through some of them by myself. On others, I needed help. Emotional support.'' His voice grew husky. ''Don't shut yourself off from people who love and respect you. They can help in their own way if you let them..."

He had said enough. More than enough, judging by her startled reaction. Thoroughly disgusted with himself and his lapse of being on guard, Linc excused himself and went to the living room. He turned on the television. The overpowering urge to reach out, to drag Brie into his arms and hold her was eating him up alive. When had any woman affected him as Brie did? Never. With a grimace, he sat on the couch, idly watching the show on television, his mind on anything but that.

For an hour Linc sat there, embroiled in an emotional quandary. Restless, he got up. He wandered into the kitchen. It was empty. He looked out the window toward the back yard. Brie wasn't there. Getting concerned, he ambled toward the hall. Her bedroom was dark, with the door still ajar. There was a light beneath the closed door of Homely Homer's room, and he walked quietly up to it. Homer was whistling softly and Linc smiled, remembering what Brie had told him earlier—the little bird was happy. He knocked softly at the door, then opened it.

Brie was sitting in an overstuffed chair opposite the door, pocket book in hand. She tried to give him a slight smile.

''This is where I do my reading,'' she explained.

Linc noted how Brie looked calmer and less out of sorts. "I just got worried about where you might be."

She placed the novel in her lap, her lips curving. "Tell me something, Tanner. Are you a great big watchdog the chief has sent to hover over me?"

He felt heat in his cheeks. If only she knew how close to the truth she was. Linc ruefully shoved his hands into the pockets of his jeans. "Nah, just my normal protective mechanism coming out. Why? Does it bother you?"

Brie shifted position, curling her long legs beneath her. "It just feels strange. I'm not used to having someone care openly about me, that's all."

Linc went over to the large bookshelf that dominated the back wall. Most of the books were on chemistry, hazardous material or fire sciences. He leaned down to the bottom shelf. "What's this? Romance novels?" His mouth quirked, and he slid a glance in Brie's direction. She arched one brow.

"That's what I happen to be reading right now."

His grin increased as he straightened. "I'd never have believed it. You, of all people."

"Now what kind of crack is that? I happen to enjoy a few really good writers, and they just happen to write for a particular category."

"Are we getting defensive?"

"Not in the least," Brie shot back, relaxing beneath his banter. "You'd be surprised to know that these books can educate."

His cobalt eyes darkened with mirth. "Yeah, I'll bet they do."

"You're such a pervert on top of being a chauvinist, Tanner."

He held up his hands, enjoying their exchange. When Brie wasn't on guard, she was delightful, making him feel lighter and happier than he'd felt in a long time. "Guilty as charged, I suppose." He walked over and took the book from her hands, studying it. "Look at this cover. And you call me perverted? With two people in a clinch like that, I'd think *you're* the pervert." He handed the novel back to her.

Brie gave him a bored look. "Typical male. You're so good at casting stones at something you haven't even made the effort to research first." She waved a hand toward the bookcase. "Read one before you hand me your assessment. I hope you don't analyze haz-mat situations in the same haphazard fashion, Tanner, or we're all in trouble."

Saucy little cat, I like your style. "That's logical of you." He went to the bookcase and squatted, perusing the section containing the romance novels. "Okay, for a first-time reader of these things, which one do you suggest?"

Brie gave him a stunned look. "You're serious?"

"Yeah. We'll discuss the issue of romance novels tomorrow morning over coffee."

A smile glimmered in her eyes. "You? Alert at breakfast? This I have to see."

He ignored her jab. "Okay, which author?"

She uncurled like a cat and came to join him, their shoulders almost touching as she knelt beside him. "Let's see...there's one author here whose books can be read by a man or a woman. You'll probably like her style. She has a lot of adventure and suspense in her books." Brie pulled one off the shelf. "This one is about test pilots. Even my brother, Steve, who's a first lieutenant in the Air Force, enjoyed it.'' She put the book in his awaiting hand.

Linc slowly rose. ''Was your brother a doubting Thomas about these things like I am?''

''Dyed-in-the-wool doubter,'' she agreed, going to the chair. ''He now reads the books by this author that I send to him. Religiously.'' She sat, watching Linc as he stared at the cover then read the back-cover blurb.

''Give me the keys to the white whale,'' he said.

Brie frowned. The haz-mat truck was always locked when they weren't using it. ''Whatever for?''

''I'm going to take some of the tools from the kit and repair that bedroom door for you.''

Her heart dropped, and she stared at him. She could find no trace of any emotion in his face. ''Well, I could repair it,'' she managed to say.

''No. I did it, so I'll fix it.'' Then he added a smile that reached his eyes, making her feel warm all over. ''And I know you can probably repair it just as well if not better than me, but you're busy.''

There was so much Linc could have said to wound her or to probe more deeply into the wounds within her, but he didn't. He was keeping the conversation light for her benefit. ''I don't call reading for pleasure busy. I'll just—''

Linc leaned down, pressing his hand firmly against her shoulder so she couldn't rise. ''I said I'll do it. Just tell me where the keys are.''

Brie avoided his gaze. ''On a hook over the sink.'' She was wildly aware of his hand, her flesh burning beneath his touch. For an instant, Brie wanted to drop her book, lift her arms, slide them around his neck and draw him close to her.

Removing his hand, Linc nodded. "Okay. Just stay here and rest."

"But—"

"Damn, woman, do you always have to have the last word?" he asked, moving to the door.

Brie watched Linc's easy gait. He was a broad-shouldered man sculpted with muscle. She felt buoyant beneath his teasing. "I guess I don't." His returning smile devastated her screamingly aware senses.

"That's more like it. I always like to see a woman who knows her place."

"Linc Tanner! You get out of here before I throw this book at you!"

Chuckling, he closed the door quietly behind him. He stopped smiling and felt worry churning within him. So, he had the ability to lift her out of her quagmire. And she was responding beautifully, like a purring cat who loved his touch. Disgruntled, Linc came to the realization that he was attracted to Brie on a personal level. This wasn't supposed to happen. He had to rise above his needs, which Brie had effortlessly tapped into. Had she done it on purpose? Or was she innocent, responding to him because she needed a little support? Linc firmly rejected the possibility that Brie was genuinely drawn to him, man to woman. Tossing the romance novel on the kitchen table, he went to the haz-mat truck and got the toolbox.

It was nearly ten o'clock when he finished repairing the bottom hinge on Brie's bedroom door. She hadn't emerged from the other room all that time, and Linc suspected she was too uncomfortable about the situation to be up and about. Later, around eleven, Linc went to the room and gave a soft knock. Receiving no answer, he gently opened the door.

Linc's heart began a slow pound as he stepped inside the room. Brie was curled up and asleep in the chair, her head resting against the overstuffed fabric, the novel barely held between her long fingers. Linc removed the book from her grip and laid it on top of the bookcase. He placed his hand on her arm. He felt the texture of the cotton blouse and her supple flesh beneath it.

"Brie?"

She stirred slightly.

Linc watched her for several moments. He didn't have the heart to wake her. Let her sleep. He slipped his hands beneath her back and legs and lifted her easily. She weighed next to nothing, he thought in alarm. Her head lolled against his jaw and he absorbed the soft curves of her womanly form against him. He was aware of the sandalwood scent to her skin and inhaled it deeply. Was it perfume? He felt her stir, her hands coming to rest against his chest.

"It's all right, Brie," he told her quietly. "I'm taking you to bed."

"Bed?" she slurred.

Linc pushed the door open with his foot. "That's right, bed." He heard Brie mumble something, but he was unable to understand it. She relaxed totally within his arms, and it made him feel good. Trust was being established.

He laid her on the bed and drew the quilt over her. Another shield enclosing his heart melted away as he watched her slide into the embrace of sleep. The urge to lean down and lightly brush her full, parted lips was excruciating. Linc pushed his fingers through his hair, agitated with all the feelings Brie was bringing to life in him. He walked to the door and left it ajar. If she was going to have any nightmares, he wanted to be able to reach her quickly. Good night, he told her silently. How he wished he was beside her....

## Chapter Five

Brie awoke, feeling at peace. She stretched, uncoiling from her position, vaguely aware of dawn light peeking through the windows. What time was it? Turning her head, she stared at the luminous dials of the clock on the bed stand. Six-fifteen. Time to get up. As she sat up and realized she was still dressed, Brie frowned. Then the events of the night before returned to her. She remembered being carried by Linc. She recalled his low, vibrating voice, the strength of his chest that her hands had rested upon and a delicious feeling of being cared for.

*Care?* Her jade eyes narrowed as she considered where that word had come from. Closing her eyes, Brie allowed all the feelings that had come to her as Linc carried her to appear. She didn't remember all their conversation, only that she felt warm and lovingly cared for. Ridiculous, she told herself. She was old enough to know the difference between love and sexual attraction. And Linc was definitely sensual. It was nothing more than physical attraction, she told herself sternly. Besides, her instincts still shouted a warning to her, and until that feeling was explained, she could never fully trust him. Rubbing her face, Brie got to her feet and went to the closet to select a clean uniform. She tried to sidestep the fact that yesterday, her opinion of Linc had altered drastically. Linc was a loner because he had never been wanted. Yet he still had the ability to reach out and try to help her. That spoke of his sensitivity and unselfishness as a human being.

The lukewarm shower helped awaken her. Brie towel dried, splashed on her favorite perfume, then dressed. She continued to dwell on her budding emotional fusion with Linc. The feelings were there, whether she wanted to admit it or not. Looking at herself in the steamy mirror, Brie wondered what he saw in her. She had mouse-brown hair, now short because it had been burned off by the explosion. There was nothing exceptional about her face except for her eyes. Her mother had always told her she had lovely eyes. She wasn't built like a voluptuous woman. Instead, her breasts were small and her hips and rear only vaguely hinted that she was a woman.

"You're not a prize, Williams," she told herself out loud. "But you have other assets." She smiled because she was content to be herself and not a raving beauty depicted in so many magazines.

Brie halted at the entrance to the living room. Linc lay on the couch, too long for it, his knees drawn up beneath the pale yellow quilt, which barely covered his lower body. Her gaze moved to his naked torso, dark-haired chest and broad shoulders. Last night, she had lain on that magnificent chest. In sleep, Linc looked vulnerable, and an ache seized her. His beard shadowed his features, making his cheeks more hollow than they actually were. The dark growth gave him a powerful look, and she trembled. Brie longed to walk over, kneel down and gently trace each of those lines that life had etched in his face. She suddenly wanted to talk at length with him and ask about each one, and how it had gotten there. She wanted to know him better.

With a shake of her head, Brie wondered if moon madness was upon her. Never had any man shaken her to the core as Linc did whenever he looked at her with those thoughtful blue eyes of his. Each time, Brie felt as if he was gazing past all the walls she had erected and was clearly seeing her. But there was something else in those eyes that held secrets, and it bothered her. Tucking all those warm and disturbing thoughts away about Linc, Brie forced herself to switch to work mode. Much had to be done today—and that wasn't including possible haz-mat calls. First, coffee. And then she'd get Linc up.

The aromatic smell of coffee pulled Linc from his sound sleep. He grimaced, his back in a knot because of the lumpy cushions he slept upon. He barely opened his eyes. At first, he didn't believe what he saw. Then he forced himself to concentrate. Brie was standing in front of him, a welcoming smile on her lips, holding out a cup of coffee to him. He stared through his spiky lashes at her soft, pliant mouth, and a stab of yearning surged through him. He wanted to kiss her, to feel just how lush her red, inviting lips really were. His brain fogged and he blinked again.

"There's no secret to how a woman gets you to wake up," she said, placing the mug of coffee on the lamp table near his head. "It's six-forty, Linc. Time to get up."

Linc watched her turn with that feline grace that fed his hunger for her. She looked so damned good in that dark blue one-piece uniform. How did any man she worked with keep his hands or his eyes to himself? The scent of the coffee delighted his nostrils, and he inhaled deeply. Brie sure knew how to cater to him. For no particular reason, a lopsided smile tugged at the corners of his mouth as he levered himself into a sitting position. He pushed unruly strands of hair off his brow and gratefully took the mug in his hands, cradling it reverently. He owed Brie one for her thoughtfulness.

After an eye-opening cold shower and shave, Linc felt semihuman. For the first time, he wore the dark blue one-piece haz-mat uniform. Last night, he had sewn on the required patches with needle and thread he found near the sewing machine. Of course, the red thread didn't match, but he didn't care. The silver name tag went over his right breast pocket and the silver badge over the left one. Linc felt strange when he stared at himself in the mirror. In reality, he was a government agent and had his real badge stashed away in his apartment in D.C. It was odd to be undercover and assuming a law-enforcement identity. It didn't dissolve the fact that Brie believed in what he was, and the misrepresentation ate at him. Maybe on another case, where there was clear demarcation between himself and those committing an obvious crime, it wouldn't bother him at all. Today it did, in a very deep and disturbing way. Brie could be a killer. He had to erect those guards to protect his life and continue to play the game with her. But where did the game begin and end? The lines were blurred, and Linc felt uneasy.

He ambled to the kitchen, cup in hand. Brie was sitting at the table, chin resting in the palm of one hand, studying a clipboard before her. Soft waves of hair caressed her brow and framed her cheeks. He thought she looked beautiful, but he kept his heated, simmering comments to himself.

"Good morning," he said, heading to the coffee-pot on the counter.

Brie met his greeting with a crooked smile. "I keep wondering what you'll be like when you have to take a call in the middle of the night."

He snorted as he poured himself another cup. He turned, saw that her cup was empty and poured her another one. Settling himself at the table near her elbow, he drank in Brie's radiant face. "You'd better have that quart thermos filled to the hilt with coffee before we leave or we'll both be in big trouble," he joked. Linc couldn't hold back the compliments that he wanted to give her. It seemed the more personal he became, the more she dropped the walls she hid behind.

"I never realized a woman could look so good without makeup," he told her in a husky voice.

Brie stared in shock for just a second, caught off guard. "Why, thank you."

His smile tore at her senses. "You're welcome. This coffee sure hits the spot. You make a good cup, lady."

She colored prettily and pretended to concentrate on the task before her. "Strictly self-preservation, believe me. I can't seem to get started without it, either."

He rubbed his jaw, content to share the quiet of the morning with her. "I wonder if it has anything to do with the stress of our jobs? High stress means a lot of adrenaline flowing. Coffee's a natural upper when you're running low on adrenaline."

"Makes sense. Trauma junkies always have their fix of coffee or cigarettes," Brie observed.

He gave her a wry look, thinking how much a good night's sleep had erased the shadows beneath those lovely green eyes of hers that glimmered with flecks of gold. "Healthwise, coffee is the lesser of two evils."

"Amen," Brie agreed fervently.

"You sleep okay last night?" he asked after a few moments.

She nodded, her heart picking up. "Yes. Thank you for tucking me in last night. I was dead to the world."

"It was a pleasure, believe me," Linc said, meaning it. He saw her cheeks turn pinker, and smiled more broadly.

"Stop enjoying my discomfort so much, Tanner. Few people get to see me sacked out on a chair."

"I thought you looked kind of nice sleeping in it." He slid her a wicked glance. "I had considered waking you up like Sleeping Beauty."

Brie pursed her full lips and barely held his gaze. How many times had she wondered what it would be like to feel his strong mouth against hers? Brie tried to ignore the yearning in her body. The man carried secrets. Until he showed all of himself to her, Brie had to try to combat her attraction to him. "The day I'm

Sleeping Beauty is the day Miss Piggy will win the Miss America contest,'' she told him archly.

Linc started to laugh but stopped when he realized she was serious. "Well," he drawled, "guess I'll have to prove to you that in my eyes, you're a Sleeping Beauty and not bacon on the hoof."

Brie rose, unable to stand his closeness. She went to the counter, hoping to hide her nervousness. "Jeff should be here any minute now."

"You start at seven every morning?"

She automatically went through the motions of making beef sandwiches for three people. She had to do something, anything, to quell her nerves. "Take a look at the clipboard. It's a list of companies we've got to check. At the bottom are the classes Jeff and I will be giving to the various fire departments in our quadrant this week."

He dragged the clipboard over to him. The number of companies listed was staggering. "I was wondering what you did with your spare time," he groused.

She put a sandwich into a plastic bag and set it to one side. The world beyond the curtained window was stained with a lovely apricot dawn. "If we don't get any haz-mat calls, we can make all of them this week."

"But you always get calls."

"Sometimes we get a quiet week."

"My luck won't hold."

She smiled absently, placing a bag of potato chips and a jar of sweet gherkins into a huge grocery sack along with the sandwiches. "I'm not Irish, either, so you can count on at least one haz-mat incident."

Linc perused the list with more than a little interest. Brie was efficient and organized. Each company had been checked at three-month intervals. He twisted his head to the left, watching her work. A blanket of contentment washed over him. What would it be like to wake up every morning with Brie? The idea was tantalizing. "On an average, how many haz-mat calls do you get a week?"

"Three."

Linc groaned.

"Now, that may include something as simple as checking out old chemicals in a high-school biology department to a full-scale incident. Saturday was considered a full-blown incident." She shrugged her shoulders and added three bright red apples to the sack.

"What are you doing? Preparing to feed an army?"

"No. Just two men who have the appetite of growing boys, is all," she answered blandly, setting the bag on the table. She went over to the coffeepot and filled her battered aluminum thermos.

"You make lunch every day?"

"Yes. Most of the time we're nowhere near a McDonald's or Wendy's. And if we get a call, no one feeds you during the hours you're working. You can't just shimmy out of your gas suit and drive down to the nearest fast-food joint and order a hamburger, then get back to the site."

Linc's eyes glimmered. "Pity. No wonder you're so skinny. You starve to death out there in the field. Jeff's built like a toothpick, too."

She laughed. "Don't worry, Linc, I'll make sure you're well fed."

"How did you know the way to my heart was through my stomach?"

"Oh, please," she said in an exasperated tone. "You're as obvious as a charging bull elephant, Linc."

He was rather pleased with the analogy. He watched her make another pot of coffee. "Thanks," he murmured.

Brie cocked one eyebrow. "I wouldn't be taking it as a compliment if I were you."

There was a knock at the back door and they both turned. Jeff waved and came in, dressed in his uniform. Before he was able to get out his greeting, the phone on the wall rang. Linc saw Brie's face close as she walked over to answer it. Jeff raised his hand in greeting and zeroed in on the grocery bag.

"Bad news," Jeff warned Linc in a conspiratorial tone, motioning toward Brie.

"Why?"

"The chief knows we meet over here at Brie's at seven sharp every morning. If something serious is up, he calls us here." Jeff grimaced. "It's gonna be a bad week if we're gettin' called by the chief this early."

Linc turned his attention to Brie, who was leaning against the wall, her features sober as she talked in a low voice. What was up? he wondered. Finally, she hung up the phone, her lips thinned.

"Jeff, that was the chief. You're to drive down to Reynoldsberg right now."

"What?" he crowed in disbelief.

Brie came to the table, pulling out three beef sandwiches and an apple. "Yeah," she answered in a clipped tone, anger in her voice. "Jim McPeak's partner, Bob Townley, just got slapped into the hospital with injuries from that train derailment near Englewood." She met Jeff's widening eyes. "You're heading south, Laughlin, so close your mouth and take this for your lunch. Where you're going, you're going to need it."

"But I haven't finished my training," he protested.

Brie tried to control her anger. The chief had already boxed her into a corner by forcing Tanner on her. Now he was taking her right hand away from her. "It doesn't matter, Jeff," she said patiently. "Come on, I'll walk you to your truck. There isn't time to waste right now. McPeak needs you." I need you, she thought angrily. Tanner knew nothing of procedures except as a fire fighter, which didn't mean much. Brie wanted to slam her fist into something just to relieve the frustration she felt. Saxon was taking advantage of her, and they both knew it. Why couldn't he have taken one of the other qualified people in Quadrant Two or Three?

Linc watched Brie leave, feeling her fury. He got up, picked up the grocery sack and headed out the door to the white whale. Minutes later, she appeared with Homely Homer in her cage, a jar of baby food and the thermos in the other hand.

Wisely, Linc said nothing as he opened the back door of the truck for Brie. She gently set the cage in a corner, holding it in place with a black rubber strap. She stepped out and he shut the doors and locked them. Until the pigeon was able to fly and hunt for its own food, Brie took the bird with her every day.

"Get in, I'll drive," he told her.

Brie glowered at him as if deciding whether to rip his head off or simply chew him out with a choice expletive.

"Come on," he coaxed. "The mood you're in, you'll get us killed." He saw Brie's eyes lighten and she lifted her chin, taking a deep breath.

"You're probably right," she muttered. "Okay, you drive."

Once on the road and heading toward their first stop, a chemical company outside Canton, Linc broke the brittle, icy silence. "For whatever it's worth, I'm sorry this happened, Brie. I know I'm not much use to you—yet. If I hit the manuals hard this week, maybe I'll be able to relieve you from some of that load you're having to carry all by yourself."

Brie's features softened, and she glanced at him. "Don't mind me, Linc. Every once in a while I need to sulk like a child and get it out of my system. Coffee?"

He grinned, giving her a tender look laced with care. "I think we both could use a shot."

She gave an unladylike snort, unscrewing the cap of the thermos with angry jerks. "A shot of something. Damn, I'm so mad I could spit nails!"

"Let's talk about it, then. No sense in bottling it up inside you." Maybe he'd get a bit more information.

Brie handed him his cup then poured coffee into it. "You don't deserve this kind of welcome into your new career slot!" She slid the thermos between their chairs, put both feet on the dash, scrunched down and glared straight ahead. "I'll tell you, sometimes, this job is the armpit of the universe. I hate getting screwed around like this by management. They should have taken a more seasoned veteran from one of those other quadrants to help McPeak."

"You don't think Jeff can handle it?"

"Yes, he can handle it. He may come off carefree, but Jeff is thorough and careful. Those two things will save your neck every time out."

"Who's Bob Townley?" Linc wanted to know.

"Him!" Brie growled. "Bob's long on guts and short on common sense. Sometimes I could just throttle him. I'll lay you odds he got too close to one of those tank cars and breathed in that stuff. He's in the hospital with lung congestion because of it.''

"How serious?"

She gave a bitter laugh. "Don't worry. Bob hasn't bought it yet, and he's been in haz-mat for almost twenty years. He takes a hell of a lot of chances, but has always walked away." Her lips compressed. "This time he didn't."

Linc divided his attention between the swelling morning rush hour of Canton traffic and Brie. "You might take Saxon's choice as a backhanded compliment to you," Linc offered, hoping to make her feel better.

Brie slid him a glare. "This better be good, Tanner. How?"

"You must be an ace at training people, or he'd never have taken Jeff over seasoned vets. That's a compliment to you."

He was right, Brie decided. "Just pretend you don't know me for the next hour or two, okay, Tanner? When I get in one of these moods, I'm a brat to everyone around me. So just ignore me."

He reached over, gently massaging her tense shoulder for a moment. "Lady, you're hard to ignore under any circumstances." Then he smiled. "Besides, I think you look provocative as hell when you pout."

She gave him an exasperated look. "Tanner, you really are a pervert!"

His laughter rolled through the van. Brie tried to hide her smile, but it didn't quite work. She'd never admit it, but Linc knew how to ease her anger. "You always this good at dealing with people?" she demanded tightly.

"Just people I like," he amended, trying very hard to remain innocent-looking.

Brie shook her head and drank her coffee. "Well, for better or worse, Tanner, you and I are stuck with one another."

"Don't make it sound as if we're married. I think I'm getting cold feet already."

She met his amused blue gaze, drowning in the warmth that he was lavishing upon her. And she hadn't forgotten when he reached out and slid his hand across her shoulder in an effort to soothe her. Hope sprang strongly in her heart as she looked at him. There was a vein of pure gold running through him, she realized. She lifted her cup toward him in toast. "I owe you one, Linc."

He nodded, his mouth quirking in a grin. "Okay, I'll remember that and collect soon."

A startling coil of heat sizzled through Brie at the inference in Linc's softly spoken words. She gave him a wry look but said nothing. "Well, the day's off to a fine start," she griped. "Let's just see how far downhill this baby is going to slide."

At nine o'clock Brie entered the office of Carter Fuel and Oil of Lisbon, Ohio, and was met by the owner, Frank Carter. Tall and lean, at thirty-five, he was a proud, handsome man. He scowled darkly from where he sat at his desk behind the counter.

"What the hell's up?" Carter demanded, standing. "You were here just three months ago."

Brie gave Carter a brisk smile meant to defuse his initial reaction. Many companies panicked when a haz-mat official walked in to inspect their premises. "Our quarterly inspection, Mr. Carter."

Frank moved to the counter that separated them. He looked at Tanner, and then focused his attention on Brie. "Look, this is ridiculous, Miss Williams."

Instinctively, Linc moved to Brie's elbow in defense of her. "Mr. Carter, I don't think you have anything to get upset about."

Carter glared at him. "I sell fuel oil, not hazardous chemicals. The fire marshal's office ought to be more interested in the chemical companies up the river from me than my small company." Out of frustration, he looked at Brie. "Don't you think this is ridiculous? Every three months you drop in here unannounced?"

Brie held on to her patience. "We realize fuel oil is low on the hazardous material list, but we'd like to check out the trucks, just to make sure they aren't leaking any oil, Mr. Carter. It won't take long."

Disgruntled, the owner turned to his office manager. "Earl, go with them. I've got too much work to do to play these silly games with the state."

Earl, who was bald and fifty, nodded and quickly got to his feet. "Yes, sir, Mr. Carter!" He gave Brie a smile and hustled his rotund form around the counter. "Come with me, Brie. I'll take you over to the garage where we keep the trucks."

They crossed the hard-packed dirt yard and out of earshot of Earl, Linc asked, "Isn't Carter a little rabid about us checking his trucks?"

Shrugging, Brie said, "No, because every company we visit gets upset. They're afraid of the fines we might levy." She gestured at the fenced-in area that contained several buildings and trucks. "He's right. Fuel oil companies are low on our list of concerns, but Carter's business is on our way to two chemical plants on the Ohio River."

Linc smiled. "Luck of the draw, eh?"

"Yes. Carter's got a clean record, but it doesn't hurt to keep fuel oil companies on their toes. Sometimes a truck will have a leak, and they get lazy and won't fix it. Oil on a road can create an auto accident."

A huge German shepherd came trotting over, wagging his tail in a friendly fashion at Brie. She leaned down, murmuring words to the animal. Linc remained alert, looking around, mentally making notes that he'd later put into his own notebook of evidence.

Just as Brie and Linc were ready to leave the office of the second chemical company, at the close of the day, Brie's beeper went off. She asked to use the phone, and the secretary nodded. Giving Linc a frustrated look, Brie muttered, "Beepers going off usually mean a major haz-mat incident."

Linc nodded. "Calling the FM?"

"Yes."

Brie heard the line connect and the chief answer.

"Chief? It's Brie. What's up?"

Saxon's voice came across worried. "Brie, is Linc Tanner with you?"

Confused, Brie said, "Yes, he's here." The unspoken why was left in the silence between them.

"Let me speak to him, please?"

She held out the phone to Linc. "Chief Saxon wants to talk to you," she said, sliding out of the booth.

Linc's scowl deepened, surprise flaring momentarily in his eyes. "Me?" Saxon always talked to Brie whenever a haz-mat spill was reported. "What's going on?" he muttered, gripping the phone.

Linc's grip tightened on the phone. Something was up. His gut knotted instinctively, and he glanced at

# WOW!

## THE MOST GENEROUS
## FREE OFFER EVER!
### From the
### Silhouette Reader Service™

**GET 4 FREE BOOKS WORTH $11.80**

Affix peel-off stickers to reply card

## NO COST! NO OBLIGATION TO BUY!
## NO PURCHASE NECESSARY!

Because you're a reader of Silhouette romances, the publishers would like you to accept four brand-new Silhouette Special Edition® novels, with their compliments. Accepting this offer places you under no obligation to purchase any books, ever!

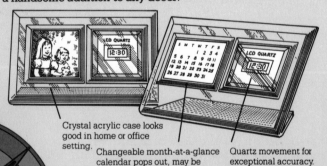

# WE EVEN PROVIDE FREE POSTAGE!

It costs you *nothing* to send for your free books — we've paid the postage on the attached reply card. And we'll pick up the postage on your shipment of free books and gifts, and also on any subsequent shipments of books, should you choose to become a subscriber. Unlike many book clubs, we charge *nothing* for postage and handling!

Brie, who stood beside him with her arms crossed, eyes reflecting suspicion as to why the call was for him.

"Linc?"

"Yes, sir."

"I want you to get over to Carol Holcomb's residence right away. I just got a teletype message from your office in D.C. via the Canton police that her house has been torn apart. It appears that it was broken into while she was gone."

Grimly, Linc listened: "I see. Burglary?"

"Not according to the Canton detectives. Nothing is missing. Carol Holcomb called in tears to report the break-in to the police department. The house is apparently a shambles. It appears as though three or four people were looking for something. Just thank God she and her daughter weren't there when they broke in."

Linc broke into a cold sweat, his eyes never leaving Brie's face. His instincts were screaming danger so loudly. "When did this happen, sir?"

"Carol Holcomb left for the grocery store at four o'clock this afternoon and returned an hour and a half later. The police were called, and after a preliminary investigation, they sent a report to your office, as they had been instructed earlier when the ATF made their initial contact with them. I was then informed via the FM as to who you were. Your boss, Mr. Cramer, wants you to get over there and investigate. Talk to Mrs. Holcomb and see if you can find anything out. Then contact a Detective Brad Gent at Canton police. He'll let you read their reports. When you're done, contact Cramer and me. I want to know what the hell is happening. I'm not so sure Mrs. Holcomb's residence being broken into is a fluke. I want Brie protected. Her house could be next. We just don't know if this is an isolated incident or not.''

Linc's jaw tightened. "Yes, sir. I'll do what I can. Goodbye." He hung up the phone, staring at it for several seconds before turning to face Brie and her questions. She couldn't know who he was. Not yet...

"The chief wants us to get back to Canton," Linc said, putting his hand on her arm and leading her out of the office. Outside, he said, "Carol Holcomb's house has just been broken into." The color drained from Brie's face. For a fleeting second, he wondered if Brie knew something about it. He opened the door for her. She stared numbly at him.

"What do you mean, 'broken into'? Are Carol and Susie all right?"

He nodded patiently, coaxing her into the seat. "They're fine. Tighten up that seat belt," he warned her.

The hour it took to get to Canton was reduced to forty minutes. Her fists were tightly clenched in her lap as she wondered how Carol really was. This was all they needed six months after John's death. Her brow furrowed as she looked at Linc's blunt features. It was on the tip of her tongue to ask him why the chief had called and asked for him. Why discuss the break-in with Linc and not her? She was too upset to think clearly and pushed the questions aside for now.

Brie's brows drew down as they approached the street she lived on. "Linc, what are you doing? I thought we were going over to Carol's house."

"We will. First I want to check something out."

Confused, Brie stared at him. He had been silent all the way back. The way he had driven, like a professional race-car driver, he had to devote all his concentration to the task. Why was he going to *her* house? Brie became even more confused when he made the van move very slowly up the tree-shrouded drive. Impatient, she rubbed her brow.

Linc's eyes narrowed as the house came into view at the end of the curve. There were no cars in the driveway other than Brie's Toyota. Everything looked peaceful and quiet. He'd know in a few minutes if someone had broken into her house. Casting a glance out of the corner of his eye at Brie, he realized she was fuming. He stopped the van.

"What are you doing parking this far from my house, Linc? What's going on? You're acting odd."

He took her impatience in stride, never allowing his gaze to leave the house. All the windows looked closed. The front door didn't look jimmied or tampered with. Maybe if they were lucky, her house hadn't been touched. "I want you to stay here, Brie," he told her, opening his door.

"What? Linc—"

He snapped his head to the right, pinning her with his narrowed cobalt gaze. "Stay here," he ordered in a low tone. "I don't want you out of this car for any reason unless I say so. Understood?"

Brie blinked, stunned by the coldness emanating from him. Her lips parted in shock, and she nodded. "All right."

A twist of a smile touched his mouth. "Just trust me."

*Trust him*, Brie thought, sitting like a caged tiger in the idling van. Why was Linc acting so odd and distant? She watched as he approached the back door to her house. The way he walked, the way he carried himself was entirely different from what she'd seen.

Brie sat there, feeling stunned, getting more and more upset by the minute. The way Linc slowly opened the screen door and carefully unlocked the back entrance made her take whatever he was doing seriously. Her heartbeat picked up as he slid like a shadow through that slit and disappeared inside.

She fidgeted. Linc came out five minutes later, some of the harshness gone from his unreadable face. As he got into the van she couldn't help snapping, "Look, I want to get over to Carol's. I don't know why you stopped here. Now if you're done, can we go?"

Linc shot her a look and said nothing, turning the van around. "We'll be there in a few minutes." Brie's home had been untouched.

Carol gave a cry when she saw Brie at the front door. Making her way through the litter of debris on the floor, Carol said, "Brie, thank God, you're here!" and threw her arms around Brie.

Brie returned the embrace and felt shock go through her as she surveyed the living room. She was barely aware of Linc coming in after her.

"My God, Carol," she stammered, releasing the blond woman, "what happened?"

Carol rubbed her reddened eyes, streaked with mascara, and made a helpless gesture. "You tell me. The police have been here for hours questioning me." She sniffed. "Come on in, although I don't know where you can sit."

Brie's heart contracted when she realized Carol was trying to make a joke of the situation. "This is awful," she said, seeing the strain in Carol's pale face. "What about Susie?"

"As soon as I saw this, I called her grandmother. She came over and picked Susie up. I just couldn't let Susie see how badly the house is torn up." And then Carol sobbed. "Oh, Brie, this is frightening! First John's death and now this...this evil thing. What have I done to deserve all this?"

Linc remained in the background, watching Brie closely as she comforted Carol Holcomb. His instincts had taken over, and he moved through each room, cataloging all that he saw. Whoever had done the dirty work knew what they were doing. There wasn't a drawer unopened and turned over to spill out its contents, a closet not empty of clothing, shoes or toys. Mattresses were yanked off beds, baring the box springs. Pillows had been slit open with a very sharp knife, the goose feathers sprinkled throughout the bedrooms. He stood in the master bedroom, surveying the professional search that had taken place. What were they looking for? Did Brie know about the break-in? Or Carol? He turned and went downstairs, his face grim.

Brie looked up from the couch where she sat with an arm around Carol's shoulder. A thread of relief flickered through her. Linc looked so capable that she automatically felt safer in his presence. He came and knelt in front of Carol.

"Look, how about if we take you out and get you a cup of coffee or something, Mrs. Holcomb? Let's get away from this place for a while. Afterward, we'll bring you back, you gather up whatever you need for the next couple of days in the way of clothes and I'll get this place back into order for you."

Carol's face sagged with relief and gratefulness. "I couldn't let you do that, Mr. Tanner—"

"Call me Linc. And I think right now, after all you've gone through, you don't need to try to get this house straightened up by yourself."

Brie's grip on Carol's shoulder became firmer. "He's right, Carol. We'll call the chief and request tomorrow off. We can clean this up for you." She wanted to cry because of Linc's generosity.

Linc saw the sunlight in Brie's wide eyes, and he managed a slight smile for her benefit. The house was a disaster area, and Brie looked so damn beautiful and untouched in it. A cold blade of terror crept up his spine. This could have happened to Brie's house. Or was Brie a part of this?

"Come on, let's get you that cup of coffee and we'll discuss what can be done to help you," he murmured, helping Carol stand.

Brie sat beside Linc in the restaurant booth, their legs brushing occasionally against each other. Linc had been right, the coffee was a good idea. Brie hadn't realized how upset she was until she felt her fingers tremble when she picked up the spoon to stir the cream and sugar. Linc saw it, but said nothing.

Carol gave them a grateful look. "I think I will take your offer of help. But I can't let you two do it by yourself."

Linc nodded. "Are you sure it won't be too upsetting?"

She shook her head. "Compared to John's death, nothing could ever be that upsetting," she murmured, "not even the house being ransacked."

"Carol," Linc began, "do you have any reason to suspect why someone might want to do this to you?"

"None. None at all. I just think it was a vicious gang of vandals. At least, that's what the police are saying."

They're lying through their teeth, Linc thought. He kept his voice low and coaxing. "Did John have any enemies?"

Carol gave him a weary look. "The police asked me the same thing. John was a good man. Just ask Brie. He loved her like the sister he never had. John didn't ever make enemies. He always made friends."

"That's true," Brie volunteered, looking at Linc's harshly set features. "I was always the hard nose collecting the enemies. He wasn't."

"What do you mean?"

Brie didn't like the edge in Linc's voice or his sudden interest in her statement. "Nothing, really," she muttered.

"No, what did you mean?"

Her nerves were frayed. "When I first started in haz-mat, I was uncompromising with chemical companies who were breaking the law. Over the years, John taught me how to be less abrasive with the people we had to deal with, that's all."

"Any names pop into your head who might have a reason to get even?" Linc held his breath.

Brie shrugged. "A few, like Bach Industries. Like I said, John smoothed the situations over and got the same things accomplished as I did, only with less abrasion. The ones that were guilty were heavily fined by the state."

Linc turned his attention to Carol, who was looking extremely fatigued. He looked at his watch. It was nearly eight o'clock. "How about if we get you some overnight clothes and you can drive to your mother's house? Brie and I can start on the cleanup tonight, and you can join us tomorrow morning.''

Carol reached out, touching Linc's hand. "I think it's a great idea. Frankly, I'm so washed out by all this that I'm ready for some sleep.''

Brie's face softened. "Come on,'' she said, scooting out of the booth and rising, "let's get going then.''

## Chapter Six

It was almost one in the morning when Brie staggered into the cleaned-up living room and flopped down on the couch. The house was quiet except for Linc working upstairs. He had asked her to put down the names of those companies who bore a grudge against the haz-mat office. Brie wrote for a short while, then gazed around, exhaustion pulling at her. She buried her hands in her face and took a long, deep breath.

That was the way Linc discovered her when he walked silently to the entrance of the room. Brie looked broken, her shoulders hunched, face buried in her hands, elbows resting on her knees. Did she know something she was hiding, and was it eating at her? He had claimed the opportunity to go through each room in the Holcomb house, looking at everything closely. Thus far, he had found nothing that indicated John

Holcomb had something to hide. What about Brie? Did she know something John knew, and was it their secret? Grimly, he walked up to her and knelt in front of her.

"Hey," he called softly, pulling Brie's hands from her face, "let's go home. You're whipped."

Brie offered him a weary smile, strengthened by his attention and unexpected tenderness. He had been so hard, cold and efficient since returning to the Holcomb house, saying little, as if he were in a totally different world as he sifted through the debris. "You're right. I am."

"Come on, let's lock this place up and call it a night."

Brie pushed away from the couch. "I hope we have a quiet night."

"So do I," Linc said. If an emergency arose, their day off could disappear.

"I don't know about you, but I'm going to grab a shower when we get home," Linc said.

"Fine. I'll feed Homer, then go to bed."

Linc managed a slight smile. "Sounds good." Right now, his focus was elsewhere. He was staring at the sheet of paper Brie had written on. Later, he would take that list to the Canton police, use their computer facilities and tie into the ATF terminal.

It was nearly two o'clock when they arrived at Brie's home. She was the last in the door and shut it behind her.

"I told you to keep that door locked, Brie. Anybody could just walk in here."

Stung, she felt her cheeks flush with anger. Linc placed his canvas bag on the floor in the kitchen and walked over to her. He hadn't meant to rip her head off as soon as he got in the door. He settled his hands on her shoulders. "I'm sorry. I didn't mean to yell at you."

Brie resisted, holding his stormy gaze. "Why are you upset, Linc? I don't understand why you're so jumpy. Ever since Carol's house was vandalized—"

"It wasn't vandalized," he ground out, releasing her. It hurt that she resisted his apology, but what else could he expect? How would he react if she had walked in the door and jumped on him? He pushed his fingers through his hair, walking around the kitchen like a caged animal.

Brie crossed her arms, watching him. "What are you talking about?"

Linc halted at a chair and glanced at the table. A sharp ache centered in his chest. There was no way Brie was going to become a casualty in this case. He said, "First, John's suspicious death. Now John's house is torn apart. Why? What was he hiding?"

"Linc, John was hiding nothing!" Brie's voice grew strained as she stared at his hard, implacable features. "I don't know why you keep digging at me with that angle. He had nothing to hide! He was always aboveboard."

"All right," Linc continued in the same tone. "What about Jameson Chemical, Cordeman Transport or Bach Industries?"

She blinked. "Those are names from the list I gave you. They've all been fined by John and me. What about them?"

"Yeah, that's what I want to know from you. What about them, Brie? Remember me asking you if anyone had made any vague threats to you or John?"

Her temper was fraying. "Yes, I remember," she said, pronouncing each word emphatically, matching his grim posture.

"I asked you if any of them had reason to get even with you. A vendetta. And you said no." His knuckles whitened against the back of the chair he was resting them on.

Brie glared at him and turned away. "I gave you the list. What else did you want?" she snapped.

Linc's nostrils flared, and his eyes turned thundercloud black. "According to your notes on these companies, Jameson has had to pay 1.5 million dollars in fines you leveled against them. Cordeman said 1.2 million, Bach 1.8 million. That is reason enough right there to want to wipe you and John off the face of this earth!" he said, walking toward her and gripping her shoulders.

A soft gasp escaped her, and she tried to twist free of Linc's capturing grasp. His sudden explosion of anger and action stunned her. "Let me go!"

"I'm not hurting you. Now stand still."

Anger warred with hurt in her as she stared at him. Suddenly, the man was a stranger to her. She felt the contained violence in him and thought it was aimed at her. He pinned her savagely with his eyes.

"Tell me about these three companies. In detail. Now." He released her and stepped away, waiting.

Brie rubbed her arm. Linc hadn't hurt her physically, but it felt like it. "You've got a problem, Linc," she shot back, her voice shaking with anger. "Earlier tonight you were sneaking around like some damn cop, and now you're giving me the third degree. Don't you think I had enough of that when I was recovering in the hospital? Don't you think I told those detectives at that time about those three companies you just mentioned?'' Her eyes narrowed. ''Just who the hell are you?''

Linc wanted to shake Brie, to tell her the truth. To tell her just how much danger he felt she was in. But he couldn't. Not yet. Not until he was satisfied she was completely innocent. She had to be hiding something! She was doing it for John because of their special relationship. His voice came out low and guarded. ''I'm going to drop over to the police department and do a little snooping around. The fines levied by the attorney general's office against those companies are public record. Anyone can get the info if they're a little persistent. I want to see if I can dig up any information the detectives might have overlooked.''

Brie had backed against the counter, standing up to Linc. ''That still doesn't explain *your* behavior. Tonight when we came back to the house, you acted as if someone was in here just waiting for us. And then you went around checking every window and door latch. You never did that before when you were here.''

''Yes, I did. Only you didn't see me do it, Brie.''

Her eyes lost their anger. ''Why are you trying to frighten me?'' The words came out soft and strained. ''Don't you think I've suffered enough? I don't need you jumpy and nervous, too.''

Linc closed his eyes and settled his hands on her shoulders. ''Brie, I'm not doing this to hurt you.'' He bit back so much of what he wanted to say. Instead, he continued on in a low tone. ''More than anything, I want you safe. I think, in some ways, you want to forget that John was probably murdered. From the drawing you did for me of the wires from the explosion that killed John and from their color, it's obvious they're the kind used by the military. That stuff is not sold on the open market." He raised his head, holding her wavering green gaze. "I know, because I've handled them in the Marine Corps. They're highly reliable in any type of weather condition, and damn near foolproof. Whoever rigged that explosion either stole the wires outright or bought them on a black market." His fingers tightened on her flesh. "Either way, Brie, it screams at me that the people who laid that trap for you were paid professionals who knew where to get the best equipment to do the job. There's no doubt in my mind that John was murdered." He dragged in a deep breath, watching his words strike Brie with force. "With Holcomb's house being a target, I feel yours will be, too, if they didn't find what they were looking for." He grew desperate. "I can't— won't risk you being here alone when or if they come."

Brie sighed, all the tension draining from her body. "My God," she whispered unsteadily. And then, "Why didn't you tell me about those wires before this?"

Linc wanted to bring her into his arms, needing her womanly warmth, her softness, some reassurance against an unknown future for both of them. But he remained where he stood. "I didn't want to alarm you, Brie. I could be wrong." He inhaled the sweet scent of her hair. "You've gone through enough. You didn't need me yelling like Chicken Little that the sky was falling in."

She stood uncertainly, suspicion in her eyes along with exhaustion. "Isn't it?" she muffled.

He released a ragged breath. "Maybe. I don't know yet." He knew. Linc stilled his anger. Pulling Detective Gent aside, he tried to convince the policeman to release a squad car to keep a watch over Brie's house when they were gone during the day, but the detective had refused. They could only spare one, and that one was going to keep watch over Carol Holcomb's residence. Linc swallowed his frustration over the idiotic move of the police department. He drew Brie into his arms.

"I'm sorry," he said huskily against her velvet cheek. "I didn't mean to yell at you."

Brie nodded, accepting his explanation. She leaned heavily against him, needing his strength right now. "It's so unreal, Linc. It's like a nightmare that never ends...." Her voice died in tremulous silence.

He heard the terror leaking through her tone and held her as tightly as he dared. "I'm here," he told her. "And until we get this situation resolved one way or another, I'm not letting you out of my sight, little cat. So don't worry, you can sleep at night."

Brie melted beneath his blue eyes, which were stormy with turmoil. "Somehow, I get the feeling you're very good at being that watchdog you were talking about earlier."

Linc nodded, feeling guilty over hiding the truth of who he really was. "You're right," he whispered thickly. "I'm very good at what I do. So don't let this break-in tear you apart. We'll be fine as long as we're together."

The tenderness of his look dissolved her tension. "For once, I'm glad you're a chauvinist," she admitted, trying to smile after he released her. "I think I'm in need of some cavemanlike protection. I'm feeling terribly vulnerable and naked." She rubbed her arms slowly, frowning, thinking of the ramifications of Linc's assessment.

"Hey, now, stop that," he chided, placing his arm around her shoulder and giving her a squeeze. "We'll go about our normal duties. You concentrate on hazmat, and I'll keep my eyes peeled." He could have kicked himself for having to disclose information to Brie. He had done it in hopes that she would reveal what she might know about John or what he was hiding. It hadn't worked, and in the end had only upset her more. Agitation and anxiety were clearly written in the depths of her jade eyes.

The phone was ringing. And ringing. And ringing. Linc rose off the couch in a stupor, stumbling toward the kitchen in the darkness. He crashed into Brie at the corner. Groggy, Linc stumbled, reaching out to stop her from falling. Myriad sensations rushed through him from the collision of her soft, rounded breasts against his naked chest, the warmth of her hand on his shoulder and the moist sweetness of her breath against his neck.

"You all right?" he mumbled, trying to orient himself to the present.

Breathless, Brie left his arms. "Y-yes . . . I'll get the phone." And she disappeared like a beautiful wraith. Linc stood dazed and touched his brow. What time was it? Three in the morning. He forced himself to the kitchen. He froze at the door, his sleep-ridden eyes widening as he drank in Brie with the phone in her hand.

The moonlight pierced the curtains at the kitchen window and back door, bathing her in a silver incandescence. The silky white nightgown clung to her body like a lover's caress, and his breath caught in his throat. Her hair, pleasantly mussed, softened her already lovely face. Her full lips looked so damned provocative. When she looked up and realized he was standing there staring at her, her eyes widened.

Linc saw something he would never have thought he would see in a woman her age—shyness. There was pleading in her eyes as she was caught and held in his hungry gaze. Turning, Linc stumbled into the darkness of the house in search of her robe. He found it at the bottom of the brass bed and brought it to her. Brie was seated at the table, hastily scribbling instructions, her voice low and still husky with sleep. Linc settled the silk robe around her shoulders and stepped back, realizing Brie's discomfort that he might have seen her twisted, red flesh a second time.

By now, the shock of running into her then seeing her clothed in that devastating nightgown was wearing off. Linc could see well enough in the moonlight and began to make them a pot of coffee. From the sounds of the phone call, he could tell it involved a haz-mat incident. The sandalwood scent of Brie lingered in the air, and he savored her scent. He leaned against the counter, allowing her honeylike voice to flow over him as she gave instructions to the caller. And when Linc realized she was staring at him, he cursed himself. Right now, all he wanted to do was walk those few steps, take her into his arms and press her length against him. He felt his body growing rigid and knew that evidence of his need would soon be visible. Concentrating on stopping this unexpected reaction, Linc pushed away from the counter and headed to the living room to dress in a clean uniform. The night was shot anyway.

Linc was sitting on the couch pulling on his socks when Brie appeared at the entrance to the living room. She had her robe on. Her arms were crossed against her breast and her face was sober. "We're going up to Cleveland. The bomb squad from their police department just called."

Linc rapidly put it together. Cleveland was where John was murdered. "What else?"

She shrugged tensely. "They got an anonymous caller telling them there were explosives in a warehouse out near the lake."

Explosives, his area of expertise. He shoved on his boots and walked over to her. Brie's face was shadowed with concern, and she was pale. "They find anything?" he asked quietly, coming to a halt inches from her.

Brie rubbed her forehead. She was achingly aware of how strong, confident and calm Linc was—and how devastatingly masculine. Her voice came out in an unexpected wobble. "Yes. A couple of bundles of TNT along with some jars with a crystal content." She raised her chin, meeting his eyes, needing his nearness. "Probably picric acid or something. Anyway, they can't identify the contents in the jar and they don't want to move it until they have confirmation from us on what it is and if it's safe to move. They can handle the dynamite easily. It's just the other stuff they're not sure about."

He settled his hands on her shoulders. Brie was trembling. His fingers tightened slightly on her warm flesh. "It's going to be all right," he told her quietly, holding her wavering gaze. Her lips parted, and Linc groaned to himself. Oh, God, just to lean down and touch her wine-red lips and take away the pain he saw so clearly in her haunted eyes.

Brie swayed toward him, and she heard a soft gasp escape him as she leaned her head on his chest. His heart was beating strongly against her ear, while her heartbeat was erratic. A quiver raced through her as she felt his hands loosen from her shoulders and his arms gently wrapped around her, drawing her close to his seemingly indestructible body. Just for a second, she cried to herself, let me forget! "Linc..." she said in a ragged whisper.

Linc brushed her hair with a kiss, inhaling her warm, feminine scent all over again. Hot, scalding fire uncoiled deep within him as he felt her arms slowly go around him and she pressed herself against his hard contours. With one hand, he stroked her silky hair. "It's going to be all right, kitten," he whispered, his voice strained. "I know what's going on inside that head of yours. I can see it in your eyes. This time, it's going to be different. No one's going to get hurt, I promise you."

A shudder ran through her, and Brie clung to his dark, healing voice. "I—I'm afraid," she said hoarsely. "It's so much like the other call that got John killed."

"Shh, I know that." Linc managed a strained smile and gently drew her inches away from him. He didn't want to, but if he didn't he knew he'd overstep the boundaries of trust he was building with her. But he wanted to kiss those trembling lips.

"Now listen to me," he said, his voice more authoritative. "My specialty is explosives. I know them like the back of my hand." He gave her a slight smile and brushed away a strand of hair that had fallen across her brow, tucking it gently behind her ear. "I also know the kinds of wires used on that stuff. If it's a setup, we'll know going in."

Her eyes rounded with terror. "But we didn't last time, Linc."

He gave her a small shake. "Neither you nor John was an expert in explosives, Brie." His face hardened. "I am. I spent sixteen months in Nam finding and detonating all kinds of explosives under the worst possible conditions. Believe me when I tell you nobody can fool me when it comes to a setup with explosives. Now go on, get dressed. I'll get the coffee in the thermos and have the van waiting for you by the time you're ready." Linc reluctantly released her, watching her closely. At first Brie swayed, then she seemed to draw on some reservoir of strength within her and stepped away. If she was a killer, this was the best act he'd ever seen put on for his benefit. It could be a trap to kill him, he realized. But one look into Brie's eyes and Linc nearly rejected the possibility. Her voice was low and tortured.

"I won't take long."

The drive would take two hours. At three-thirty in the morning, the interstates were free of all but a few cars. Red lights flashing, the white haz-mat van moved at a steady sixty-five miles per hour toward its goal on the lakefront of Cleveland. Linc glanced at Brie. She had been silent since they had gotten in the van.

"Tell me one more time about those wires leading from the drums that you and John saw."

Brie stared out into the darkness. "They were gray wires, four of them leading to the center drum. They had red things on them." She rubbed her brow. "I drew a picture of them for the investigating officers and one for you.''

"Draw them again for me now?"

Without a word, Brie took a pen from her pocket and the clipboard from the dash and painstakingly drew him the picture he requested. Her lips tightened as she bore down on the pen. "I've always thought that, since John was murdered, I would be next."

The admission came out so low that Linc barely heard it. He snapped his head toward her, his eyes narrowing. "What makes you say that?"

Brie shrugged. "Just a gut feeling, Linc. Nothing I can prove."

Frustration curdled in his throat. "Who do you think did that to John?"

She closed her eyes and tipped her head back. "That's like asking me to find the needle in the haystack."

"Look, you've got to be more specific with me, Brie. Who holds a grudge against you? You leveled fines against a lot of companies. Certainly there has to be a specific company. Who's really angry about being caught? Could they have put a contract out on you two? Have you received any threatening phone calls? Letters?"

"Slow down, Linc. I can answer only one question at a time." Again, his eyes had that look in them, and Brie wasn't sure if he was friend or foe. She hadn't even had time to ask him about his odd and unexplained behavior over the break-in at Carol's home, or the fact that the chief talked to him about it, and not her.

He grimaced. "Sorry. It's just that I'm worried, that's all." He almost said I care so much for you,

Brie. I'm not going to let anyone even get close to harming you. No matter how hard he tried to see her as a suspect, his heart kept insisting the opposite. He swallowed all that, concentrating on her halting answers.

"We never got threatening calls or letters. A few company officials hinted that we'd be sorry if we had the state attorney general go after them."

"Are there any other names beside the ones on the list you already gave me?"

She gave him a disgruntled look. "Now you sound like those damned investigators."

He ignored her sudden sarcasm, not understanding it. "Just think."

Brie placed the clipboard on her lap and rubbed her temples gently. "Linc, I was barely out of my coma and in so much pain I didn't know who I was, where I was or what happened, but those investigators were in there, hour after hour, grilling me the same way you're doing now. And what has it gotten us? Not a damn thing." Her eyes were bright with hurt. "John's dead, and the Cleveland police are no closer to who did it than months before."

Linc's mouth flattened into a single line. "They shouldn't have questioned you like that. With those kind of deep burns, you had to be almost out of your mind with pain." He glanced at her, his eyes turning tender. "I'm sorry they did that to you, Brie, for whatever it's worth." The bastards were unprofessional in the worst way. If he'd been in charge of the investigation, he'd have waited until she was at least stabilized.

Her heart ached with humiliation. What was happening to her? Brie had never spoken about her three months in the hospital to anyone, not even her parents. She gave Tanner a confused look. "How do you know so much about burns?"

His smile was cold, matching the glitter in his darkened eyes. "Remember, I was in Nam." His voice was lowered. "My best friend, Captain Dick Martin, got third-degree burns over fifty percent of his body from a booby-trapped line of explosives. I was the first to reach him and I rode out with him in the med-evac helicopter." His tone grew hoarse. "My tour was up in two weeks. As soon as I made it to the Philippines, on the way home, I stopped by the burn unit at the Navy hospital there. Dick was like a brother to me. I decided to take my thirty days' leave and stick it out with him. I saw his agony, Brie. I heard his screams as they soaked him in that water, filled him full of morphine then peeled that burned flesh from him."

Brie shut her eyes and turned her head to one side, feeling nauseous. "Then you know..." she whispered rawly.

He reached over, sliding his fingers across hers, which were curled tightly into a fist. He massaged her hand until he felt her fingers loosening. Her flesh was damp and cool. "Yes, I know, kitten. That's what I wanted to tell you the morning you woke up screaming from that nightmare. I understand your shyness and not wanting anyone to see those scars." His voice deepened, and he gripped her hand firmly in his. "More importantly, I know what courage it takes to fight back from something like this, Brie. I saw the psychological damage it inflicted on Dick. They gave him support and therapy, but he was never the same. But you—" he swallowed hard against a sudden overwhelming torrent of emotion "—you're whole.

You're functioning despite the burns. And the loss of John. Believe me when I tell you, lady, you are brave in a way I've seen few people be in my life.''

Tears pricked her eyes, and for a moment, Brie thought she was going to cry. But the tears just stayed there, and so did that huge, clawing sensation in her chest. Without a word, she lifted Linc's hand and pressed her cheek against the back of it. "Thank you."

Silence returned to the van. Brie held his hand for a long time, his touch giving stability to the world falling apart around her. Linc understood in a way few ever would. At times, she could feel his gaze upon her, but it didn't bother her as it did before. There was so much she wanted to blurt out and share with him, but the time and place were wrong. They were going to Cleveland. To a warehouse very close to the location where John had lost his life. And this time, Linc was with her. A searing pain ripped through Brie. What if Linc was killed? That would mean the loss of yet another partner. Brie couldn't stand the avalanche of pain that followed. She bit down hard on her lower lip, afraid that she would cry out.

The garish lights provided by a fire engine washed over the area. Brie walked at Linc's side, careful to make her face devoid of any emotion as they made their way toward the huddled group of fire fighters, police and reporters. Linc's presence shored Brie up enough so that she could think and act coherently. He stood to her side and slightly behind her, saying little as she covered all the salient points with the officials.

Linc stared at the aging warehouse made of wood; its roof was sagging. The full moon rode high in a sky tinged from light gray to terrifying total blackness. Linc kept his ears on Brie's conversation with the police bomb squad while his gaze swept the area. Except for the red and white lights flashing against the warehouse, the place looked like a scene from someone's worst nightmare.

A plan was made. Linc would make a careful, thorough investigation with Brie at his side while the rest of the officials remained at a safe distance. With Brie's drawing of the wires from the previous explosion and powerful flashlights in hand, they began a painstaking inspection of the outer perimeter of the warehouse. From time to time, Linc would stop and show Brie certain items, teaching her his trade. He didn't tell her, but in his mind they were no longer in Ohio. Right now, they were out in the jungles of Nam looking for a hidden trip wire that could blow them all away.

Sweat glistened on Brie's tense features as they completed the inspection of the perimeter, satisfied no wires led outside from the warehouse. She looked up at Linc's hard, unreadable face.

"We have to go inside." It was a statement, not a question.

"Yes, but I want you to wait out here for me, Brie." She was still a suspect and could possibly put him in a situation where he could be killed.

Her eyes widened enormously. "No!" It was just like before—John sending her away while he moved closer to investigate. She wouldn't do it again!

Linc gave her a patient look. "You have to trust me, Brie. There's no sense two of us going in there. I've got your drawing. That's all I need."

Stubbornly, she shook her head. "I won't let you go alone. We're a team. I won't stay out here."

His mouth remained compressed. Using all his instincts and experience, he studied her ruthlessly. Brie didn't have the face or eyes of a killer. All his senses told him she was scared to death. If she came along, he'd have to be on guard toward her and toward the situation. A double-edged sword. Damn. The look in her eyes told him she wasn't going to be left behind. "All right, let's go. But stick close. If I tell you to hit the deck, do it."

"Fine," she answered faintly, taking a better grip on the flashlight.

He took her arm. "Let's go."

Brie's heart pounded without letup. Her chest was aching and her throat so tightly constricted that it hurt to breathe. She and Linc headed toward the area where the explosives had been located. The beam from the flashlight stabbed through the pitch blackness, and Brie slipped her hand through Linc's arm. There was no sound except for her harsh breathing and the scrape of their boots against the dusty, cracked concrete beneath them.

Linc froze. "There." He moved the light down slightly.

Brie swallowed hard. There were five sticks of dynamite on the floor between two stacks of crates. Next to the dynamite was a mason jar with a blue lid.

"Kneel down," he ordered quietly.

She knelt, keeping her trembling light focused on the explosives. Brie watched in fascination as Linc shone his beam at different angles. Finally, he slowly got to his feet. He turned, his face grim.

"Stay here," he growled.

The cold command rooted her to the spot. This was a different Linc Tanner than the one she knew. Brie watched as he moved like a cat, no sounds coming from his heavy boots as he approached the explosives. Her breath caught as he stood only a few feet from them, carefully searching for wires that might lead from them. Tears stung her eyes, and Brie wanted to call out for him to be more careful than he ever had in his whole life. Her limbs froze, and her stomach shrank into a fierce, white-hot knot.

Linc dropped to his belly, all his awareness focused on that lone jar. He was a foot away from it. Sweat ran down his tense face, and he narrowed his eyes as he studied the contents. The bomb squad was ten feet away when it had first discovered the explosives and had backed away. There was a tattered label on the side, and he gently slid forward, his breath lodged in his throat as he read the faded label: picric acid. Swallowing, he gauged the crystals with even more respect. One jolting movement and he'd have his face blown off. If one crystal fell and struck another, it would set off an explosion that would level one third of the warehouse. He didn't forget that Brie was only ten feet away. She would probably be killed, too. The thought made his mouth go bitter with bile. He got lightly to his feet, the front of his uniform filthy with dust.

Brie watched him walk back to her as if he were on eggs. He reached out, lifting her from her crouched position, his hand firm on her elbow. He didn't know who was more scared in that moment. Brie's eyes were wide with terror. The moment he touched her elbow, he saw some of the fear drain from her eyes, and he was thankful that he had such a profound effect on her.

"It's picric acid," he told her softly. "There are about four ounces of it."

"Crystallized?" she croaked.

"Yes. Enough to blow this warehouse to hell and back. Come on, let's get out of here. We'll leave through the opposite entrance. I don't even want to risk walking by that stuff."

Brie agreed, her fingers at the base of her aching throat. Her knees were suddenly wobbly, and it took all her remaining strength to walk under her own power. Once outside, the cool night air hit them. Linc shut off his light, and darkness engulfed them.

"Come here," he grated softly, taking her into his arms, realizing she couldn't possibly be acting. In that instant, Linc knew she was a victim, not a suspect. As he folded her into his arms, he realized that all that remained to be done was to prove that to the satisfaction of everyone else.

She came without question, and his arms went around her, drawing her against him. A ragged sigh broke from her lips as she nestled her head beneath his hard jaw. The silence cloaked them, and all she was aware of was his sweaty male scent, the roughness of the uniform beneath her cheek and the drumlike beat of his heart. Brie sensed that some sort of emotional bonding was taking place between them. Time wound slowly to a halt as he held her tightly, his cheek against her hair. Nothing else mattered in that minute. Finally, Linc released her. She could barely make out the features of his face as she looked up at him. He gave her a grim smile.

"Come on, we've got our work cut out for us."

* * *

They greeted the rising sun with bloodshot eyes. Brie watched as the bomb squad trailer, bearing the jar of volatile picric acid in a sand-filled metal case, slowly pulled away. Taking out the dynamite had been easy in comparison. Brie was grateful that the bomb squad removed the jar. She had lost count of how many times she had removed the liquid and crystallized form of acid. It took incredibly steady hands and no fear of dying. She had neither right now. She lifted her chin, meeting Linc's weary eyes, aware of the warmth that continued to throb between them.

"What do you say we go home and get some sleep?" she asked.

He pushed several strands of dark hair off his brow. "I'd say it sounds like one hell of an idea."

Brie nodded. "You want to drive? I'll go to the fire chief and sign the last of the forms."

"Yeah, I'll do it." Linc started to turn away, then hesitated. "What about Homely Homer? Shouldn't she be hungry by now?"

A softened look came to Brie's features. For someone who knew little about animals and professed a dislike for them, Linc was turning out to be suspiciously different. She would ask him about that change some time. "Yes, there's a jar of baby food next to the cage. Just put it in there for her. And don't get alarmed if she starts nuzzling you with her beak when you do it. She'll think you're her mother."

He snorted and turned. "First time I've been a mother in that sense of the word," he grumbled, walking away. There was more to digest. As Linc fed the pigeon, he assessed Brie's actions throughout the crisis. There were several times she could have endangered his life and hadn't. Grimacing, Linc realized that Brie was a victim, and he disliked the sham he had to continue to play with her. Linc would rather have had Brie be a suspect. That way, he could continue to fight his attraction to her. Now that she was a victim, all his overprotective feelings would emerge, throwing an entirely different light on his relationship with her.

"A mess," Linc growled, putting the bird back in the cage.

Brie handed Linc the last of the coffee from their thermos. The interstate highways were heavy with rush-hour traffic into Cleveland. Thankfully, they were leaving. She felt an inner glow as Linc gave her that heated look that always suspended her breath for an instant.

"When you finish your coffee, why don't you stretch out in the back and catch a few winks," he suggested.

Brie sipped the coffee. "No, I'll stay up here and help keep you awake."

His mouth quirked. "Anyone ever appreciate how the haz-mat people go beyond and above the call of duty?"

"No. It's an expected part of our job, Linc. I warned you about putting in long hours."

He nodded. "All I want is a shower. I smell."

"Far be it from me to say that."

"You're a saucy cat for this time of the morning."

Heat stole into Brie's cheeks as she met his smiling blue eyes. "Jeff accused me of having a sense of humor at the worst of times. I guess it's true."

Linc squinted against the rising sun. "I like your humor. In my business I've found the people who can keep it in the worst situations are the ones who are the most reliable. They won't buckle under the stress."

Brie agreed. "I think our brand of comedy is labeled black humor at best."

"To an outsider hearing us, I'm sure it is. What they don't realize is that it's a way to relieve the stress and pressure we're feeling."

"Speaking of stress, did you manage to feed Homely Homer?"

He smiled, and she noted how his teeth were white against his growth of beard.

"Yeah."

"You like her?"

He gave a slight shrug. "She's okay for a pigeon, I guess."

Brie was watching him closely. "I think you like animals a lot more than you want anyone to know."

"Just never was raised around them much as a kid," he mumbled evasively.

"What happened, Linc?" Brie asked in a softened tone. "You try and make me believe you're a big, pushy bully who hates women, children and animals. I know you don't hate women too much, or we wouldn't be working so well as a team. I haven't seen you around children, so I'll reserve my opinion on that. The other night when you met Homely Homer, I saw the look in your eyes."

Linc shot her a disgruntled glare. Brie was too damn good at people watching. Much better than he gave her credit for. Agents had that knack of noticing the most minute of body language signals, not someone like Brie. "What look?" he growled, trying to bluff his way out of the situation.

Brie chortled delightedly, putting both feet on the dash and relaxing. "What look?" she mimicked. Her green eyes, although ringed with exhaustion, were filled with tenderness. "Despite all your growling, I think you wanted to pet and hold her."

"You have an unnerving habit of being insightful, Ms. Williams," he muttered.

"But I'll never use it against you, Linc."

"My experience has been different with women, Brie."

"Time will prove me on that point. You're stuck with me whether you like it or not."

Now she was teasing him, he was sure. "Am I complaining?"

Brie met his smile, drowning in the warmth she saw in his face. "So, tell me about the animals in your life, Linc Tanner. Why are you so afraid to reach out and share yourself with that little bird?"

He sobered abruptly, twisting beneath her laserlike insight. "You missed your calling," he muttered. "You should have been a shrink."

Her laughter was spontaneous and lilting. "Oh, please! Why should it bother you that someone besides you has the ability to see past walls and facades of another human being? Do you think I'll use that information against you, Linc? No, on second thought, don't answer that."

"The more someone knows about you, the more vulnerable you become to them," he stated stubbornly. "You bare your soul to another person and you're practically telling them where your Achilles heel is located."

Brie had the good sense to remain sober beneath his assumption. "You're right."

"And I don't think either of us is the kind of individual who gives much of himself away to anyone."

She was quiet for a moment, digesting their conversation. Linc was right, as usual. Gently, Brie steered him back to the subject she wanted him to talk about. "Who took the joy of loving animals away from you as a child, Linc? I can tell you like Homely Homer or you wouldn't have remembered to feed her or offered to do it."

Linc rubbed his face. "A long time ago, when I was about eight years old and living in the Bronx, I found this little gray kitten under a cardboard box by a trash dumpster outside an Italian restaurant. He couldn't have been very old, because his eyes were barely open. The family I was living with at that time had six foster kids, including me." His voice turned grim. "The old lady was getting a hefty allotment check for keeping the six of us. She spent it on new clothes and a car while she fed us cheap junk food.

"The kitten was mewing, and I rummaged through the boxes around the bottom of the dumpster until I found him." He smiled softly. "He was the furriest little thing. I'd seen cats before in the neighborhood, but they always ran when you tried to go up and pet them. Not that I blamed them. A lot of the kids hated cats and would throw anything they could get their hands on at them. I guess he thought I was his mother or something because he kept crying and sucking my fingers when I held him. So I tucked him inside my shirt and went to the back door of the restaurant.

"There was a cook there by the name of Davis. He always knew I hung around. I got up my courage and pounded on that back door until someone answered it. Thank God, it was him. I showed him the kitten and he broke into this big, toothy smile and told me what I had to do. He came back about ten minutes later with some warm milk and a glass eyedropper. He showed me how to fill the eyedropper and feed the kitten. So, before school, I'd race over to the restaurant where I had a box by the back door, feed the kitten and barely make it to class on time. After school, I'd run back there and feed him again. And at night, I'd sneak out the window in our bedroom where we all slept, and feed him a third time."

Brie swallowed, her eyes luminous. "That was wonderful. And Davis... the man had a heart."

Linc nodded grimly, keeping his eyes on the road before them. "Yeah, things went pretty good for a while. The kitten grew fast. He had big yellow eyes and long gray fur. And it got so he'd hear me coming and meet me. I couldn't believe an animal would do that. He'd begged to be lifted and carried. And when I would pick him up, he'd lick my chin and purr like crazy. I really liked that."

Brie heard the pain in his voice. "Something happened to the kitten, didn't it, Linc?"

He nodded his head. "It seemed like everything I touched, no matter how much I loved it, was taken from me. At one foster home I was happy. The man and woman really loved me. And then she finally got pregnant and they reluctantly gave me back to the orphanage because they just didn't have the money to support two children. Then I landed in that viper's nest where the woman used us to obtain extra money." He shook his head, silence settling between them. Finally, Linc said, "The kitten was hit by a garbage truck. When I found him that night, I just sat huddled against the brick building in that alley holding him and cried my eyes out. After that, I swore no one would ever hurt me again. I wouldn't let any human or animal get close enough to me to make me cry. I just couldn't accept it anymore, and in my eight-year-old mind, it was the only acceptable solution to the situation.''

"And that's when you joined one of those street gangs?''

He turned, aware of the compassion written so clearly in her face. "Yeah. I became a real hard nose. Started skipping school, getting in trouble with the cops, and finally I got dumped into juvenile court. The only good thing out of that was that the viper gave me back to the orphanage because she didn't want to have to keep coming down to the police station to pick me up.''

Brie felt the ache widening in her breast for him. Their lives were so completely different from one another. "And yet, you've made something decent out of your life despite a bad start. I think that says something about your caliber as a human being, Linc.''

"Don't put me on any pedestals, Brie. I still carry a lot of that inner toughness around with me on a daily basis. At age fourteen I met this parish priest who used to walk the worst alleys of the Bronx. He changed my life. He took me under his wing and straightened me out to a large degree. Father O'Reilly got me a scholarship to a local university and told me I had to have a degree in order to make it out in the world. So I scraped up the funds by working at a restaurant at night and going to college by day. I got a BS in chemistry.''

"So your unimpressive grades weren't from the girls and partying? They were from working until odd hours of the morning, getting a few hours' sleep, studying, then going back to class."

He grudgingly nodded. "If it hadn't been for Father O'Reilly's belief in me, I'd never have gotten through. At the time, I felt so proud of myself. I'd made it. I'd made something of myself. I was no longer a pawn someone could push around. I wouldn't be known as 'that orphan' or 'foster brat.' From then on, I was a graduate. I had respect, Brie." His brow furrowed. "I don't know if you can understand that. I was raised in Italian neighborhoods where respect was the thing. If you didn't have respect, you didn't have anything."

"You've come a long way."

"Now don't get moon-eyed over my life. There's no such thing as a happy childhood for any kid. I don't care if he was born with a silver spoon in his mouth or was a ghetto rat."

"I wasn't getting moon-eyed, to use your words," she defended swiftly.

"You're such a marshmallow. I should have known better than to tell you about myself."

A smile touched her lips, and she reached out, placing her hand on his broad shoulder. She enjoyed the strength she felt beneath her fingertips. "I'm glad you told me, and I promise I won't cry. Okay?"

"You're still a marshmallow, Williams. Through and through."

She allowed her hand to slip off his shoulder. "If you call being kind to animals and people being a marshmallow, then I guess I am."

"My definition of one goes further than that," he muttered. "You wear that heart of yours on your sleeve."

"Nothing wrong with that, Tanner."

He snorted and rubbed his watering eyes. "Like hell there isn't. Every vulture in the world can spot a patsy like you a mile away and take advantage of the situation." Like he was doing, and it ate him. Brie didn't deserve to have her trust twisted like this, and manipulated.

Brie groaned. "You're such a pessimist! Thus far, I'm still alive and in one piece at age twenty-nine. Now, I call that surviving."

His grin was wry. "I call that lucky." And then he wondered how many men had taken advantage of Brie's open, honest nature. Maybe she had learned to protect herself by remaining private. But beyond those walls of privacy, where he had already found himself, she was a sitting duck for an emotional bullet that could wound her gravely. At that moment, Linc didn't like himself very much. Brie was open to him, not even realizing he held the bullet that could destroy the trust she shared with him. A bitter taste coated his mouth, and he looked away, unable to meet her warm, vulnerable eyes.

## Chapter Seven

$F$ive days of working together, Linc thought, as he gathered several manuals from the rear of the white van. Another day on the road inspecting chemical companies was at an end. Brie took Homely Homer into the house. It's gone too fast, I want it to slow down. And then he laughed at himself. If he was honest with himself, he would admit how he liked living with Brie, even though they slept in different rooms.

His mind ranged over the clues he had picked up over the week. Brie had given him a more thorough list of companies who had threatened John or her in some vague way. Cramer was pulling the records on those companies to check the number of violations they had, if any. The company who had the most reason to kill would most likely be the one with the most fines. And Linc had continued to pry information from Brie, who was totally unsuspecting of his motives. She was taking his probing curiosity in stride, thinking all his questions were normal for someone who was breaking into the job.

In a week, they had stopped at fifteen different businesses that used or manufactured some form of chemicals that, under improper conditions, could create a hazardous material situation. Linc found these inspections enormously interesting. He cataloged every company representative's reactions to her request to go over files of transported chemicals to and from the business. And when he asked to accompany Brie to check where the contents were located she was delighted, having no idea that he was looking for totally different reasons. Brie had been pleased with his careful investigation of each of the businesses they dropped in on, commenting that he had the earmarks of a fanatic. He had only smiled and mentally logged in the nuances of each establishment. Every night, after Brie had gone to bed, he had taken out his notebook, written out thorough descriptions of the types of chemicals carried and the reactions of the reps. Cases were broken by dogged thoroughness, not luck, and Linc had the patience of Job when it came to collecting all the seeming loose ends to the puzzle. He was very good at putting evidence together after a certain number of leads had been investigated.

Linc followed Brie inside their home. He smiled at himself. He thought of her house as their home. Well? Wasn't it? Two people in a house, both fairly content with one another's presence, constituted a home. He scowled. How had Brie grown on him in five days' time? Linc found himself loath to leave her home and move into his new apartment. He would miss her bright morning humor, her coffee, her laughter, which was coming more and more easily each day they were together, her natural warmth and sensitivity, and yes, even Homely Homer. Linc grinned. Brie and that ugly duckling of a bird of hers. Even when he had been married to JoAnne, his home life was never as it had been in the past five days. The basic difference was that Brie actively sought a part in living life, and JoAnne had been content to let it pass by her. If Brie wasn't out dutifully weeding her garden, she was mowing the lawn, sneaking enough time to bake a cake, read one of her silly romantic novels and staunchly defend their value to him, cut some of those bright tulips and sweet-smelling hyacinths and place them in a vase near the couch, or so many other little, important things. He would miss her. A lot.

"Just think," Brie said, turning on the Tiffany lamp in the living room. "Your last night on that old, lumpy couch. I'll bet you're happy about that."

"I was getting kind of used to it," Linc protested, managing a smile. He sat down on the couch, unlacing his boots and taking them off. It was almost eleven, and he was tired. Brie looked fresh, despite the twelve hours they had put in that day. She took Homer's cage and carried the bird to the sewing room.

In five days, they had fallen into a routine in the evenings. Brie would shower first, stick her head around the corner and tell him the bathroom was free, then disappear into her bedroom. Tonight, he didn't want her to disappear so soon. He yearned to stretch their last hours together. Linc found himself hungry just to sit near Brie and talk with her. Those times were so rare between phone calls, haz-mat incidents and her heavy lecture schedule. They would stagger in late, wash, then fall asleep.

Linc brightened. Since he had been at the house, Brie had had no recurrence of her nightmares. He had deliberately not talked to her about them, saving it for a time when they wouldn't be pressured by external demands, when he could devote himself to helping her work through that trauma. He knew he could help Brie; it was simply a matter of patience and timing.

"I'm going to bed now, Linc. The bathroom's all yours."

Linc frowned and rose just as she disappeared. "Wait, Brie."

Brie reappeared, dressed in the appealing apricot robe that brought out the color of her complexion. Her hair was mussed, and Linc had the urge to tame those strands into place. He saw her eyes widening as he walked over to her. Even in his stocking feet, he towered over her. What was she feeling? Longing? He took a deep breath, thankful that there was no longer the fear he had seen in her eyes when they had first met. No, during this week trust had jelled between them.

"Yes?" She stood uncertainly before him, hands clasped in front of her. Her mouth went dry as she saw the naked hunger in Linc's cobalt eyes.

"What time are you waking up tomorrow?" He wanted to reach out and bury his fingers in her soft, velvet mane of hair.

"Six. Why? You don't have to get up." She smiled. "You get to sleep in as late as you want, for once."

That was the truth. Up at six, home around eleven every night. And no time for themselves. It was wearing on him already. "Wake me, okay?"

"Well, why?"

He reached up, lightly brushing her flaming red cheek. "Because I enjoy having coffee with you in the morning. Is that reason enough?" he asked huskily.

Brie's heart pounded in her breast, and she stepped away from Linc. "Okay. I'll see you in the morning then. Good night." She turned, walked down the darkened hallway and quietly shut her bedroom door.

Linc stared at the door for a long time. Give her time, he cautioned himself. Don't push her. She wasn't the type of woman who could be bulldozed into a— What? One-night stand? Linc even felt a twinge of guilt. Brie was worth more than that. How much more? Disgruntled, he picked up his pajama bottoms and headed for the bathroom, lost in his own thoughts. What did he want from Brie? She was supposed to be protected. He was a glorified guard dog.

Brie jerked up in bed, a scream ready to tear from her lips. Disoriented, she gasped for breath, trying to get control of the unleashed emotions threatening to overwhelm her. The room was dark, the light of the moon making her surroundings gray and forbidding. Shakily getting to her feet, she slipped the robe over her shoulders. Her mouth was dry and her throat constricted. She needed a drink of water. The clock on the bed stand read three o'clock. Deluged with harsh emotions over John's death and questioning her own fear, Brie went to the kitchen.

A sliver of moonlight sliced through the curtains as she picked up the glass she always had sitting near the sink. Her fingers trembled badly, and it slipped from her hand, shattering loudly in the porcelain basin. Brie stood frozen, hands over her pounding heart, staring at the jagged pieces of glass. That was how she felt—

so many parts and pieces of herself torn and mangled beyond any hope of repair. A sob caught in her throat, and she took a step away from the sink.

"Brie?"

Linc's sleep-thickened voice sent a quiver through her. Brie turned jerkily, her gaze moving across his dark-haired chest to the powerful width of his shoulders and up to his concerned features. His eyes were dark and alert with a trace of fear in them. She swallowed.

"I—" Her voice was barely a raw whisper.

Linc moved forward. "What's wrong, Brie?" He saw her eyes turn luminous with tears. "Those dreams again?" he guessed.

Brie nodded, needing to be held badly. Twisting her head, she looked at the fragments in the sink. "I—I broke it," she cried, burying her face in her hands.

"Come here," he said roughly, his voice charged with emotion. He settled his hands on her shoulders. She was trembling badly, the gown damp beneath his fingers. A soft groan came from deep within him as he brought her into the safe harbor of his arms. Her hair was cool silk against his chest, her velvet cheek like a brand on his flesh over his pounding heart.

Brie tried to take a deep breath and closed her eyes tightly, burying herself deeply in Linc's arms. "I—I'm so afraid...out of control..."

He winced as he heard the anguish in her voice. Gently, he framed her face between his fingers, lifted her chin up so their eyes met. "Listen to me," he said thickly. "You need to let it go, Brie. Let all of what you're feeling go. Do you hear me?"

Brie's lips parted as she felt the heat of his hands against her cold flesh. "B-but if I do...I'll fly apart...I'll—"

"No," he whispered harshly, his fingers tightening. "Let those tears fall, kitten. Cry for what you've lost and for how much you hurt. Come on, I'll be here for you. You aren't going to lose control. Trust me, Brie. Trust me."

The ragged thickness of his voice tore away the last of the fears that had held her tortured emotions at bay. Tears formed and slowly rolled from the corners of her eyes. Then came a low moan. Brie clutched at his hard, solid arms, clinging as if she were going to fall. She saw his face lose its hard lines and soften. The moment his thumbs brushed away the first of the tears, an explosion of pain and anger burst within her.

Linc braced himself. Brie's lips, now wet with tears, formed in a helpless cry, and he crushed her to him, burying his head against her hair. The sobs racked her body, the sounds torn from deep within her, and he felt every one of them. She had tried so hard for so long to be brave and in control when any other human would have capitulated to the terror and trauma long ago. Linc felt her knees giving way as she surrendered to her pain. In one motion, he gathered her up in his arms and carried her through the dark house to the couch where his blanket and sheets lay in twisted disarray.

He sat down with Brie on his lap, her head buried beneath his jaw, her fists on his chest. He held her and rocked her. His voice was raw as he urged her to get it all out. Her anguished cries slowly died down, and after a while she lay silent against him. An occasional spasm passed through her. She hiccuped, and Linc smiled. Brie was so soft and warm, her breasts were grazing his chest, her hip nestled against his. The sandalwood scent teased his nostrils, and he inhaled her feminine scent, which made him heady with desire for her.

His mouth rested on the damp strands of hair clinging to her wet cheek. Don't kiss her! a voice screamed in his head. He was taking advantage of Brie's lowered guard. Linc had urged her to trust him enough to allow him to help her and now... He groaned, feeling her fingers uncurl and flatten out over the mat of hair on his chest. His mouth moved down the curve of her cheek, and he tasted the salt of her tears. Linc pressed her urgently against him, savoring her velvet-smooth flesh beneath his questing mouth. His heart thundered heavily as he felt Brie move a mere fraction of an inch so that he could kiss her.

He didn't know why her action caught him off guard. Brie was a woman so different from his experience that it had never entered his mind that she might also be drawn just as powerfully to him. And yet, as his mouth barely brushed her trembling, wet lips, an incredible surge of joy went through him, stunning him with its intensity.

Her mouth was like a lush flower opening to his tender advances, he thought as he traced the curve of her lips. Her breath was broken and ragged, and he was vaguely aware of her fingers curving around his neck, drawing him closer, melding to him. His breath caught as he gloried in her shy response to his mouth. She tasted sweet, so very sweet. Her lips were yielding beneath his pressure, and achingly feminine. Sensations roared through Linc, and he fought for control. He wasn't sure who needed to be kissed more. What he did know was that they had kissed for different reasons—Brie, because she needed human contact and care in the aftermath of grief; he, because... Linc opened his eyes and stared down at Brie's pale features.

Gently, he caressed her lips one more time before pulling back. His heart was a drum beating heavily in his chest. Everywhere Brie touched him, he was on fire. His body was rigid, and he knew without a doubt that she had to be aware of his need of her. His fingers trembled as he stroked her hair. Words were useless as he sat with Brie in his arms in the quiet living room. Linc was aware of her breathing and her heartbeat slowing.

Brie closed her eyes, too devastated by the stormy release of her bottled-up emotions, needing, wanting Linc's touch. Each time he caressed her hair, he took away a little more of her pain. His wiry hair beneath her cheek tickled her nose, but she paid it no heed. The thudding beat of his steady heart promised her that there was constancy in her shattered universe. Her world centered on Linc, his arms providing her protection against the emptiness she felt in the wake of her tears. Brie took an unsteady breath, a tremor passing through her as she vividly remembered Linc's mouth moving searchingly across her lips. His tenderness opened the doors to her heart, flinging them open, and helpless, she drowned in his strength.

"Linc..." Her voice was wobbly.

His hand stilled on her hair. "Don't try to talk yet, Brie," he coaxed, pressing a kiss on her damp brow. "Just lie there and rest. We have time, kitten." Or did they? Guilt seared through him. He'd just committed a terrible error in judgment. His heart didn't think so, but his head did. Linc was getting involved. What would Brie do when she found out he'd lied to her? Abused her trust in him? Suddenly, Linc panicked.

Obediently, Brie closed her eyes, sinking into the throbbing silence, Linc's breath flowing across her brow and cheek. How long she lay there, Brie didn't know. Had she fallen asleep with Linc's chest as her pillow and his heart providing the balm she needed? The wonderful masculine scent of his body, the warmth of his flesh and the wiry mat of hair beneath her cheek and hand soothed her further. Was there anything more special than care and love shared between a man and a woman? Brie thought not, nuzzling her lips against his corded neck.

Linc changed position slightly so he could tip his head back. Had he dozed? He wasn't sure until he lifted his head and looked at the clock. Four o'clock. "Feeling better?" he asked Brie, his voice gravelly.

Brie nodded, not trusting her voice, her throat raw and dry from her wails of pure anguish. Linc's hand settled on her hair, and he gently raked his fingers through the silken mass. The sensation was utterly drugging to her.

"You slept for a while," he murmured. Linc should have been groggy, but he wasn't. His awareness was hotly centered on Brie and how good she felt in his arms.

"W-what time is it?"

"Around four."

She didn't want to stir from his arms. "I'm sorry..."

"I'm not. That's been a long time coming, kitten." His fingers brushed her cheek. "And I'm glad you shared it with me."

Brie was silent for a long time, staring into the darkness, focusing on the beat of Linc's heart. "You're a good man."

Linc managed a slight chuckle. "JoAnne would tell you differently."

She ran her hand across his collarbone, aware of the muscled strength that lay beneath her palm. "I'm not JoAnne."

"No, thank God, you're not." He gently moved her as he sat up, keeping her deep in his embrace. Looking down at her, Linc held his breath. She was gazing up at him, her eyes dark and luminous. Fragile. The word slammed home to him. He had to try to tread a fine line with her, keep his distance and continue to provide her the stability she needed. A faint smile touched his mouth as he reached down to brush some strands of hair away from her brow.

"You're good in a crisis, Linc."

"I've had a few myself." There was self-deprecation in his voice.

Brie closed her eyes again, allowing his voice to flow through her. "I've been wanting to cry for such a long time," she began tremulously. "And the tears just wouldn't come. I cried when I came out of that coma and Chief Saxon told me John was dead." Her fingers tightened on his arm. "I couldn't even make the funeral. I cried for Carol and Susie, because I knew just how much they loved John."

Linc kissed her hair. "But you never cried for yourself, did you, Brie?"

She turned, burying her face on his neck and shoulder, her arm slipping around him. "It was awful," she muffled. "Awful."

He began to rock her as the tears came again. "You endured three months of pain in that burn unit all by yourself, didn't you?"

"Y-yes," Brie said, choking. "H-how could I let my parents or my brother see me screaming like that?" She shuddered in memory of those times when she had to soak in warm water and they had torn dead flesh from her healing wounds.

Linc tightened his embrace, burying his head against hers, eyes tightly shut. "Listen to me, kitten. You're a woman of tremendous strength and courage. I've seen that rare kind of combination in some men, but never a woman before. And with that steel will, you can hold a lot at bay that ordinary people would have been forced to release a long time ago. In some ways, you've carried an even greater load because of that." He inhaled the silky scent of her hair, fighting to keep himself on a tight rein. "There's nothing wrong with crying, Brie. And there's nothing wrong in letting others see you be human. Stop trying to be Super Woman. Just be yourself. That's enough."

Brie struggled to sit up. She remained sitting next to him, his arm draped in a relaxed manner around her waist. Sniffing, she wiped the last of the tears away, giving him a shy look. The tenderness she saw in Linc's features staggered her. Was she looking at a different man? Then Brie realized that he, too, hid behind walls, just as she had. How many sides were there to Linc? A smile pulled at her lips, and she reached out, trying to dry his chest of all her tears. He caught her hand, pressing it where his heart lay.

"Don't erase what we shared," he told her in a low voice, his eyes stormy.

Her fingers tingled wildly upon contact with his hard flesh, and Brie was achingly aware of Linc as a supreme male. The black hair on his chest intensified his rugged looks; the planes in his face were etched sharply against the shadows of the retreating night.

"We've shared nothing but my pain in the five days since we met, Linc."

A gentle smile tugged at his mouth. "Am I complaining?"

His teasing was back, and Brie rallied beneath his cajoling. "No. But I can't help thinking what you must think of me."

"I accept you, Brie. *All* of you. I kinda like the way you are."

A tentative smile stretched across her lips. "You really are a masochist."

He dislodged himself from her and rose. "Stay there," he told her in an authoritative tone. Brie gave him a questioning look as he disappeared into the kitchen. He returned a few minutes later, and she noted how his thin cotton pajama bottoms hung from his hips, showing a dark line of hair that disappeared beneath the loosely knotted drawstring. Linc knelt in front of her, placing a shot glass in her hand.

"Here, drink this," he said gruffly, one hand resting on her silk-covered thigh.

Brie stared at it. "What is it?"

"Apricot brandy. Found it the other night when I was digging in the refrigerator for that last piece of lemon pie you made. Now, go on, drink it. All of it."

She tipped the small glass to her lips and gulped it down. A fiery sensation spread rapidly down her throat into her stomach; relaxation flew through her almost immediately afterward. Linc took the glass from her hands and placed it on the lamp table.

"Okay," he said, lifting her in his arms. "It's time for you to go to sleep."

Brie gasped softly as he picked her up and brought her against him. Automatically, her arms settled around his neck, her head resting on his capable shoulder. "I can walk," she protested.

"I know you can. I just like having an excuse to stay close to you."

She closed her eyes, trusting him completely. "You're good with people, Linc Tanner."

He carried her to the bed and gently laid her down. Brie looked so small and helpless in that huge brass bed. He forced himself to cover her, drawing the quilt up around her shoulders.

"Just with certain special people," he corrected quietly.

The brandy was having a powerful effect on Brie. She tried to keep her eyes open, but it was impossible. Reaching out, her slender hand hanging off the edge of the mattress, she murmured, "Thank you, Linc. I don't know what I'd have done without you..."

His eyes softened as he heard her exhausted words. How could she be anything but a victim in all this? Against his better judgment, Linc leaned over and brushed her parted lips with a kiss. "Good night, Sleeping Beauty. You're one hell of a woman in my book."

Linc glowered at the packed and unpacked boxes lying at his feet in the center of his apartment. His boss had sent them as part of the ruse Linc had to continue to play. It was Sunday night, and he still wasn't moved in! As he glared at the nondescript beige walls, the ivory drapes and ivory furniture, he thought how dull the room looked in comparison to Brie's living room. His mood had deteriorated since Saturday morning, when he woke up at eight to find Brie had made coffee, left him a note and had already gone. Throughout that day, while helping Jeff move his furniture from a third-floor attic apartment into a van, Linc wondered if Brie had left him asleep because she was too embarrassed to face him.

Hands resting on his knees, he sat in the middle of the carpet, damned unhappy. And he knew why. He missed Brie acutely. He'd never missed another woman in his life as he did her. Before, he had always been able to separate business from pleasure, work from play. This assignment was turning out all wrong, and it left him feeling nakedly vulnerable. Linc got to his knees and began to unpack the last box of books, which would go up on the bookshelves on the opposite wall. He itched to pick up the newly installed phone and give Brie a call to see if she was home yet. He didn't like the idea of her going anywhere without him! But how was he going to lie his way out of moving into an apartment just so he could stay in her home to guard her? She'd misinterpret his motives, and that could be just as disastrous. No matter what happened, Linc had to try to keep a certain distance from Brie.

It was almost nine o'clock when the doorbell chimed. Linc frowned, getting up and making his way through discarded packing boxes. Who could that be? He wasn't expecting anyone. He opened the door, and his heart began pounding. Brie stood there with a small cardboard box in her hands. Just seeing her smile melted his bad mood, and Linc grinned.

"I didn't expect you."

Brie tried to tame her thumping heart, remembering all too clearly Linc's tenderness and his kisses. She had been able to concentrate on little else. She was thankful there were no haz-mat calls, and she could do the workshop for the various fire departments with her eyes closed.

"By now I thought you might be ready for another home-cooked meal." She held the box toward him. "Supper. Are you hungry?"

Linc groaned, eagerly taking the small box. "You've got to be the world's best lifesaver. Yeah, I'm starved. Come on in. At least the kitchen is in decent shape," he muttered.

Brie tried to ignore her vivid awareness of Linc as she followed him. She put her hands in her pockets and looked around the rectangular room. Linc had put the box on the table.

"Nice," Brie approved. She pulled open a drawer by the sink and found silverware.

He snorted. "Compared to your house, it's nothing."

Brie felt a twinge of happiness when she saw Linc's face soften as he opened the foil-wrapped meal.

"I don't believe this. Stuffed pork chops, rice, gravy, peas and a salad."

With a laugh, Brie pulled out a chair for him. "Come on, sit down before you faint, Tanner. You'd think no one ever made a home-cooked meal for you the way you're behaving."

"Wait, there's one more. Is this dessert?"

Dessert is kissing you, Brie thought. "Yes. Why don't you save opening it for later? A surprise."

Unable to wait, Linc lifted out the plate and carefully unwrapped the foil around it. "A cherry pie. I'll be damned." He looked at her as she sat down. "How'd you have time to make all this stuff?"

She enjoyed his pleasure over the food. No wonder women liked cooking for their men when they made a meal seem as if it were a treasure. It would be easy to cook for Linc on a daily basis because he was grateful for her efforts. "I got home at six tonight and got to thinking that you've probably been subsisting on Wendy's and McDonald's hamburgers."

Linc sat down, eager to eat. "Ask me where all the fast-food places are now and I can tell you," he muttered. He was about to dig in when he looked at her. "Have you eaten?"

She had come to expect that of Linc—the ability to share with another. "Yes." Brie looked down at her uniform. "As you can tell, I didn't even change. I got home and started cooking."

Between bites of the succulent stuffed pork chops, Linc asked, "How'd the class go?"

"Good, as usual. The guys really got into the tactics and strategy sessions on Sunday. They had a good time and learned something in the process.

"Brie, this is delicious."

She smiled, resting her chin on her clasped hands. Just for you, Linc. For all your kindness and understanding. Through her lashes, Brie wondered how she could have thought Linc was such a bastard. Of course, they had gotten off on the wrong foot, but things were changing now, rapidly.

"How come you let me sleep Saturday morning?"

Brie roused herself, addressing his question. "I was going to wake you, but you looked so tired, Linc." She gave him a slight smile, meeting and holding his probing blue gaze. "I didn't have the heart to wake you. I was groggy from being up that night. Why should I have made you as miserable as I felt?"

He spooned a portion of rice and gravy into his mouth and was silent for a moment. "Oh, I don't know. I think we're pretty good being miserable together."

She smiled softly, meeting and drowning in his tender gaze. "Yes, yes we are. I still haven't thanked you for holding me . . . helping me through all that, Linc."

He had finished the dinner and got up to set the plate on the counter. Then he sat down. "You'd have done the same for me," he told her.

"Yes."

He folded his arms on the table, holding her wavering gaze. "How are you feeling since it happened?" Linc had worried about the deception he was playing on her. It wasn't time yet to tell her the truth because he felt she was still under too much strain. And besides, the more Brie trusted him, the more she was readily volunteering things about herself. All the scraps of evidence would eventually yield an answer.

Brie looked at the ceiling. "Fragile. As if I've had a baby-bottle brush wipe me clean inside." She lowered her head and pointed at her tear-filled eyes. "I also cry at the drop of a hat now."

Linc saw a tear drift down, leaned over and brushed it away with his thumb. "That's a good sign," he murmured.

"Is it?"

"Yeah. It means you can begin to heal now. Holding all that stuff inside was stopping you from healing, Brie. Until you get rid of the poisons you're holding, you remain raw."

She sniffed, took a Kleenex from her pocket and dabbed at her eyes.

Linc saw the frail quality in Brie's face and heard it in her voice. The cleansing had left her more vulnerable than she was comfortable with. As much as he wanted to reach out and take her into his arms or kiss her, he knew he didn't dare. Right now she needed a good friend to talk things out with. *Friends.* He laughed at himself. Another first. He'd never tried to establish a friendship with a woman before. Now it was happening.

Brie closed her eyes, resting her brow against her clasped hands. "I feel so awkward, Linc. You're almost a stranger. My parents, my brother and Carol have all reached out to try to help me." She lifted her lashes, staring blindly at the kitchen wall. "And I was afraid. Embarrassed. You should see the stack of letters I have to answer, the phone calls I have to make. I've avoided so much in the past three months."

Linc forced himself to reach for the cherry pie and begin eating it. Guilt jabbed him sharply. He'd already read those letters. How would Brie feel if she knew that? Linc didn't want to look too closely at the answer. His stomach knotted in fear. "Part of healing is getting back into contact with the world, you know. Why don't you go home and if you're up to it, give your mom and dad a call? Maybe pen a few letters. Sort of get back into the swing of living again." The last thing he wanted was for Brie to leave so soon after she had arrived.

"I know you're right. But I feel so...breakable right now, Linc. I feel as if any moment I'll just burst into tears. Thank God, I didn't do it in front of today's class. If I start crying on the phone with my mom..."

Linc gave her a steady look. "It's normal, Brie. Take my word for it."

She gave him a tender smile. "The voice of experience speaking?"

He nodded, not tasting the cherry pie. "You don't need another sad story tonight. Why don't you get your nice-looking rear out of here and go talk to some of those people who love and care about you so much?"

He lay in his own bed, with its nondescript wooden head and footboard. Nothing so individualistic as brass, he thought, like Brie's bed. Hands behind his head, Linc stared at the ceiling. There was no fan gently whirling to move the air as there had been at Brie's home. He scowled. Dammit, he missed her. And her house. Was he missing married life? Linc snorted with disgust. He'd never shared with JoAnne what he had with Brie in the past five days.

Brie was bringing out surprising and unknown facets of him. Why hadn't JoAnne? The difference between the two women was stark. Brie was assertive, JoAnne utterly passive. Brie took life by the throat, JoAnne allowed it to flow by her. Brie was highly emotional, making him feel as if he were on a roller-coaster ride. JoAnne was like a steady beacon, favoring peace above everything. She would rarely respond with a raised voice. Come to think of it, JoAnne never once lost her temper. If he and Brie were married, she would never stand still for his long absences. He wouldn't, either. He'd want to come back to Brie more than once every three or four months.

Linc rolled onto his side and stared at the white curtains covering the window. A streetlight cast unnatural brightness into the bedroom. He missed the moonlight falling through the pale green sheers of Brie's living room, giving everything a softened, almost magical quality. His mind revolved to JoAnne. In all fairness to her, she wasn't at fault. He'd simply married the wrong type of woman. He needed someone of Brie's volatility, openness and assertiveness. She made him come alive. She *was* life, he admitted. She felt deep and hard. And so did he, he was discovering, because Brie was bringing out all those stored emotions from him.

All right, little cat, we have time, he thought. Time. He was getting a lot of pleasure out of waiting for her and he'd never felt that before. He liked the idea of getting to know her before taking her to bed and making love to her....

Linc rolled on his back, hands behind his head again, the sheets in a twisted tangle around his naked body. No. I'm going to make love *with* you, little cat. He wanted to give her as much as he knew she was going to give him in return. Linc shut his eyes, dwelling on that last pleasant thought. Yes, Brie was a giver. And he, by nature, was a taker. Or was he? What was this driving need to give back to her, then? He'd never wanted to do that with another woman.

When this investigation was completed, what was he going to say to Brie? How could he defend his deceiving her to get her trust?

With a groan, Linc rolled on his belly, shoving the pillow off the bed with one dark-haired arm. Go to sleep, pal, he ordered himself. You've got another tough week in front of you. Then he thought of how he'd be spending that week with Brie. He could tolerate anything as long as she was with him. Anything.

## Chapter Eight

Linc had just stopped the white whale in front of Brie's home when their beepers went off. A week had passed since Brie had appeared on Linc's doorstep with a home-cooked meal, and they had just had a long day on the road. Brie groaned as she stepped out of the van to go inside the house and make a phone call to the FM's office.

She came out scowling. "There's a report of a Bach Industries tanker dumping chemicals at the edge of a farmer's field up in Ashtabula. If we hurry, we might catch him," she told Linc breathlessly.

It was another haz-mat incident. Feeling grim, Linc nodded. They changed clothes and grabbed food in case they were stranded on a long call. Brie checked on Homely Homer in the back of the van; the bird had to take another ride with them. Then they were pulling out of the driveway. Linc drove as Brie pulled out a map of northeast Ohio and spread it across her lap.

"What's the name of the farmer who made the call?" Linc questioned. There hadn't been time to discuss the call before.

Brie traced the quickest route to the reported area. "David Reynolds. He owns a farm up in Ashtabula County, close to Lake Erie." She pulled the folded paper from her breast pocket where she had written the farm's address as well as directions on how to get to it. "He said he saw a big tanker truck with Bach on the side of it stop near a roadside ditch and start pumping something out. When he went to investigate, he said the driver warned him away with a sawed-off shotgun."

"Wonderful," Linc muttered darkly.

"This isn't the first time that's happened with Bach," she said softly.

Linc remembered Bach had the best reason to kill John and Brie. The largest fine in the United States had been levied against the company a year ago, and John was killed three months after the fining. He felt fear and didn't want Brie out on this dangerous assignment. "Does Reynolds know what was being pumped out?"

"No."

"Did he see any placards on the truck that might give us a number so we can trace it through one of our manuals?"

"No."

"Great. This is stacking up to be quite some call."

Brie's mouth thinned. "Yes, it is."

Linc swore softly. "We'll be getting back at midnight at the earliest."

She nodded. "And that involves only driving time, not handling the incident itself," she reminded him. Brie reached over, placing her fingers on his shoulder, reveling in his powerful build. "Welcome back to the real world, Tanner."

He shot her a look. "I've been working on this job for only three weeks and I've got a gut full of this being called out twenty-four hours a day, seven days a week. I'm burned out already."

She gave him an understanding smile, tiredness shadowing her eyes. "Try three years of it. Or, like John, five years."

Linc shook his head, wanting this case broken open and solved. This job was killing. How had Brie managed to stay on top of the mental strain, the hours, and yet remain alert and capable of handling incident after incident without making an error? It was phenomenal. She was phenomenal. All the more reason to protect and keep her safe, he thought.

By the time they reached the area, it was dark. It was a moonless night, and the country highways had no streetlights to help them find the small roads given in the directions. Using a flashlight, Brie found wooden signs with peeling paint. Linc was holding on to his anger and frustration as he took the haz-mat truck slowly down the road that would lead to the Reynolds farm. The road was heavily rutted and potholed, and he had to put the truck in low gear.

They went seven miles into the countryside before Brie pointed to a farm sitting high on a hill. "This has to be it. Hold on, let me go out and look at the mailbox and see if Reynolds's name is on it."

Linc waited, always alert, his gaze perusing the dark countryside. There was no sign of a tanker, and relief sizzled through him. Brie climbed in.

"Success! David Reynolds. Okay, let's go up there and talk with him.

Dogs barked and bayed as they slowly drew to a halt in front of the old stone farmhouse. Brie quickly got out, anxious to talk with Reynolds and get something done about the situation. A porch light came on, and a man in his seventies went out to meet her.

Brie smiled and held out her hand. "Mr. Reynolds? I'm Brie Williams from the hazardous material unit."

The man's silver hair glinted in the yellow light above them. His pinched and weathered face drew into a smile of relief.

"Glad you're here." He produced three Polaroid shots. "The Bach tanker's gone, but I got these pictures of him dumping, miss."

Excitedly, Brie showed Linc the photos. Reynolds had wisely moved far enough away not to get shot at, but close enough to show the tanker dumping the chemicals into the roadside ditch.

"These are wonderful, Mr. Reynolds. I'd like to file a report on what you saw."

"Surely, come right in."

Maybe this was the break they needed, Linc thought as they walked into the home filled with antique furniture. He hoped so. By midnight, they should be home, getting some badly needed sleep. But his night was just beginning. As soon as Brie filed the report, he'd take a copy over to the Canton police and send it to the ATF and Cramer. Bach Industries was going to be scrutinized by every law-enforcement agency computer, and their board members run through an FBI check. Nothing was going to be overlooked after the Holcomb break-in.

It was midnight when they arrived at Brie's home. Linc frowned. Something looked wrong. The screen door was ajar. He knew Brie had closed it before she came back to the van. He shut off the engine, the hair on his neck rising.

"Stay here," he warned her quietly.

Brie frowned, half asleep.

"What . . . ?"

"Your back door is open."

Immediately Brie sat up. She became aware of Linc's on-guard stance. "Oh, no..." Memories of the break-in at Carol's house returned to her. "It had to be the wind that pulled the door open," she stammered.

Linc got out, telling her with a look to stay in the van. "I hope you're right." He approached the door with extreme caution. As he pulled the screen open, he saw crowbar marks on the door. With a gentle push, the door swung wide into the darkness of the kitchen.

Linc heard no sounds, only the hollow ring of emptiness as he stepped into the kitchen and switched on the light. What met his eyes sickened him. The entire kitchen was in shambles, nothing neglected, everything torn out, opened and spilled on the floor, table and counter. The pit of his stomach knotted as he cautiously went through the rest of the house.

Whoever had done this was gone. He stepped over the clutter, frantically trying to find the words to tell Brie. He knew how much love she had put into this home. His heart was pounding with pain—her pain. As he stepped toward the van, he saw her wide, questioning eyes, as if she already had guessed what had happened.

"Linc, what is it?"

"Your house," he croaked, opening the door for her, gripping her by the arm, "has been broken into."

He measured his words slowly. "Whatever it is they're looking for wasn't found at Holcomb's house, Brie. They think you have it."

Brie's fingers rested on her aching throat. Her house. Her beautiful house, which was a magical, healing place, had been broken into. She shut her eyes tightly, fighting back the tears that wanted to come. She had spent three years lovingly painting, wallpapering and adding just the right appointments that would reflect her private self.

"Did you hear me?"

Linc's voice grated over her nerves, and she realized she had been holding her breath. "Y-yes, I heard you. Linc, do you think they tore up my house as badly as Carol's?"

He heard the anguish in her soft voice and kept his firm grip on her arm as he led her to the back door. "Yes." He was lying. Brie's house was in worse shape than Holcomb's. Whoever was looking for something tore Brie's place apart and went over it with a fine-tooth comb. He felt her icy fingers clutch at his hand and he felt her terror. "Just hang in there. We'll get to the bottom of this."

Brie stood numbly in the living room. She heard Linc call the police, and minutes later, she watched several uniformed and plainclothes detectives wandering in and out of the rooms. She saw a man with powder and a brush at the front door. He's looking for fingerprints, she thought. Linc went to her, and his hand encircled her shoulder. Brie leaned against him, needing his silent strength.

Linc was watching her closely. He felt a tremble go through Brie. He was nauseated by the destruction. There wasn't one dish left in the cupboards; all of the dishes lay shattered on the kitchen floor. The paper that lined the cupboards had been torn away, exposing the wood. Linc recognized Detective Gent, who stood at the entrance to the kitchen.

"Come on," he coaxed Brie hoarsely. "Detective Gent wants to talk with us, Brie."

Brie stood in what was once her wonderful, jungle-like living room. The trees had been turned upside down, the catch pans torn off the bottom, as if someone was looking for something small enough to wedge between the pan and pot. Each of her expensively framed photos of African wildlife had been torn off the walls, slit and torn out. The back on the television had been removed, the cushions on the rattan couch ripped open. Nothing was left untouched in the raping of her house. As Brie stood in Linc's arms, she felt stunned and in shock. Carol's house had not been as brutally mutilated as hers.

It was almost three in the morning when the detectives finished questioning her. Brie was dazed, unable to think any longer. She had sat on the floor with Linc beside her, answering Gent's long list of questions in a monotone. Finally, the police said they would come back tomorrow. Silence swelled around Brie as all the men left in their black and white cruisers. Woodenly, she had gone to her bedroom and stood beside her bed, staring at the goosedown mattresses torn open and the feathers scattered everywhere. With trembling fingers, Brie touched the cool brass of the foot-board.

Linc found Brie standing there, head bowed, her hand pressed against her closed eyes. "Let's go," he urged huskily, taking her into his arms.

"Go? Where?"

He winced at the vacant expression in her eyes and her voice full of defeat. Linc studied her intently, feeling her despair. His arms tightened protectively around her.

"Home," he said thickly. "With me."

Brie's heart somersaulted. Only this time, it was with warmth, not dread. She studied his dark gaze that said so much and rested her head against his chest, allowing the beat of his heart to smooth the ragged edges of her composure.

"Yes, I'll go home with you..."

Fighting to contain a caldron of untapped feelings, Linc could only nod. He gave her a brief squeeze, looking over at Detective Gent.

"We'll be in touch," Linc promised grimly.

Gent nodded. "You bet."

"I'll call your office tomorrow morning."

"Fine, Mr. Tanner. Until then."

Centering all his attention on Brie, Linc led her through the clutter in the rooms and to the kitchen door. There was an awful darkness in her jade eyes that frightened him. All Linc wanted to do was take her to bed with him, hold her and drive away all the pain.

As they slowly walked to the van, Linc decided that somehow, Brie was at the center of the case, even if she was the victim. And even after what had taken place at her house, she honestly still didn't seem to know why. Taking a last look at her as she climbed into the van, Linc silently promised her that he would put an end to this case—soon.

In silence they drove to his apartment. Linc led her inside. "Listen, you take the bedroom," he told Brie. He opened the door and gestured toward the dark interior. "I'll sleep on the couch."

Despite her bone-deep exhaustion, Brie resisted. "Linc, you'll be more comfortable in your own bed—"

Leaning down, he pressed a kiss to her sable hair. "Don't fight me, little cat. Get a good hot bath, change into your gown and sleep."

It was a gruffly spoken order. And it sounded heavenly to Brie. A bare hint of a smile tugged at the corners of her mouth. "Okay. I'll see you in the morning."

"Fine." As soon as she was in bed, Linc was going to the Canton police to get in touch with Cramer.

Eyes burning with fatigue, Linc entered his apartment. It was nearly five o'clock. The time at the police station, much of it spent on a computer terminal connected to the ATF office in D.C., had turned up little.

Linc took a quick shower and put on his pajama bottoms. He opened the door that led to his bedroom to check on Brie. He saw her sleeping, the covers having slipped from her waist and bunched around her legs. Smiling tenderly, Linc padded softly to the bed. His eyes adjusted to the semidarkness, and he could see that Brie's face was clear of all tension. Her lips were slightly parted, and alluring.

Dragging in a deep breath, Linc carefully pulled the sheet and blanket up to Brie's waist, tucking her in. She stirred but didn't awaken. He stood there for long, torturous moments. Linc didn't want to leave. The urge to lie next to Brie and hold her throughout the long night was overwhelming. The couch in the living room was waiting for him. He should go....

Brie stirred, stretching. She felt someone nearby. When she dragged open her eyes, she realized Linc was standing by the bed, his features harsh and lined with worry.

"Linc?"

"Shh, go back to sleep, little cat. You're exhausted."

A slight smile tugged at her mouth as Linc ran his hand across the crown of her hair. "I'm feeling better."

Swallowing hard, Linc nodded. "Good." His voice sounded strangled. Brie's sounded like velvet. The ache in him grew. How he wanted just to hold her close to him. Her eyes were clouded with sleep, and he knew she wasn't really that awake at all. He ran his fingers through her silky hair. A soft sigh came from her.

"My mom used to do that," she whispered, closing her eyes again.

"Yeah?" He never wanted to stop, his trembling fingers lightly brushing the curve of her cheek. Brie was so soft, so womanly that a keen hunger swept through him.

Brie nodded, snuggling into the pillow. "When I was scared, she'd come and hold me. Then she'd make me feel better," she murmured, her words barely audible.

His throat constricted. "Are you scared?" His voice was barely above a whisper.

Raising her lashes and meeting Linc's gaze, she nodded. "Y-yes..."

"Do—do you want me to hold you?"

She captured Linc's hand and held it against her cheek. "Will you?"

Taking a shaky breath, Linc nodded. "As long as you want."

"All night?"

He managed to smile. "All night," he promised huskily, removing his hand from her's. Linc moved to the other side of the bed. His heart was pounding heavily in his chest. As he slid into bed, he realized that Brie had already sunk back into sleep. He moved to take her into his arms, knowing she probably wouldn't recall their conversation in the morning. It didn't matter. All he was going to do was hold her, give her that feeling of safety so she could continue to heal herself.

"Come here," he murmured softly. A groan escaped him when she turned over and blindly sought his arms. He felt the warm sleekness of her silk nightgown. Brie rested her head against his shoulder, hands pressed to his chest. Her scent entered his flared nostrils, and Linc's heated blood rushed with throbbing urgency throughout him. He had to strangle the urge to wake Brie and make slow, delicious love with her....

Memories of her house being broken into flooded Brie's awakening mind, and she burrowed more deeply into Linc's arms. His naked chest was warm and firm beneath her cheek. As she lay there, listening to his heartbeat, her arm wrapped around his torso, she admitted how much he'd come to mean to her on a strictly personal level. Was it love?

With a sigh, she closed her eyes, feeling Linc's arms coming around her as he awakened. She had nearly married once, but the emotions she'd felt then were not as strong and vibrant as what she felt toward Linc. His heartbeat quickened, and she knew he was fully awake.

Wanting to erase the terrible events that were stalking her, Brie pressed herself against his entire body, wanting to lose herself in Linc.

Linc levered himself upward on one elbow, gazing down at Brie in the early morning light. Her eyes were lustrous with invitation, lips parted, begging him to kiss her. He'd waited so long for her silent invitation to love her. He'd done right, and it felt good, knowing that she wanted him at last. He threaded his fingers through her silky hair, and she responded with a sigh. Her fingers moved across his shoulder and back.

"I've waited a long time for this," he told her, pressing his lips to her hair, inhaling her feminine scent. Linc ignored what his mind was screaming at him, that Brie didn't know he was an agent, that he had come to her in deception and cloaked with lies. Shoving that reality aside, he trailed kisses from her temple, across her cheek and to her awaiting lips, feeling her unfettered response.

"So have I," she said, sighing, raising her lashes, drowning in his cobalt eyes, which burned with hunger.

Linc nodded. "That night I held you on the couch and caressed you, I had wanted to carry you to the bed. I wanted to do a hell of a lot more than just hold you after you cried." His voice lowered to a gritty growl. "I wanted to make love to you, Brie. I wanted to erase all that hurt that was left in you from your storm of tears. I wanted to be there in the morning and have you wake up in my arms, knowing that I was there for more than just a one-night stand." He shook his head, mystified at the depth of his feelings for her. "I didn't even want to leave you from that moment on."

Brie stared at his rugged face and the grim set of his mouth. With a thrill, she realized Linc was revealing another part of himself to her, and elation soared through her. This was the Linc she had always known existed beyond those walls he had set around himself. "So you felt the best way to help me was to create distance between us, of a sort?"

His gaze rested on her serene features. "I want to love you," he said thickly, his body going hard with need of her. He saw and felt Brie arch against him.

"Linc," she said huskily, "I don't want that distance between us any longer."

With a groan, he brought her to him.

Brie closed her eyes, opening her arms to receive him. The instant his mouth molded firmly over hers, a small moan of pleasure escaped from her. Her arms followed the curve of his shoulders. The white-hot shock of need uncurled heatedly in her as she felt him shift so that she was lying beneath him. His breath was moist and ragged against her cheek.

"Open your mouth," he rasped, "I want to taste you, Brie. All of you..."

Another bolt of pleasure unwound through her as his tongue gently explored her mouth. An ache, so intense and startling, made her gasp as his hand trailed a path of fire around her breast. She felt her nipples

growing hard, throbbing, begging to be touched by
Linc. Her breathing became uneven, and she hun-
grily returned his fierce kiss. Brie ran her fingertips
over his back, reveling in the movement of his mus-
cles.

She was totally unprepared when Linc tore his
mouth from her lips, captured one of her nipples beneath the gown and sucked it gently. A cry of need tore
from her, and she arched toward him, filled with the
ecstasy of pleasure. Another cry tore from her as Linc
gave the other nipple equal attention, easing the ache
there. His trembling fingers pushed the straps of her
gown aside, and Brie froze. Her eyes flew open and
she lay staring up at Linc, feeling a mixture of shame
and shyness. He leaned down, kissing her lips, and she
knew it was a kiss meant to give support, not ignite
passion. He was breathing harshly as he rested his
hand upon her injured shoulder.

"I'll be gentle," he told her.

His hand had begun to push the fabric away to expose the angry red flesh that Brie was so ashamed of.
She tensed, her eyes going wide with pleading. He
leaned down, kissing her lashes, nose, cheek and finally her mouth.

"Listen to me." Linc breathed thickly against her
ear, holding her close. "It makes no difference to me
about your burns. They aren't the whole of you. It's
only skin, not your heart, that's been wounded." He
brushed a kiss on her cheek, sensing she was beginning to relax and accept his touch. "It's what I see and
feel from your heart that I want you to share with me.
Your warm, giving, loving heart." He shuddered when
she pressed herself to him. "I ache for you. I want you
so bad that I would tear this world apart to be with

you." He gently pulled down the strap. "What you have is in you. In your heart, Brie. Give that to me. Let me drown myself inside you . . ."

Tears clung like shimmering diamonds to her lashes. Then she opened her eyes, wrapped her arms around his neck and met his burning gaze. "Yes," she whispered unsteadily. "I'm not afraid anymore."

He smiled tenderly. He leaned down to place moist kisses in the valley between her breasts as he released them from the captive material. She was so beautiful, he thought, after he'd undressed her. He quivered as she lay before him on the dark wine-colored blanket, her body a creamy white with graceful curves. Pleasure sang through him when she sat up and with trembling fingers of her own helped him shed his pajamas. He liked her participation, finding it provocative. And when she came to him, settling on her knees between his legs, pressing her lips to his, his surprise melted into a caldron of fire.

He ran his hands down her torso, rested them on her hips and drew her to him. His body throbbed with heat and growing fire. A small moan of pleasure broke from her parted lips as he suckled her nipples, hands cupping their curved roundness. She was magic. She was a dream. And so much a woman. Dazed by her ability to take and to give in return, Linc brought her down upon him. He knew that because of Brie's burns, he shouldn't lie on her and have the sheet and blankets rub against her tender, recovering flesh.

Brie's heart thrashed wildly in her breast; her body screamed to be freed of the torture of needing Linc. Hot flames were burning inside her, and Brie was barely aware when he lay back, taking her with him. He lifted her easily, as if she were a feather. The instant she settled against his hips and the hardness of his body pressed against her soft, womanly core, a sweet quiver rippled through her. It was so exquisite, so shattering that Brie could only grip his arms. And when he arched against her, a sob tore from her lips and she felt need as never before. Fire spread through her belly down to where she needed to join with him. As if he had sensed her need, Brie felt herself lifted, and in the next second, she welcomed him into her.

Sensations overwhelmed her as he moved against her in the way only a man can with his woman. Liquid heat built rapidly through her, and Brie tensed. A shattering explosion roared through her, robbing her of breath, stealing her senses and hurling her to the edge of an unnamed universe. She rested her head on Linc's shoulder and called his name over and over again. His hands gently caressed her back and hips and he called thickly to her, moving, bringing her into fiery rhythm with himself once again. This time, she was aware of his power, his maleness and strength as never before. His hands tightened against her hips and he thrust deep and hard into her. Brie felt their universes collide, then fly apart in an eruption of golden light as they shared the ultimate with one another, the gift of themselves.

Linc lay there long afterward, breathing raggedly, his heart thudding savagely in his chest. Brie lay against him, her head on his shoulder. He could only feel. Thought was nonexistent, banished into exile. He ran his hands lightly down her body, which was slick and hot. Her heart was skittering, and he smiled. She was boneless, her giving, spent body molding and curving to the harder planes of his own. His hand settled on her velvet brown hair and he ran the strands between his fingers.

"You're like a feline," he said in a gritty voice, "purring and rubbing against me."

Brie couldn't open her eyes, wrapped in euphoria. "I've never thought of myself as a cat," she admitted, her voice wispy.

Linc opened his eyes. "You're the first woman I've met who reminded me of a cat. There's something about you..." He groped for words that refused to come because he was still held in the glowing, throbbing spell of what they'd just shared. He cupped her face, staring into her half-closed eyes fringed with dark lashes. Her lips were slightly swollen, and he immediately felt regret, not wanting to have hurt Brie. But she had come to him with her fire to match and mate with his, and it had torn away all his best intentions.

"Any regrets?" he asked her.

Brie closed her eyes and gave a small shake of her head. "No." She opened them and stared at him. "And you?"

Linc warmed to her. No other woman had ever asked him that. Or perhaps, cared enough to ask. For her, physical union went far beyond physical needs. But he had always known that. For Brie, the union was a nonverbal commitment of herself to him, and he was suddenly moved by what had occurred between them. He managed a slight smile, thinking how beautiful she looked after their loving, hating himself for having to keep a lie between them. "No. No regrets," he told her softly. He saw the smoldering gold flame in her eyes suddenly die, and his hands tightened on her jaw. "What is it?"

Brie placed her lips against his palm, aware of the roughened texture of his flesh, then rested her head in the crook of his shoulder. "I'm scared, Linc," she admitted.

His hand came to rest on her uninjured shoulder. "About what?"

"Us. Me, rather." She took a breath and rushed on, her words coming out in a torrent. "I know your kind. And I accept that. But it's the first time I've accepted it. I'm used to a one-to-one relationship where more counts than just the bedroom scene. I want...no, need that depth of sharing with a man." She swallowed hard. "And I know from the way you've talked in the past that a woman is pleasure. That's all. I knew all that before we made love with one another, and I accepted that about you. I'm not going to play a game with you and try to get you to change."

She had courage, Linc thought. And she was clear-headed. She was right—women were to be enjoyed in bed. But he had enjoyed Brie in and *out* of bed. "In the past three weeks you've taught me something, little cat—what it's like to be a friend to a woman."

There was disbelief in her voice. "I have?"

He smiled and kissed her hair. "I've changed my mind about women because of you." He sighed. "And it's got to be due to you. I like you as my friend, too. I like all the things we do together." Then he added as she raised her head, hope in her lovely green eyes, "In and *out* of bed."

Tears scalded her eyes as she held Linc's tender gaze. "You mean that?" she asked. His answering smile caressed her.

He wiped the tears from her cheeks. "Yes, I mean that. You're different, Brie. And it's hard to put into words what I'm talking about. You aren't like other women. You're unique, one of a kind.''

Brie leaned over and kissed his roughened cheek, then nuzzled her lips near his ear. "No, I'm not so unique, Linc," she whispered. "All I did was refuse to allow you to put me into that mold. And you had no choice because we worked together. There are many other women out there like me. Circumstances just haven't been there for you to see or discover that."

He buried his face in the curve of her neck, tasting her sweetness and the saltiness of her skin. "There may be, but I'm interested only in you, woman. Now, come here . . ." He gently rolled her onto her back, levering himself beside her. Just the sound of her voice and the brush of her fingertips on his skin sent his body into rigid awakening once again. He wasn't sure who was more surprised by it—him or Brie. But if she was surprised, it didn't show in her welcoming green eyes. He leaned down and cherished her full lips, and he knew—she loved him. Brie was incapable of hiding her real feelings, and Linc felt a powerful current of fear and joy jag through him. His new awareness made the kiss he gave her that much sweeter. Brie deserved happiness. She deserved to laugh. He had seen life dancing in her eyes. She was like the sun, touching and coaxing life from the earth.

And what was he bringing her from himself? Lies, deceit and distrust. His heart felt as if it was ripping in two. How could he tell her? When? What would happen to this fragile joy they now shared? Linc didn't want it destroyed. But how could he make Brie believe him? That his feelings for her were genuine? That he never meant to hurt her? Oh, God, he was going to, and he'd never felt as miserable.

## Chapter Nine

"So what now?" Brie asked quietly over breakfast with Linc.

"I called the FM when I was at the police department, and McPeak and Laughlin will fill in for our quadrant while we push this investigation on who's after you."

"Linc, if they want to kill me, why haven't they done it yet?"

"They may have tried with that second explosive device up in Cleveland we answered."

Brie nodded. "It might have been. But they're tearing up our homes, not firing shots at us. Or me."

Linc agreed with her. "Whoever it is is looking for something, Brie. Some tangible piece of evidence that was either in your possession or John's." He shook his head and scowled. "Believe me, I've been through all your paperwork and John's, and I can't find anything that would incriminate any company except for Bach. I just can't figure it out. When John died, did Carol give you anything of his?''

Brie thought for a moment. "I was in the hospital when she called up one day. Carol was in tears, I remember that much.''

"What else?'' Linc asked, hoping against hope that she could provide a clue or lead.

"I was on painkillers at the time, Linc. I think...I think she was going to throw out all his haz-mat books and manuals. I told her I'd take them, because John had some old ones that were out of print that had valuable information in them.''

"Did you pick them up when you got out of the hospital?''

She shook her head. "Carol had a key to my house, and she said she'd take the boxes over there. When I got home, there were three boxes in the living room near my bookcase.''

"What were in those boxes?''

"Books and manuals." Brie looked at him. "I can show them to you if the person who broke into the house didn't take them. What will you do with them?''

"Well, whatever they're looking for is probably small and could be tucked away. It means sifting page by page through all of John's books.''

Sudden excitement coursed through Brie, and she sat up. "Linc, I'll know if any of his books are missing!''

"How?''

She clapped her hands. "I have a Rolodex that has every title and author of the books I own. That was one of the things I did right after I got out of the hospital. The books that belonged to John, I made a notation on each card. We can find out right away if all his books are there. And if they aren't, we'll know within a couple of hours, and that would give us a lead!''

Linc resisted her enthusiasm. "It's a lead," he admitted gravely. He reached out, caressing her hair. "The house is a mess, Brie. Are you up to going over there?"

She gave him a tender smile, sliding her arms around his shoulders. "I'm ready to tackle it."

He ran his thumb across her flushed cheek. "From now on, I want you to be extra careful. Just stick close to me. If I tell you to hit the deck, do it without question. Okay?"

Brie swallowed hard, seeing the military part of Linc surfacing. "Yes, I'll always listen to you."

He grinned, trying to relieve some of the strain he saw appearing at the corners of her mouth. "You mean you'll stop being bossy at haz-mat spills?" he taunted.

Brie managed a smile, loving him for his ability to ease the pressure from her. "That will never happen, Tanner."

With a groan, Linc got to his feet, pulling her along with him. "I was afraid of that."

As Brie walked through her home, she felt the strong urge to start cleaning immediately, but she knew how important it was to find the Rolodex. So instead she merely waded through the overturned furniture in the living room.

Linc spotted the Rolodex on the carpet next to the cherrywood desk. He gestured for her to come and sit next to him. "Take a look at this and give me the titles of John's books and I'll make a list of them." Everywhere Linc looked, books were scattered like leaves off an autumn tree. There were hundreds of books to search through. It was going to take a long time to find them all—if they were still in the house.

Several minutes later, with thirty-five books stacked in piles, Brie called off the last title. She looked at the miniature towers that surrounded them.

"They're all here, Linc." Triumph was in her voice.

He took five books from the first stack. "That's a good sign, little cat. Now comes the hard part—going through them page by page, looking for a clue."

She joined him on the couch they had righted. "If there is one," she groused.

Linc nodded, opening the first book. "Right. But judging from the break-ins, there's probably something in one of these books that might point a finger. It's the only link I can think of between you and Carol and John."

Almost three hours later, Brie got up. "Nothing," she groaned, rubbing her neck, which she had held in the same angle for so long. The sun had changed position, leaving a muted light in the living room that she loved so much. "Come on, let's take a break and I'll pour us some coffee." At his apartment, she had wisely filled both their thermoses with coffee and brought them along with some cups.

Reluctantly, Linc followed her into the kitchen, taking the book he was thumbing through with him.

"John was one for highlighting things in yellow and making notes in the margins, wasn't he?" Linc made himself comfortable at the table.

"Yes, he was very thorough," she answered, filling the cups and sitting down opposite him.

Linc thanked her for the coffee and settled back with the book, slowly turning page after page. John's handwriting was clear and precise compared to his own hen scratchings. He read every margin note and highlighted sentence trying to figure out if they had any significance to the case.

He sat up, frowning. "Come here, look at this," Linc said, placing the book on the table.

Brie stood and leaned over Linc's shoulder, looking at where he held his finger. In the margin John had written, "PCB in #2. See Earl."

"What do you make of it?" Linc asked. "This is a chapter on polychlorinated biphenyl—PCB."

She rested one hand on Linc's shoulder, studying the cryptic note. "PCB in number two could mean a lot of things. Number two tank or tanker?"

"Earl? Who's that?"

Brie searched her memory. "Linc, I don't know when John might have made that note. He was forever making notations. Earl might have been one of his teachers in college, for all I know."

Excitement surged through Linc, and his mind began to work. "Number two could be a fuel oil grade, too. Couldn't it? You know, the oil people use to heat their homes."

"Yes, it could." Her brow wrinkled. "But PCB in fuel grade oil is illegal because PCBs are known to cause cancer."

Linc got even more excited and snapped his fingers. "Wait a minute! A certain level of PCB is found in the oil of older transformers. It could refer to an electric company, one of the companies you gave a hefty fine to—Ohio Utility."

"By law and EPA regulations, that oil is to be drained from the transformers and trucked to disposal sites."

Linc nodded, putting his finger on the name Earl and tapping it. "I'm going over to the police department." He'd call Washington and get their computers to check on all the company representatives that John and Brie had checked in the past five years to see if an Earl showed up.

"Okay, go ahead," Brie said. "I'm staying here to clean up."

After working six hours nonstop, Brie sat at the kitchen table. Slowly, her home was taking on a familiarity once again. Her mind returned to Linc and his keen interest in her problem. Every time she thought of him, her body felt like a simmering caldron of fire. Brie tried not to think of the obvious, that she was possibly falling in love with Linc. There was nothing not to like about him, she decided, feeling serene for the first time in nearly six months. He was honest, hardworking and loyal, attributes she applauded.

Linc came back four hours later. He entered the room, a look of triumph on his face.

"We may have struck pay dirt," he said, sitting down next to her on the couch. "Earl Hansen, the representative from Carter Fuel and Oil, was coughed out by the computer.''

"Oh, Linc, he couldn't possibly be a suspect!"

"Everyone is at this point, Brie."

Brie shook her head, not wanting to believe it. "Linc, he's a dear, sweet man." She grimaced, seeing the implacable set of Linc's jaw. "He used to bring me wildflowers from around the corner of the office," she muttered defensively. "How can a man who is that thoughtful and sensitive be contaminating fuel oil?"

He reached over, capturing her hand. "Believe me, little cat, people will do anything with enough reason," he murmured. Linc saw the genuine distress in Brie's eyes and felt badly.

"What are we going to do?"

He held her cool, damp hand in his, trying to soothe her. "I think I'll pay a visit to Carter Fuel under cover of darkness, take a few samples from their underground tanks and get the oil analyzed. If they are mixing PCB with good fuel oil, it isn't going to be in their office records, you can count on that."

"And if the PCB shows up?"

"Go to the authorities and have them arrest Earl and Frank Carter."

Tears gathered in Brie's eyes. "Earl is innocent! He just isn't the kind of man who would do something like that, Linc."

His mouth tightened. "Don't forget, John was murdered, and someone tried to kill you, too," he told her quietly. His words had a chilling effect on Brie. He hated shattering her illusions about people.

"All right, then I'm going with you."

"What?"

Brie got up. "I said I'm going with you."

"No way. This could get dangerous, Brie. How do we know Carter doesn't have a security guard who patrols that place at night?"

"Carter has a huge German shepherd that's loose within that fenced area." She gave him a slight smile of triumph. "And I just happen to know the dog, Captain, very well. If I'm along, I doubt if he'll bark or attack you when we go over the fence to get those samples."

Linc chafed, he didn't want Brie along. But a dog was harder to fool than a sentry, and dogs barked, alerting everyone.

"Besides, Linc, if Carter does have PCB in the fuel oil, how do we know it's in the underground tanks? Why couldn't it be in any one of the five trucks in his garage?"

She was right. That would mean taking several samples and spending a lot of time collecting them. The possibility of getting caught was doubled because of the time factor. If Brie did come along, that time could be cut in half. "Okay, you're coming along," he said gruffly, standing. "First let me contact the police." In reality he'd contact Cramer at ATF, apprising him of everything, in case something went wrong. That he had to put Brie in a potential line of fire agitated Linc. It would be so much simpler if he could walk in with a search warrant. If he did, Carter would get suspicious, legally stall for time, then remove any evidence before they could get their samples. And then where would they be? Dammit!

* * *

Brie crouched next to Linc, her heart hammering away in her throat. She checked the time on her watch: three o'clock. Linc had made her get into her dark blue uniform and wear a long-sleeved black sweater beneath it to cover her arms. Then he had produced a tin of black substance and she had had to smear it all over her face until only the whites of her eyes showed. She wore a thin black knit cap over her hair. Linc had on a different outfit: a body-molding black nylon suit. He looked frightening, Brie thought. This was the military part of Linc Tanner with which she was now dealing. Every piece of equipment he carried on his person had a use, including the 350 magnum in the black shoulder holster. A shiver crawled up her spine. When she questioned his expertise, he muttered something about learning it in Vietnam. She believed him.

"There goes the cruiser," Linc whispered, nodding to a Litton police car that crawled by the facility, which sat at the edge of town. "He won't be back for another hour. Okay, go get Captain."

Brie gave him a frightened look, felt his hand gripping hers and rose. They had been sitting for a while near the brush along the creek behind the fuel oil company. They had made sure no one was inside the compound and that the police cruisers passed by at regular intervals. She was amazed at what Linc knew about this sort of activity and was a little in awe of him as a result.

She stumbled going up the sandy incline. Quickly recovering, Brie walked with a confidence she didn't feel toward the fence. Captain was on his feet, his hackles rising, his huge yellow eyes becoming wolf-like slits.

"Captain!" Brie called softly, whistling to him. "Come on, boy! It's Brie, remember?" What if the German shepherd didn't recognize her? He had always followed her around when she visited before. Brie crouched down by the wire fence, calling the dog. Sweat popped out on her upper lip and her mouth went dry when Captain began an ominous growl. He approached her in long, graceful strides. It was a moonlit night, and Brie could see the feral glitter in the animal's eyes. She shoved her hand through the wire and held it out to him, wondering if he was going to bite her. A choked sound came out of her throat as Captain opened his mouth, revealing his white fangs.

"Captain!" she called more firmly.

The German shepherd halted a foot from her.

"What's the matter with you? You know who I am. Brie, remember?" She worked her hand farther through the fence, the flesh pinched by the wire. "Now come here! Come on!"

Captain hesitated then gave a friendly wag of his tail. Relief surged through Brie as she felt Captain's welcoming tongue on her fingers. She slowly got up on wobbly knees, the dog whining and remaining where he was. In a moment, Linc was at her side.

"Grab his collar and keep him occupied." Linc put down a small satchel, then pulled out a hypodermic needle filled with a clear liquid.

Brie's eyes widened as she saw him sink the needle into Captain's hindquarter. Moments later, the dog slowly sank to the ground. Brie uttered a cry.

"You didn't kill him, did you?"

Linc threw the satchel over the fence. Gripping her by the waist, he said, "No, he'll be unconscious for about an hour if I've guessed the dose correctly. Okay, up you go. Remember, swing one leg clear."

The six-foot-high fence was no problem with Linc's help. Brie jumped to the dusty ground and watched as Linc took the fence like a black panther. He gently picked up the dog and placed him in the shadows, making sure he was in a comfortable position.

Brie's mouth was dry, like the ground they treaded lightly upon. Her heart was hammering without pause. Each sound, no matter how far away, made her freeze. They reached the garage, and began to take samples from each of the five trucks. Linc, collecting from the underground tanks, was out in the open, visible to anyone. Would they be discovered?

Her hands trembled and she spilled some of the oil from the last truck over her gloved hand. She placed the cork in the plastic test tube and quickly made her way out of the garage, quietly closing the door behind her. A hand closed around her mouth, and Brie struggled, a scream strangling in her throat.

"Quiet!" Linc hissed into her ear, dragging her against the building.

Her breast rose and fell sharply. Linc slowly loosened his hand, and Brie gulped in several breaths of air. Then she froze. She heard it too. Men's voices, two of them. She twisted to look up at Linc's hard, sweaty face. What should they do? The sounds of the chain-link fence padlock being opened and the gate swinging wide grated on her exposed nerves. Linc pulled her behind him, signaling her to stay silent.

Brie had never felt so helpless. Or in so much real danger. Haz-mat incidents were nothing compared to this. She saw Linc slowly unsnap his holster, draw out the lethal-looking magnum and hold it ready. They were crouched at the far corner of the building with the fence and stream directly behind them. Brie saw two policemen enter the area, their flashlights moving through the darkness. They had mistimed the cruiser. She shrank against Linc as the officers walked up to the office door, tested it, then went back to their cruiser after locking the gate.

Linc turned, looking at Brie. Despite the blackness on her face, he could see the strain in her wide eyes. Without a word, he slipped his arm around her shoulders, drawing her close, needing her warmth. He helped her stand, realizing she was shaky. So was he. He always trembled after the danger was past. Keeping his hand on her elbow, he guided Brie to the fence and helped her over. As they were walking down to the bank, they heard Captain groan and flail around. Brie halted, watching the dog to make sure he would be all right. Linc waited patiently. He knew how much she cared for animals, and as Captain groggily got to his feet, shaking himself unsteadily, Brie looked at Linc, gratefulness evident in her eyes. He smiled and placed his hand on the small of her back. He led her toward the stream and to the van parked in a grove of cotton-woods.

"What's next?" Brie asked tiredly as Linc swung the van into the driveway of his apartment building.

He glanced at her. "A shower and bed for you. I'll take these over to the Canton police and have them analyzed by their lab."

Bed and sleep. Both sounded wonderful. Brie realized she felt more than exhausted. She didn't want to believe that Earl Hansen would do something as horrible as mixing PCB in people's fuel oil. "It has to be Bach Industries, Linc, not Carter Fuel."

"I hope you're right," he murmured. "Come on, I'm going to grab a shower, change, then leave."

Linc quietly unlocked the door and slipped inside. The sun had been up since six-thirty, and he'd greeted it with bloodshot eyes at the police station. It was almost eight o'clock before he'd returned home to Brie. While he dealt with the details of this investigation in the past hours, he had thought of her—and their fragile relationship built upon lies and deceit. Linc had already seen the tears in Brie's luminous eyes, her belief in mankind eroded.

Linc stood in the bedroom doorway, drinking in Brie's sleeping form like a man dying of thirst. Only he was aching to take her into his arms where she belonged. He walked to the bed and gently sat on the mattress. When he pushed back several strands of hair from her brow, she stirred, and a tender smile pulled at his mouth. You respond so beautifully to just the slightest touch, he told her silently. Linc leaned over to place a warm kiss on her parted lips.

Brie awoke in his arms, and with his name on her lips, she pulled him down upon her. She welcomed his kisses down the length of her neck and over her collarbone. Nestling his face against the soft firmness of her breast, inhaling her feminine scent, he groaned.

"This is the way it should be," he said.

With a sigh, Brie murmured, "Always."

Linc rose up on one arm, keeping a hand resting on her hip, drowning in her slumberous green eyes. "Are you awake enough to talk?"

Brie nodded, feeling the sweet ache of wanting Linc. "Yes. What time is it?"

"A little after eight," he murmured, running his fingers through her hair.

"Did you find out anything?"

"Plenty. One tanker you took a small sample from has a level of more than fifty thousand parts per million of PCBs. That's extremely high levels, not to mention illegal."

Brie struggled to sit up, the covers falling away to reveal her white silk nightgown. Disappointment clouded her features. "Now what?"

"Well, we illegally obtained those samples, so we can't use them as evidence. So now we have to get a search warrant. Of course, Carter will fight that."

Brie pushed her hand through her hair, trying to wake up. "Linc, what if we go talk with Earl? My gut says he's just not a criminal. Maybe if we can get a confession from him or something..." Her voice trailed off.

"It's worth a try," Linc admitted slowly. "If we could get Hansen to turn in evidence to us, he might be able to plea bargain his way out of this mess. I don't know. I'm not the attorney general."

Hope sprang to her eyes. "You mean, if he testifies that Carter is doing this, Earl might not have to go to jail?"

Linc nodded. "Whoa. As I said, I'm not an attorney. I can't promise him or you anything, Brie."

She slipped out of bed and put on her floor-length robe, her eyes alight with excitement. "Let me get dressed, then let's drive down to see him."

Exhaustion was lapping at Linc. The bed felt so good to him right now. All he wanted to do was crash for a few hours. "Okay, little cat. Get dressed, and we'll go have a chat with your friend." He scowled. "But you realize that Earl could have been the one who tried to have you killed?"

Brie halted at the bedroom door, the possibility sinking in. "Y-yes, I realize that, Linc." Her fingers curled around the doorknob. "I just don't want to believe he would do such a thing."

Linc lay down, arms crossed on his chest after Brie had disappeared into the bathroom. She had every faith in the world in that untarnished heart of hers. How he hoped for her sake that Earl was innocent. But wasn't that one of the many facets of Brie he loved? Her view of people, that they weren't all bad or had ulterior motives.

But would she be able to feel that way about him after the case was solved? After she knew who he really was, and how he'd lied to her? Throwing an arm over his eyes, he sighed loudly. In the past week, he'd fallen in love with her. Once he'd made up his mind she was the victim and not the killer, all the held-back feelings in his heart rampaged through him.

Linc knew their love hadn't stood the test of time in order to become stable enough to ride out problems. His lies were more than a problem, though, and he knew it. *God, let her be understanding with me. Please. I need her, want her.*

Dragging his arm off his eyes, he stared numbly at the white ceiling. He didn't know he was going to fall in love with Brie. And neither did she. Love was the wild card, and when she knew the truth, there was every possibility of it being destroyed. No! He'd just found her. If Carter Fuel and Oil turned out to be a red herring and the investigation had to continue, when could he tell her? And how? Linc decided that there was no good time to inform Brie he was an agent. When he did, all could be lost. No, it was best to keep his cover until the case was solved. Maybe, by that time, their love for one another would have grown enough to take the traumatic shock in stride instead of getting destroyed. He certainly hoped so.

"Mrs. Hansen?" Brie called, knocking at the screen door of the small, single-level dwelling. She cast a glance at Linc, who stood there stoically. She knocked again. It was ten-thirty on Saturday.

Flora Hansen walked to the door, her thin body covered in a cotton shift that had been washed and worn many times over, the colors faded from the material. Her hazel eyes held a look of confusion as she stood looking through the screen at them. "Yes?"

"Hi, I'm Brie Williams, Mrs. Hansen. And this is Linc Tanner. We're with the Hazardous Material Bureau of the fire marshall's office. Is Earl home?"

Flora frowned. Although she was probably in her early fifties, she looked nearly ten years older. Her hair was almost white, in need of a combing and some care.

"Well, yes, Earl just got home. May I see some identification, please?"

"Of course," Brie murmured, pulling out her badge and holding it up to the screen. Brie had decided that they should come to see Earl in civilian clothes so they wouldn't scare him any more than necessary. She wore a silky, short-sleeved orange blouse and a white cotton skirt with sandals.

"Flora?" It was Earl's voice floating through the house.

Flora turned. "There's some people here to see you."

Brie watched Earl's face turn ashen as he approached the door.

"Brie? What are you doing here?" he asked in amazement.

Linc stepped forward, his hand moving to the handle of the screen door. "Mr. Hansen, we need to talk with you privately for a few minutes. Would you like to come out here on the porch?"

Flora knew when she was being politely asked to leave and did so, but only after settling her paper-thin fingers on her husband's pudgy arm. Earl's eyes rounded, but he did as Linc suggested. Linc motioned to the porch swing, taking an old chair that was in need of sanding and a new coat of paint.

"Sure. What's the problem, Brie?" Earl asked, sitting down, clasping his hands between legs.

Brie swallowed, her heart aching for Earl. The man was so frightened, his darting brown gaze moved back and forth between her and Linc. She deliberately kept her voice soft and opened her hands in a gesture of peace.

"Earl, we need your help."

Earl flinched visibly, color draining from his florid features. "About what?"

"About the PCB we found in truck number three, Earl."

He reared back, as if struck. He turned to Linc and waited and watched. He licked his lips then mopped his brow with a handkerchief. "PCB?" he whispered, his voice cracking.

Brie was dying inside. "You know about them, Earl, and so do we. Please don't try to play games with us. I don't want to see you go to jail."

Linc's voice broke the brittle tension surrounding them. "If you turn over state's evidence, it might mean that you'll be granted immunity, Mr. Hansen. Tell us what we want to know and maybe you can stay out of prison."

For a moment, Brie thought Earl was going to faint. The man bowed his head then looked toward the screen door to make sure his wife wasn't standing there. He twisted the handkerchief between his short, thick fingers, as if waging war within himself. "My wife has cancer, Brie."

"Oh, no. Oh, Earl, I'm sorry. I didn't know." Automatically, she placed her hand on his shoulder.

Linc quickly added up the weight of Hansen's admission. "How would you like to be in prison and your wife alone here? By herself." It was a cruel question, but it had the effect on Earl that Linc had hoped for.

Hansen snapped up his head, his eyes filled with tears. "Okay, okay...yes, there is PCB in the grade-two fuel oil. But it was Carter who did it!" He got up, hand pressed against his glistening brow, terror in his eyes. "Carter said if I didn't go along with it, he'd fire me. And where would I be? My wife needs continuous chemotherapy. I don't have enough medical insurance. He said if I didn't keep a second set of books, he'd let me go. Do you understand? I can't let my wife get worse because I don't have the money to pay the doctor bills. Carter promised me that if I went along with this, he'd see that I had enough to help Flora." He turned away, burying his head in his hands, sobbing.

Brie was up in an instant, tears glittering in her eyes, her hand coming to rest on Earl's rounded shoulder. "Oh, Earl," she whispered, "why didn't you come to us? Do you know what PCBs are? What they'll do to people?"

Linc got up and led Hansen back to the porch swing. Brie sat down with him. Linc took the chair, and he waited for Hansen to compose himself. The man raised his head, his reddened eyes filled with anguish.

"I don't know what they are," he admitted miserably. "Carter said it was nothing to worry about. He said he was just doing some friends a favor by taking the oil off their hands instead of having to transport it to a chemical dump where it would cost a lot of money to dispose of."

Brie clenched her hands in her lap. "Earl, PCBs, if inhaled for a long enough time, can cause cancer. By law, any oil with PCBs in it has to be disposed of and the EPA notified. It's illegal to do what Carter's been doing."

Hansen stared at her. "My God, no..." Then his face turned an angry plum color, his voice wobbling. "Carter's been putting PCBs in the fuel oil people have been burning for the last three winters."

A gasp escaped Brie, and she met Linc's stormy gaze.

"That bastard!" Hansen cried hoarsely, getting to his feet. "Carter lied to me!"

If Linc hadn't caught and held him, Hansen would have gone after Carter. Brie watched the two men struggle briefly on the porch, Linc's superior strength and height quickly subduing Earl. Linc forced him to sit down.

"Tell us what you know, Hansen."

Brie sat there for the next half hour, listening to the horror story. Carter had made a contract with a New Jersey firm to haul the PCB-laden fuel oil to Litton where it would be mixed with clean fuel oil. He had been selling the contaminated mixture for three years.

Linc's face became grimmer. "Earl, do you know if Carter hired some professionals to murder John and Brie?"

Earl tried to wipe his eyes of his tears. He glanced at Brie. "Yes, he did. Honest to God, Brie, I didn't know about it until later. If I had known before, I swear, I would have warned you."

Brie forced back all her emotions. Even though she hadn't been killed, she hadn't completely escaped Carter's greedy, inhumane deed.

Linc leaned forward. "Where were these hired professionals from, Earl?"

"Some guys from New Jersey," he said bleakly. "Or maybe it was New York. I don't remember."

"Why did he want John and Brie killed?"

"John came in seven months ago to check the books like he always did. I had been working on the second set of books, the one that kept track of the PCB oil being trucked in. At the time, I didn't realize the mistake I'd made. John had asked for a copy of those two pages with the information on them, and one of the secretaries ran the copies for him. I had been on a phone call and just told her to give him copies. He thanked me and left." Earl took a deep breath. "When I realized what I'd done, I lived in terror of Carter finding out. I knew John was onto something when Brie came back two days later. Normally, I keep the second set of books in the safe, and even the secretaries didn't know what was going on." He glanced at Brie. "When Carter saw you come in two days afterward, he got suspicious. He was upset. He wanted to know why you had visited us again so soon. He thought you suspected something.

"Carter started threatening me with losing my job and letting Flora die. I finally broke down and told him that John had two pages from the wrong set of books." Earl closed his eyes, taking a deep breath. "He flew into a rage, then he picked up the phone. He ordered me out of his office and I left. When he came back out, he was calm. He said not to worry, that everything would be taken care of and we'd get those copies back." Wringing his hands, he stared at his feet, his voice raw. "And when I saw in the papers a couple days later that John had died in an explosion and you were in the Cleveland burn unit in critical condition, Brie, I died inside. I knew then that Carter had called someone."

"He put out a contract on them," Linc growled through clenched teeth. He got up, moving his shoulders to relieve the tension in them. He turned to Brie, and his heart contracted. Brie looked devastated. He wanted to protect her from all this, from Earl's complicity, but he could not. "Okay, Hansen, I want you to come with us. The Canton police will want your affidavit. You'd better get yourself a lawyer while you're at it. I'll do everything in my power to see that you get immunity, but I can't promise anything. Do you understand?"

Earl held Brie's luminous gaze. "I never meant to harm anyone, Brie. You've got to believe that."

"I—I believe you, Earl. And I'm sorry for Flora. For you."

He shook his head. "What a mess." He slowly got to his feet, as if in a daze. "Give me a few minutes, will you? I've got to think of something to tell Flora. I can't just tell her the truth and then walk away for a couple of hours."

Linc nodded. "Take as long as you need," he said softly.

Brie stood after Earl went into the house. She went to Linc and pressed her cheek against his chest, needing his love, his embrace. "So many things are falling into place, Linc," she said in a strained tone.

He kissed her temple. "They are," he agreed. "Why did you go back to Carter's two days after John was there?"

"I was sick the day Earl gave John those copies. The only reason I came back was because John had left his clipboard with our list of contact companies on it. And I remember Carter giving me a funny look when I came in. Normally, he's civil and cool. That day, he looked like a rabid dog who wanted to bite someone."

Linc took a deep breath, rocking her gently in his arms. "That also explains why John's house was ransacked. Carter obviously had someone hired to look for those copies."

"John never showed them to me, Linc. I was never aware of them. It was three days after he got those copies that the explosion occurred and he died."

"Maybe he wanted to do more investigation before he told you about it, Brie. I don't know. We'll never know. But John did put those notes in that one book, so he must have suspected something."

"I'm sure he did," she said tiredly. "John was never one to jump to conclusions, Linc. He was very careful about compiling evidence against any company we were investigating. The reason he probably put those notes in the book is that he was doing further study on PCBs. I'm sure he was suspicious, but waiting to gather more information before he said anything to me." She managed a painful laugh. "John also knew how much I liked Earl."

"Maybe, in his own way, John was trying to protect you, little cat."

Brie shut her eyes tightly, tears squeezing out. "Knowing John, he probably was."

"Like me, he had a soft spot in his heart for you," Linc murmured, kissing her damp cheek. "Just hang on, this is almost over. We've got most of the case solved. Now it's just a matter of getting Earl's statement and having the cops pick up Carter." Dread filled him. The case was solved, and now he had to tell her the awful truth. With a ragged sigh, Linc held her tightly, afraid to let go.

The phone was ringing when Brie and Linc entered his kitchen. They had just come from her house where Brie had fed Homely Homer. Wearily, he picked up the receiver, expecting it to be another haz-mat call. Instead, it was Carol, asking for Brie.

"Is everything all right?" Brie asked, concerned. It was nearly midnight and totally unlike Carol to call at that time.

"Everything's fine, Brie. I'm sorry to call you at Linc's so late, but something just struck me. Remember when you asked me the other day about those boxes of things I brought over to your house?"

Brie rubbed her brow, groggy with exhaustion. "Yes. The three boxes of books that belonged to John?"

Carol's voice became excited. "There were four boxes, Brie, not three. I was in such a stupor when I brought them over to your house. I remember putting three in your living room and the other smaller one down in your basement. It has a red diagonal slash on the top. It didn't contain books, just pamphlets, brochures and photocopied stuff. I didn't think you'd want that in your bookcase, so I took the liberty of putting it in the basement.''

''My basement?'' Brie shot a look at Linc's weary features. He had been up for almost forty-eight hours. ''Thanks for telling me that. I'll go check to see if it's there, Carol. Good night.''

Brie hung up the phone. ''Come on, we're going to the basement. If we're lucky, we might find those two photocopied pages,'' Brie said breathlessly.

## Chapter Ten

My basement looks like a rat's nest," Brie apologized, descending into the damp cellar. A lone yellow bulb flickered as she stood at the bottom of the stairs. Linc joined her, staring at the wooden crates and cardboard boxes piled helter-skelter. He frowned, moving with his flashlight toward the far wall.

"Many of the older homes around here don't have real basements. The people just dug out the dirt. Mine is one of those." Brie looked around. "I wonder if the men who broke in got down here and looked through this stuff?"

"It looks like it," Linc muttered.

"Let's see if we can find that box."

Linc handed her the flashlight. Exhaustion was making him almost dizzy. "You hold the light, and I'll lift some of this stuff out of the way," he muttered. To his surprise, the box had been on the bottom of a pile. They took it upstairs, setting it on newspapers on the table.

Brie opened the box. "It doesn't look disturbed, Linc. Maybe they missed it in their hurry."

"Could be." He scooped out half the contents and handed them to Brie. "Let's sit down and go through it, then. For once, maybe lady luck's on our side."

She glanced at him. "I don't know why you're putting so much importance on finding those copies. Earl said there's a second set of books."

"Yes, but what if Carter destroys those books and records before the police can get to him? We won't have any proof then."

Glumly, Brie agreed with his faultless logic. For an hour, the only sound around them was the movement of papers and opening up of manuals and brochures. Brie got up at one o'clock and made some fortifying coffee. Her eyes softened as she looked at Linc. A day-old beard darkened his face, making his cheeks look hollow. The shadows beneath his eyes told her of his weariness, and all she wanted to do in that moment was take him into her arms and hold him.

"Brie?"

She turned, coffee in hand. "Yes?"

Linc slowly removed two neatly folded papers from between the pages of a manual. "Come here. I think we might have found it."

Her heart leaped as she walked over to Linc. He opened up the papers, which were damp and moldy smelling. "It's them," she confirmed hoarsely, taking a closer look.

There was satisfaction in Linc's voice. "Now we've got that bastard right where we want him." He traced his finger across the page. "Look, the name and address of the New Jersey outfit." His eyes glittered. "John didn't die for nothing, Brie. With this kind of information, we're going to crack this nut all the way up to the kingpins. I promise you."

Brie's eyes widened in surprise when she saw Chief Saxon at the Canton Police Department. She and Linc had brought Earl Hansen in for a statement. Brie decided to talk with Saxon while Linc went upstairs with Hansen.

"What are you doing here?" she asked.

Saxon smiled. "I got the call from ATF that Linc and you had busted the case." He gripped Brie's arm. "Congratulations—"

"ATF?" Brie interrupted, frowning.

Saxon's brows rose. "Didn't Linc tell you yet?"

"Tell me what?" Her heart started a heavy, warning beat in her chest.

"That Linc Tanner is an ATF agent who went undercover, posing as a haz-mat technician to find out who murdered John." Saxon smiled sadly. "I'm sorry we couldn't tell you at the beginning of all this, Brie, because ATF thought you were a suspect. Until ATF was satisfied you didn't set up John, Tanner had to treat you like a possible enemy. You understand, of course?"

Brie closed her eyes, sagging against the wall, leaning against it for support. Linc Tanner was an agent. An undercover agent! He'd lied to her! She tried to breathe, but it was impossible. Pain, like a knife, sliced through her.

"Oh, God," she whispered hoarsely. Then her eyes filled with tears. "No."

"I'm sorry, Brie. I thought Tanner had already told you at this late date. Stupid of him not to." Saxon came over, placing a hand on her shoulder. "Are you all right?"

She choked down sobs, her anger over Linc's deceit rising. She loved Linc unequivocally, honestly. His love, if it could be called that, was nothing more than cover. Lies and deceit, that was all he'd given her.

"Brie?"

Brie brushed the tears from her eyes and shoved away from the wall. Breathing hard, she turned on Saxon. Her words came out in hurt, punctuated snatches. "You knew. You knew all along. And you thought I killed John! How could you?"

"Well—"

"You thought I was capable of killing John!" She was almost screaming.

"I didn't, but Tanner couldn't be sure," he sputtered. "Look, I didn't mean to upset you like this, Brie. You've had a rough six months, and I haven't helped—"

With trembling hands, Brie jerked open her purse. "No, Chief, you've just helped me make a decision I've been straddling the fence over since John was killed." She jerked out her badge case. Shakily, she pulled the silver badge out and gave it to Saxon. "I quit."

Stunned, Saxon looked at the badge he held in the palm of his hand. "But—"

"No," Brie began in a low voice, struggling to shut the purse because her hands shook so badly. "This has been a long time in coming. Too many hours, too little help from the main office. John did it for five years. I did it for three. I can't take it any more, and I'm not ashamed to admit it. There are other priorities in my life I want to pursue."

Saxon shook his white-haired head. "Please, Brie, think this over. I know you're disappointed that our office planted an ATF agent with you, but it was necessary."

Her nostrils flared with anger. "It was unnecessary to think I was a suspect!" She brushed past him. "I'm going home to get my place and myself in order. And tell Tanner I don't ever want to see him again! Do you understand?"

"Yes."

Whirling toward the doors, Brie almost collided with a police officer. She muttered an apology and headed into the sunlight. She hailed a taxi. Damn Linc Tanner! He'd used her emotions to get her trust, then her heart. All along, he was just waiting for her to spill whatever she knew.

Linc was always asking questions, always super alert. Why hadn't she seen it? Recognized it? He'd abused her love just to find out if she was a suspect or a victim! Clenching a handkerchief in her fist, Brie bowed her head, a small sob finally escaping.

Linc watched Saxon make his way toward him where he stood with Detective Gent and Hansen. The chief looked strained.

"Chief?" The man's features were positively gray.

"Linc, may I see you privately for a moment?"

Detective Gent gestured to Hansen to take a seat next to his desk. "You're done for now, Linc. If I need anything else, I'll give you a call at your apartment."

"Fine." Linc managed a slight smile at the sweating Hansen. "Earl, just cooperate, and I believe things will go a lot easier on you."

"Of—of course."

Linc followed the chief out the door. "Where's Brie?" he asked, looking around.

"Gone," Saxon said flatly. And then he muttered, "I thought she knew you were an ATF agent, Linc, and she didn't." He opened his palm, showing him her badge. "Brie's quit the department." And then, more quietly, he added, "She's upset and said she didn't want to see you again, either. I'm sorry, Linc. I really blew it."

Linc sucked in a sharp breath, pinning Saxon with a glare. "You what? You told her?"

"I'm sorry. I blundered."

Linc clenched his fists. His worst nightmare had just come true.

"She's mad and hurt, Linc."

His anger turned to frustration, then anguish. Dammit, he loved her! "No kidding," he snarled, heading for the stairs.

"Wait! Where are you going?"

Tanner jerked a look up at the chief. "Where do you think? Over to her house to try to explain things."

"But she said she didn't want to see you."

Wiping sweat off his brow, Tanner shrugged. "Tough. I love her, and there's no way I'm walking away from her or this situation."

*   *   *

Brie stood just inside her living room, looking around. Her home had been in a shambles, and now her life was. Tears dribbled down her cheeks, and she sniffed, wiping them away. She walked around. Linc had held her on that couch while she cried out her heart, trusting him, learning to reach out once again and express her feelings. They had shared their first kiss on that couch....

With a little cry, Brie turned away. She had trusted Linc, had given him her life, and all along he'd suspected her of being a killer. His tenderness, his kisses were all an elaborate sham to get her to spill whatever she knew.

Brie stumbled into her bedroom, the only room in the house that had been completely returned to its original state after the break-in. She sat on the mattress. When had she fallen in love with Linc? It didn't matter; her heart was aching so much that it felt as if her entire chest was being shattered.

She heard the back door being opened and then closed. Trying to blot the tears from her eyes and wondering who it was, Brie reached for a handkerchief.

"Brie?" Tanner stood tensely in the bedroom door, his face filled with anguish.

"You!" she cried, leaping to her feet. "Get the hell out of here!"

He winced at the anger in her voice. "No way," he growled, moving toward her. Before she could escape, Linc grabbed her by the arm, forcing her toward him.

Brie struggled to get loose. "Let me go! Let me go, you liar!"

Tanner saw the pain in her huge green eyes. He didn't want to hurt her, he'd hurt her enough. "Settle down," he said softly. "Listen to me, Brie. Just take one minute and listen to me. I can explain everything."

Fury goaded her into trying to throw off his hold on her arms, but it was impossible. "Explain what?" Brie cried hoarsely. "You *lied* to me, Linc. I was a suspect! You thought I was the killer all along! Everything you did... your kisses... your tenderness, was a sham, a lie!"

He gave her a little shake. "No, Brie, I love you. That was never a lie—"

"No!" she wailed, throwing off his hold. She staggered backward, caught her balance then moved around the bed, keeping distance between them. "Everything you did was an act, Tanner. Everything! How do you think I feel?" She struck her chest. "I loved you! I fell in love with you. I don't know how or when it happened, but it did. And what I feel—felt was real. I didn't lie. You did!"

He stood there, every breath fiery agony. Brie loved him. "I love you, too, Brie. That was never a lie." Holding out his hand, Linc pleaded, "Please, you've got to believe me. Falling in love with you wasn't something I planned on. Yes, you were a suspect. But put yourself in my shoes. Wouldn't you have done the same thing if you were a stranger coming in on a case like this? I had to get enough evidence one way or another to make a decision about you."

Brie glared at him. "I'm sorry," she said, "but I can't put myself in your shoes."

"Please, Brie, hear me out," Linc begged softly. "Maybe I wasn't honest with you on a lot of things, and believe me, I feel badly about it, but my feelings for you were never a lie. They're real." Linc touched his heart. "You have to believe me, Brie. I love you. Can't we hold on to that one fact, that truth, then sort through the rest of this stuff together?"

Brie suddenly felt dizzy. She closed her eyes, touching her damp brow. "I don't know where truth and lies begin and end with you," she whispered raggedly.

"Come on," he coaxed. "Sit down on the bed. Let me explain, little cat. Please…for both our sakes, hear me out."

Trying to assess Linc through the wall of pain she felt over his betrayal, Brie finally moved. Tensely, she sat on the edge of the bed.

"Good," Linc said in a trembling voice, going to sit on his side of the bed. Where to begin? How to convince Brie? Never had Linc wanted anyone more. Never had he felt the fear of loss as sharply as now. Linc hadn't prayed in years, but he did now, remembering prayers Father O'Reilly had taught him. Wrestling with words, phrases, trying to get them into some kind of coherent order, the minutes passed, the silence brittle between them.

"When I first came on this case," Linc began in a low voice, "I was burned out. I tried to get out of it, but my boss in D.C. promised me a long-overdue desk job if I took it." He held Brie's gaze, loving her more than he ever thought he could love anyone. "I'd almost been killed on that last case, and coming on to this one, I was very jumpy. And I did treat you as a suspect.

"But, as I got to know you and saw you in all kinds of different circumstances, I began to feel differently, Brie." Linc grimaced, unable to hold her gaze. "The first night I went through your desk, reading some letters from your family and friends."

Brie gasped. "You what?"

Wincing, Linc nodded. "Yeah, I feel pretty bad about it, Brie. I'm sorry." Forcing himself to look at her, he saw the sparks of anger in her jade-colored eyes. "It was the first evidence I had that you hadn't set up John. Then, after that, I waited to see if you really were genuinely affected by John's death, or if it was just a cover and you were playing a part with me."

"I never once playacted," Brie whispered. "Every emotion, every feeling you saw in me was real, Linc. And that's more than I can say for you."

Hanging his head, he nodded. "Yeah...I know." Closing his eyes, feeling as if Brie was slipping away from him, he went on. "Somewhere along the line, I started falling in love with you, the woman, not the haz-mat tech. Sure, I respected your knowledge and what you did, but the more I was around you, the more you affected me on some unknown inner level of myself." Lifting his head, Linc held her gaze, seeing very little anger left in her eyes. Groaning to himself, he remembered the luster in them after he'd made beautiful love with her. The ache in his chest widened.

"Little things you did, like fixing me homemade meals and desserts...and Homely Homer..." Linc cleared his throat, watching her face lose all its tension, replaced with tenderness. "You made a house a home, Brie. I never realized it until I was living with you those first five days. I never had that feeling with JoAnne. It's you, how you are, the way you see the world, that made me realize a lot of things." He absently picked at a loose thread on the quilt thrown across the bed. "I found myself telling you about me, something I'd never done. It actually felt good to talk to you about my growing-up years. JoAnne never knew about them. I was...ashamed of where I'd come from."

Brie bowed her head. "Oh, Linc..."

"No, let me finish. Please. That night you broke the glass in the kitchen and I held you on the couch...kissed you..." Linc took in a broken breath. "At that point, I knew you had been the victim, and weren't the killer. All I had to do was prove it to the FM and ATF."

She lifted her chin, staring at him, tears in her eyes. "Then why didn't you tell me?"

Linc held her wavering gaze, aching to reach across the bed and pull her into his arms. "Because you were so fragile. I didn't want to upset you any more than you already were because you were trying to recover. It was a lousy judgment call on my part, Brie." He ran his fingers through his hair. "Remember. This is Linc Tanner, the tough kid from the Bronx who had shielded himself from any kind of emotional involvement. To tell you the truth, I didn't know how to deal with you. I'd fallen in love with you, Brie, and I was limited by my inexperience. I didn't know what to do or how to do it."

"I failed you. I can't tell you how many sleepless nights I spent because I was lying to you. I was afraid to tell you, because I knew you liked me a lot, and I loved you." He shook his head. "I didn't know you loved me . . . not until just now . . ."

Linc's torn admission was dissolving her anger and answering her questions. His features were drawn in agony, his eyes reflecting his panic and fear of having lost her. "Then your childhood was real, it wasn't a lie."

He cleared his throat, unable to hold her compassionate gaze. "At no time did I lie to you about my past or about my marriage to JoAnne. Brie, I just didn't tell you who I was, that was all. How we got along, our feelings, my thoughts and what I shared with you, were real. Please believe me." His voice cracked.

Brie turned away, staring numbly at the flowered wallpaper, the silence weighing heavy in the room. Linc had no reason to lie now that he'd told her he was an ATF agent. He was here, trying to salvage what was left of their relationship, which had been shattered by his lie. Turning, she studied him in the silence.

Linc forced out, "You're like that kitten I found, Brie. You bring out all the good things I've been hiding from myself."

Brie sat, finally understanding Linc and what she meant to him.

Linc forced himself to move, to get to his feet. He'd done what he could to try to convince Brie of his love for her. "I'll get going now, Brie. I've made a mess of your life. I'm sorry, I didn't mean to hurt you. I only meant to protect you, and in one way I did. In the other way, I screwed it up.''

Linc made his way out of the room and down the hall. Misery suffocated him. Well, what did he expect? For Brie to forgive him? Slowing down, he gave the living room a longing look. Brie always had living trees and plants in there, symbolizing life. She was life, he thought. Brie had given him life by simply being herself. She had brought the gift of knowing he wasn't the cold robot JoAnne had always accused him of being. Brie had brought out his softer, more vulnerable side, and he liked himself and what he was becoming.

''Linc?''

He halted, hearing Brie's strained voice. He turned and saw her in the hall, her face pale. He braced himself, knowing he deserved whatever she was going to tell him. He had lied to her. He had been deceitful. ''What is it?'' His voice was hoarse.

Brie made a gesture toward the living room. ''I need some help getting this house cleaned up. Do you think you could hang around a few days and help me before you leave?''

He saw the hope burning in Brie's green eyes. His mouth dropped open and he snapped it shut, not believing his ears. ''Stay? Here?'' There was disbelief in his voice.

Managing a strained smile, Brie nodded. ''Yes.''

Risking everything, Linc said, ''If I stay those few days, I'm not leaving, Brie. Do you understand that?''

She took in a ragged breath. ''I don't want it any other way.''

Linc closed his eyes, feeling dizzy with elation. Brie had believed him! He loved her, and now he was going to get a chance to prove it. Opening his eyes, he managed a sour grin. "Sure?"

"Very sure," Brie answered, opening her arms to him.

## Chapter Eleven

The lap, lap, lap of water against the boat nearly lulled Brie to sleep. She heard Linc casting out again with his rod and reel, the nylon singing through the air. The combination of sun, the sweet smell of the lake and the incessant breeze tempted her to give in to the fingers of sleep. She lay on the bottom of a fourteen-foot wooden boat, which was anchored near the edge of a huge island of lily pads. Good bass fishing, Linc had told her earlier in a conspiratorial tone. And she had laughed, throwing her arms around him. Where had the weeks gone?

After finding John's evidence, which had put Carter behind bars, it seemed as if her life had speeded up. Earl Hansen was granted immunity because he was going to testify for the prosecution. The ATF was following up on the New Jersey end of the investigation, which had already ballooned into scandalous proportions. And Linc had protected her from the press when the story finally broke. He had remained at her side when both state and government law-enforcement officials had questioned her for days on end.

A soft sigh escaped Brie. She had drawn even closer to Linc, if that was possible. Throughout the investigation, they had turned to one another for support and love. Suddenly, she felt the entire boat jerk, and her eyes flew open.

"I got one!" Linc crowed triumphantly, the rod bending as he played the fish who had taken the bait.

Brie sat up, sleepily rubbing her eyes. Life with Linc had been a miracle. The house was back in order; so were their lives. Days had melted into weeks, and then into six months. Homely Homer had grown up and spread her wings. She was free and happy.

Shortly after the trial in which Carter was sentenced to prison, Linc had presented her with two airline tickets to Calgary, Canada, and a brochure on mountain cabins two hundred miles from the Canadian city. He humbled himself to ask and not to tell her that she was going with him for two weeks to escape. And she loved him for his thoughtfulness and said yes.

Watching Linc, she noted how his face reflected excitement as he reeled in his catch. For two days now, since their arrival, he had been trying to get a huge wide-mouthed bass that was so much a part of the blue lake's fame. No stranger to fishing, Brie had counseled Linc on what type of equipment he should use. Being a city boy, he felt he knew better. Instead of using a plastic frog and jiggling it in the water, he had decided on a night crawler dropped to the bottom of the lake.

"This is a big one, Brie. Look at it pull. This is going to be the biggest bass that's ever been—"

Suddenly, Brie broke into laughter. What surfaced wasn't a bass, but a turtle. Linc scowled as he stared down at the dark green amphibian floating peacefully beside the boat.

"I'll be," Linc muttered. Then a grin cracked his mouth and he turned to see Brie holding her stomach because she was laughing so hard. It was so good to see her relaxed and happy again. It was worth hooking a turtle instead of a bass.

Brie slid an arm around his neck and rested her head against his. "You're one of a kind, Tanner. You really are. I told you if you used worms and fished off the bottom that you'd get garbage."

He pressed a kiss to her jaw. "You never said anything about turtles. Now help me get that hook out of that poor critter's mouth so we can let him go about his business."

"City boy," she teased, expertly sliding the hook free with pliers and giving the turtle a pat on its broad-shelled back. She sat up and handed Linc the hook minus the worm.

He set the rod and reel aside and pulled Brie into his lap. "I'm done fishing for today. I'm glad you didn't pick up that camera and catch me with my 'bass.'"

Brie pressed her mouth against his clean shaven cheek, inhaling his male scent. "You're going to have to bribe me to keep quiet about this, Tanner. This is one fish story that's too good *not* to be told."

His blue eyes darkened. "Why you little—"

Brie wriggled out of his arms and sat in the bottom of the boat where she had spread a sleeping bag for comfort. She watched Linc's expression as he came after her. The dangerous glint in his cobalt eyes sent her pulse skyrocketing and her body crying for his touch. She wasn't disappointed as Linc took her into his arms, pressing her against him, and began a slow assault of kisses.

"You know," he said, "you are getting out of hand."

Brie sighed as his tongue traced her mouth. "You're reverting back to your chauvinistic cave-man tactics again," she reminded him huskily, staring up at him through half-closed eyes.

Linc nipped her lips, then relished her feminine softness. "I know. You just bring it out in me, Ms. Williams. Mmmm, you taste good, like a salty and sweet marshmallow." He saw the look of pleasure in her eyes.

Brie caressed his cheek. "I love you."

"How much?" he wanted to know, kissing her fingers.

"With all my heart."

"How about for the rest of your life?"

Her arms tightened around his neck. "Linc..."

"Do you love me enough to spend the rest of your life trying to change me and my chauvinistic ways?"

"Oh, Linc, I never thought you'd want to..."

He heard the wobble in Brie's voice and knew he had surprised her. "Open the tackle box," he said after a moment.

"What?"

He gave her an amused look. "Open the tackle box."

It sat near her, and she flipped the latch, slowly opening the lid.

"Now what?" Brie asked, not quite sure what he was up to.

"The third plastic box. The one with the big hooks. Take it out and open it up."

Her hands trembled slightly as she picked up the case and slid the cover off. A gasp escaped her. There, amid hooks of shiny brass, was an engagement ring. Only it wasn't the usual diamond ring. Brie stared at it in awe. The ring was gold, but the oval stone was the most beautiful color of forest green she had ever seen.

"Let's see if it fits," Linc murmured next to her ear. "The stone is a green tourmaline from Brazil."

Brie watched with widened eyes as he slowly slipped the ring on her fourth finger.

"Perfect. Well, what do you think?" She heard the satisfaction in his voice.

"I—it's lovely, Linc. So lovely..."

"Want to wear it for a while and see how it feels?" he asked, his lips against her cheek.

She managed a choked sound. "Wear it for a while and see how it feels?"

He shrugged, holding her captive in his arms. "A modern woman like yourself might have to get used to wearing something that might make her feel like she was losing her freedom or whatever."

Brie didn't know whether to cry for joy or laugh at his taunting. "Linc Tanner, how can you tease me at a time like this!" The sunlight made her ring sparkle, as if it had a thousand emeralds.

"Actually, my joking is to cover up my terror at your saying no."

She turned, seeing doubt in Linc's eyes. "I love the ring," she said in a low, trembling tone, "but even more important, I love you. And I will for the rest of my life."

Linc gave a ragged sigh, as if a huge load had been lifted from him. "Good," he said roughly, taking her into his arms. "Because I didn't know what I was going to do if you said no."

She gave a soft laugh, feeling deliciously giddy with joy. "You wouldn't have given up that easily, if I know you."

He grinned and kissed her hair. "You got that right, little cat. I'd have pursued you—"

"And badgered me."

"Hey, that's unfair!"

"And browbeat me."

"How can you say those kinds of things? I'm a nice guy."

She gave him a playful jab in the ribs. "You conceited male animal." Suddenly, she frowned. "Why on earth did you put an engagement ring in a tackle box?"

His grin widened. "I thought I'd hook you on marriage. I know I'm not the biggest fish in the pond, the wealthiest or even the most successful. I guess I'm sort of like that turtle—not what you might have expected."

Brie closed her eyes. "You were unexpected," she began quietly. "As far as success or wealth, that doesn't matter to me, Linc. I love you for yourself."

He nodded, at a loss for words—for once.

Brie opened her eyes, her fingers wrapping around his solid arms. "Linc?"

"Yes?"

"I'm not going back to haz-mat work."

He sat very still. "All right. I understand. We all have our limits, Brie. Don't feel ashamed."

"I don't. I'm twenty-nine, Linc. Professionally, I'm pleased with what I've done and accomplished. I've suddenly discovered I want to settle down and make home-cooked meals every day. I want children."

"At least two." Linc turned Brie to face him, and he thought how young and beautiful she looked. "And since the desk job Cramer promised me has come through, it'll be no more undercover work for me. I'll be punching the clock in Canton, Ohio, from nine to five every day and have weekends off. How does that sound?"

Relief shone in her eyes. "Wonderful. That means you won't be risking your life anymore, either."

"Neither of us will. Believe me, it's a big load off my mind, little cat. You were good at your job, but I'd have lived in absolute hell wondering day in and day out if you were safe."

Tears blurred Brie's vision. "We'll just risk our lives with one another."

He smiled. "You're all the challenge and excitement I'll ever need."

\*     \*     \*     \*     \*

*Silhouette Intimate Moments*®

# It's time . . . for Nora Roberts

There's no time like the present to have an experience that's out of this world. When Caleb Hornblower "drops in" on Liberty Stone there's nothing casual about the results!

This month, look for Silhouette Intimate Moments #313

## TIME WAS

And there's something in the future for you, too! Coming next month, Jacob Hornblower is determined to stop his brother from making the mistake of his life—but his timing's off, and he encounters Sunny Stone instead. Can this mismatched couple learn to share their tomorrows? You won't want to miss Silhouette Intimate Moments #317

## TIMES CHANGE

Hurry and get your copy . . . while there's still time!

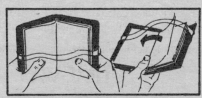
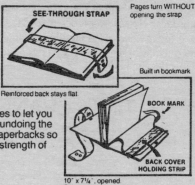

# SILHOUETTE DESIRE™
### presents
# AUNT EUGENIA'S TREASURES
## by CELESTE HAMILTON

Liz, Cassandra and Maggie are the honored recipients of Aunt Eugenia's heirloom jewels…but Eugenia knows the real prizes are the young women themselves. Read about Aunt Eugenia's quest to find them everlasting love. Each book shines on its own, but together, they're priceless!

### Available in December:
### THE DIAMOND'S SPARKLE (SD #537)

Altruistic Liz Patterson wants nothing to do with Nathan Hollister, but as the fast-lane PR man tells Liz, love is something he's willing to take *very* slowly.

### Available in February:
### RUBY FIRE (SD #549)

Impulsive Cassandra Martin returns from her travels… ready to rekindle the flame with the man she never forgot, Daniel O'Grady.

### Available in April:
### THE HIDDEN PEARL (SD #561)

Cautious Maggie O'Grady comes out of her shell…and glows in the precious warmth of love when brazen Jonah Pendleton moves in next door.

SD-AET-1R

Wonderful, luxurious gifts can be yours with proofs-of-purchase from any specially marked "Indulge A Little" Harlequin or Silhouette book with the Offer Certificate properly completed, plus a check or money order (do not send cash) to cover postage and handling payable to Harlequin/Silhouette "Indulge A Little, Give A Lot" Offer. We will send you the specified gift.

Mail-in-Offer

### OFFER CERTIFICATE

| Item | A Collector's Doll | B Soaps in a Basket | C Potpourri Sachet | D Scented Hangers |
|---|---|---|---|---|
| # of Proofs-of -Purchase | 18 | 12 | 6 | 4 |
| Postage & Handling | $3.25 | $2.75 | $2.25 | $2.00 |
| Check One | | | | |

Name _____

Address _____ Apt # _____

City _____ State _____ Zip _____

ONE PROOF OF PURCHASE

To collect your free gift by mail you must include the necessary number of proofs-of-purchase plus postage and handling with offer certificate

SSE-3

Harlequin®/Silhouette®

Mail this certificate, designated number of proofs-of-purchase and check or money order for postage and handling to:

INDULGE A LITTLE
P.O. Box 9055
Buffalo, N.Y. 14269-9055